Praise

Magical Realism often goes two ways. Either the author has a strong idea or the author uses beautiful language.Carol Parker is one of the few who combines the two. She has strong ideas and clothes them in beautiful language.

> Abigail McGrath, Founder of Renaissance House, A Retreat for Writers on Social Issues

In her debut novel, Carol Parker takes the reader on an inner journey through past lives: mystical, heartfelt, and wise. A one of a kind dress, a one of a kind novel, the adventure of a lifetime.

> Dan Pope, Author, *HOUSEBREAKING*.

Being a born and raised Mainer until a decade ago, I attest to the authenticity of life on the Harbor depicted in The Fish Dress. Reading the details of the holiday festivities in Chapter 15 harkened me back to holiday magic of days gone by, where I too enjoyed browsing the shops of Rocky Harbor. Carol Parker has masterfully woven life lessons amid the mystical journey of Nora and her affinity to the Fish Dress. Readers will be unexplainably pulled in and journey with Nora through love, lost love, broken relationships, forgiveness, courage, restoration and finding oneself buried beneath the sea of past mistakes.

> Dr. Mel Tavares, Author, Speaker

The Fish Dress is proof that the right dress can change your life. A heartbreaking and beautiful story--raw and emotional--filled with real magic.

> Jamie Cat Callan, Author, *Parisian Charm School*

To Judy, Welcome to the realm of all possibilities!

Carol Parker

THE
FISH
DRESS

Carol Parker

Kat Biggie Press

Columbia, SC

ISBN: 978-1-948604-70-3 (Paperback)
ISBN: 978-1-948604-84-0 (Ebook)

Library of Congress Control Number: 2020912412

Published by Kat Biggie Press
Columbia, SC
www.katbiggiepress.com

Cover Design by Fresh Design

Photography Credit: Roslyn Carrier-Brault and Brad Snow

To my children:

Greg Parker, Jr.—Poet. Friend. Gone too soon.

Stephanie Peña—Beauty. Optimist. Nurturer.

To my grandchildren:

Gabriella Taylor and Edward Nelson III

Rocky Harbor, Maine

Chapter 1

Rocky Harbor, Maine is a tourist town with an ebb and a flow that marks the passage of time. Every May, the first wave of sightseers arrives for the Fisherman's Festival. Tourists stand on the sidelines, clapping and cheering as locals compete in games that have a maritime theme: lobster crate running, where contestants race on a bridge of floating lobster traps tied together in the harbor, and cod relays down Main Street, with high-schoolers dressed in classic yellow slickers and rubber boots carrying slippery four-foot fish.. Following bar room tall tales, tug of wars, and the crowning of a shrimp princess, the festival culminates with a lighted boat parade and fireworks over the harbor. It's as if the carnival comes to town and lasts all summer.

An influx of tourists continues as the town swells to the size of a city. In June, Windjammer Days honor shipbuilding, and whale-watching vessels cruise the sea. Tall Ships grace the harbor in July, and the Navy comes ashore. August sees tourists flood the streets, loaded with shopping bags and spilling into restaurants, souvenir shops, and boutiques.

As the tide comes in, so it recedes. Locals experience the ebb of the tourist flow around Labor Day, with the great exodus signaling the end of summer jobs. Fewer people walk the streets, traffic jams subside, and retirees amble the peninsula in their RVs. A brief upturn happens around Columbus Day, when leaf-peepers savor the last of fall, which dots the landscape like a Prendergast painting.

By Halloween, boarded-up businesses with *See You Next Spring* signs appear, except at the Lobster Claw and the Ark Tavern, where the doors stay open year-round. The police force shrinks to one, the library closes on weekends, and the pizza shop stops delivering. A single gas station serves the town, and the grocery store slashes its hours.

The thermometer's red line plummets and the bitter winds howl, signaling winter and the end of a work season for many—restaurant and hotel workers, fishermen, their once-overflowing nets-turned-empty, and carpenters, whose building and remodeling jobs no longer stuff their pockets.

Idle time frequently proves dangerous, and few escape the doldrums that settle over Rocky Harbor during winter. Some call it the curse of "winter weirdies," for it stirs strong urges to drink, drug, and lose selfcontrol. By mid-February, the "weirdies" reach full bloom, and in the eyes of many, full doom. Husbands cheat on their wives, and wives have sex with their husbands' best friends. Teens without licenses take joy rides, speeding along icy roads and crashing into trees.

But the "winter weirdies" aren't all doom—seagulls are seen flying backwards, and Larry the town drunk actually stops drinking and is seen by the water, talking to fish.

With April, the North wind softens over the water, signaling recovery. Boots that have crunched and picked their way through arctic ice and snow welcome the vernal equinox and bird song. Spring arrives, and before the town knows it, summer unfolds and the cycle repeats itself. Year-round residents are held hostage by the tourists who feed and then abandon the town.

Summer 1999
Rocky Harbor, Maine

Today she was thankful for a day off.

Still in her nightgown and robe, Nora settled on the living room couch with her journal. Writing grounded and rooted her, helped her to ride life's rogue waves, though sometimes she felt as if she were drowning. Her journal lived and breathed confessions, professions, and fantasies.

She was just starting to write when she heard barking out front.

"That goddam Jack Russell terrorist!" A voice joined in the commotion outdoors.

Nora peeked out the window and saw her neighbor patrolling his yard, wearing a bathrobe and slippers, glaring in the direction of her house.

It was a new arrival that had the dog's attention, not the neighbor. Nora shoved the journal under a cushion. From the living room window, she watched Thomas, his silver hair shining in the morning sun, heft himself from the 1989 Crown Vic she called his land yacht. He wore his usual creased khakis and a pressed polo shirt, unlike most of her friends, who dressed in old T-shirts and torn jeans.

He opened the trunk and pulled out a jumbo-sized green trash bag, which he dragged across the driveway. She knew what was in the bag: things considered junk by Thomas's employer, Mrs. Carver. The elderly woman told Thomas to take them to the Salvation Army, with orders to have the donated goods shipped overseas. Instead, he would spread the castoffs among Nora, their friend Katrina, and until recently, Grace, who'd always had first dibs. God, how Nora wanted to tell her sister she should have stayed with Thomas.

Nora opened the back door. "What a pleasant surprise!"

"Good morning. Where's the coffee?" Thomas extended his filigree-embossed *Carver* mug.

She poured the last of the pot into the cup and eyed the trash bag. "Santa's come early," Thomas said. "Mrs. Carver's been on a rampage, you wouldn't believe what she's getting rid of."

Nora knew all about the Carvers and their luxurious homes, one in every time zone. The family had hired Thomas as a housekeeper in Rocky Harbor eight years earlier. Over time, the job morphed into a 24/7 personal assistant position. Now he also took care of their social obligations, posing as everything from a butler at their dinner parties to a chauffeur for their cultural arts fundraisers. He even had to placate their grown daughter, tend to the spoiled grandchildren, and care for Pippette, a rare yip-yap Belgian breed of dog. He was overworked and underpaid but dedicated to his employers. Grace had frequently complained she never saw him.

Dragging the bag, Thomas followed Nora onto the open porch which overlooked the side yard. She waved to the neighbor who was still scowling, and unhitched her own noisy dog, Margo, from the run before shushing, cuddling, and carrying her onto the porch. Nora settled in the white wicker settee, with Margo nestled in her lap. Thomas joined them, the heavy green sack on the floor in front of them. He set his coffee next to a citronella candle on the lobster trap table.

"Thanks for the gifts," Nora said. "I love that you let me rummage through Mrs. Carver's castoffs."

"I thought you could use some cheering up," said Thomas. "The last time we talked, you were making a career out of blaming yourself."

Nora frowned and teared up.

"Don't be so hard on yourself. Your daughter's mistakes are hers and hers alone."

He had said it before, many times, and like every time before, she hugged him for his reassurance.

"You're a good friend," Nora said, settling back on the settee.

"Glad somebody appreciates me," he said, looking glum.

"You'd still be with my sister if you'd said 'yes' to getting married. Don't you think five years is long enough to wait?" Nora saw his frown deepen and added, "Sorry, I shouldn't have said that."

"You're just being a good friend, too." Thomas jerked his chin at Nora's feet. "Open the bag."

"Ah, yes! The treasure trove!" Nora looked around, saw her neighbor still lurking and said, "On second thought, let's bring it inside."

Once inside, trash bag on living room rug, and Nora and Thomas on the couch, Nora began pawing through the treasure trove. Margo sniffed around it until she was distracted by her own wagging tail.

"Aren't we the materialistic junkie," Thomas joked.

"Look around, do you see a palace?" she asked, waving her hand around the room.

"You and Grace, both incurable bargain hunters. Your happy place is the thrift shop."

Nora chuckled. "Don't forget yard sales."

"But I *do* see the same hungry look in your eyes as in the Carvers'."

"They're all about impressing others with their money," Nora said dismissively.

"And you're in it for the beauty of the bargain," Thomas teased.

Nora had thought more than once that Thomas fed the Carvers' dependence on him, which cost him Grace, who got fed up with Thomas doing everything for the Carvers and very little to sustain their relationship. But she'd told him that at least as many times as he'd told her to stop feeling guilty, so she didn't bother to voice it now. Instead, she thought to include him in her discovery game.

"Here Thomas, you pick something out for me."

He finished the long swig of coffee he was taking, set his mug down, and reached into the bag. "How about these rose petal sheets? They smell like real flowers. I'll bet they've never been slept on." He handed Nora the tightly-folded linens.

She pressed them to her nose and smelled roses, which reminded her of the pink and yellow roses her mother loved when Nora was younger. The ones that climbed the backyard trellis and interwove among its waffled spaces. Mother's flowers and gardens had been her world, one that had never fully included her daughters.

Nora eyed a set of Egyptian cotton bath towels, emerald green, with the tags still on. "I could use some new towels."

Thomas held up several pairs of women's boots and shoes, size 9.

Nora waived them off. "Too big."

Next, she pulled out a shiny purple one-piece bathing suit with spaghetti straps and a plunging neckline.

"Do people donate swimwear?" she asked with a frown.

Then she withdrew a cling-to-your-body-roll-up-in-a-ball-and-needs-no-ironing metallic jumpsuit.

"If I can ever afford to travel, this might come in handy." She tossed it over the back of the couch. At the bottom of the bag, Nora lifted a medium-sized box and shook it.

"What's this? Why is it addressed to a church in Spain?"

"Damn. I was supposed to mail that." Thomas's brow wrinkled. "Mrs. Carver wrapped it herself. Whatever's inside, she wanted no one to know, otherwise it would've been my job." He impersonated his employer in a stern voice and reached for the box.

Nora tightened her grip. "I wonder why she kept it a secret. You'd think she'd want everyone to know." This time Nora impersonated a haughty voice adding, "What do-gooders the Carvers are. Why, we're sending something *valuable* to an overseas church."

Rubbing his chin, Thomas said, "I think this is different. Her hands were shaking when she gave me the package."

"Let's open it," Nora whispered. "She'll never know."

"Don't even think about it, Nora."

"I'll wrap it back up and mail it out tomorrow." Nora stood up and pulled the box further away from Thomas. "Come on. You've told me how crazy she is. Let's make sure whatever's inside is safe to send." Nora circled the couch, putting distance between Thomas and herself. "You don't want to get outed in the post office for trying to send something toxic. Or flammable. Or worse, pass something bizarre and inappropriate to a church."

"I really don't think it's that interesting," Thomas said.

"What if it's underpants? And the priest opens it and dies of shock? That's bad karma, Thomas. You don't need that in your life."

He shrugged and settled back into the couch. "You mean any more than I already have."

She knew he was referring to Grace and couldn't hold it in any longer. "Thomas, I'm just being honest. You shouldn't have strung my sister along for five years. She loved you and wanted to get married, but you wouldn't commit. And now you come here all hangdog about how sad you are, when it's your own damn fault."

The room got quiet. Nora bit her lip, came back around the couch, and sat down next to Thomas. His eyes were closed and she waited a beat before saying, "I'm meeting her at the Lobster Claw this morning. You should come."

Thomas grunted, opened his eyes, then rolled them and said, "Okay, Miss Nosypants, go ahead and open the damn box."

Nora was careful not to tear the cardboard while sliding her nail under the packaging tape and breaking the seal. Inside, tucked between tissue layers, was a folded piece of dark fabric.

Thomas squinted. "What the hell? An old blanket?"

Nora held it up to get a better view. The material cascaded down, as if it were relieved to be out of the box. The carboard clattered to the floor. Margo barked at it.

"A dress!" Nora's voice was reverent with awe.

Made of black linen, the dress was imprinted with a collage of white fish skeletons and sea creatures with dorsal and tail fins, gills and eye sockets. Beyond their basic structure, the creature frames differed in shape, size and direction. The fish were the only definable, recognizable shapes, while other objects looked like ancient tribal symbols, some circular, some squarish, and others crisscross. Nora's fingers tingled as she traced the cryptic designs. She couldn't tell how old the dress was, but she had the same sensation touching it that she felt walking along Maine's wooded paths, where she sensed the spirits of generations past.

Nora stood up and removed her robe, pulling the dress on over her night-gown. She pushed her chest out, placed a hand on one hip and threw her head back, letting her hair fall over her shoulders and down to her tailbone. *Is this really me?*

"This must be one of Mrs. Carver's Caribbean cruise dresses," Nora mused. "It makes me feel adventurous."

Thomas grunted again, leaning over to retrieve the item's box from the floor.

"Don't get too adventurous with that dress, Miss Nosypants. Remember, you're mailing it out tomorrow. Mrs. Carver thinks it's halfway to Spain by now."

"I just want to wear it for a few more minutes. It feels amazing." She pushed her hands down over the fabric, the tingling sensation now on her fingers and thighs.

Suddenly Margo was barking and nipping at Nora's ankles.

"Even the dog knows you shouldn't be wearing it." Thomas reached down and rubbed Margo's head but the animal would not be deterred. She growled at Nora who ignored her.

"Just a little longer."

Thomas made a face. "Not a good idea. Come on. Take it off."

Nora moved to the couch and snuggled up to Thomas with a coquettish smile. "Please?"

Thomas cringed away from her, cleared his throat and said, "Taking the dress out of the box was your doing, and it's your karma, not mine. Plus I hate to burst your bubble but it's probably not a Caribbean cruise dress if she's sending it to a church in Spain." Thomas scooted toward the edge of the couch, getting further from Nora as he did so. "What kind of church would want a dress like *that*?"

Batting her eyelashes at Thomas, Nora replied, "Maybe it's the outfit Mrs. Carver wore when she snagged Lawrence. He's at least fifteen years younger than she is, and plenty rich. Maybe if I wear it, I'll get lucky, too."

Thomas stood up. "What are you talking about? Since when do you even want a man?"

Without warning, Nora felt light-headed and closed her eyes, leaning back and resting her head on the couch.

"What did I just say?" she asked, running her fingers through her hair.

"Are you okay?" Thomas was edging toward the door, reaching for his abandoned coffee mug, and watching the dog who hadn't stopped growling at Nora.

A few seconds passed before Nora opened her eyes and sat up again. "Of course, Thomas. And Margo." Nora looked down at the dog, who whimpered. "Why wouldn't I be? Tell me more about Mrs. Carver and the dress."

Thomas glanced out the front door like he wanted to be somewhere else. "Maybe it's the dress she was wearing when she tripped over her first husband's dead body on the living room floor."

"What?"

"She found him when she came home from the hairdresser."

"You're making that up." Nora wrapped her arms around herself.

"What's gotten into you? First you're opening someone else's mail then you're getting all…" Thomas cleared his throat. "Fresh. Or something. You're like a dog with a bone."

"I'm not usually like this, right?" Nora reached for Margo, who had stopped growling but now sniffed the hem of the dress. "But, really, what would a church want with a dress?"

Thomas scrubbed his palm over his head, as if maybe he wanted a hat for it.

"I don't pretend to know why Mrs. Carver does what she does.."

"What about the needy people in Rocky Harbor, like *me*," Nora said. "Don't we deserve pretty fish dresses as much as any church?"

"Mrs. Carver thinks there's no poverty in America, let alone Rocky Harbor."

"It must be nice to live so insulated."

"Right? Okay, well I'm out. Nearly time to take Mrs. C for her pedicure and walk Pippette. See how hard they're working me? It's a tough gig," he said, chuckling a little but not without some leftover concern in his voice as he watched Nora trace the fish patterns on the dress.

"High status equals high maintenance," Nora said. "Thanks for thinking of me and lifting my spirits. I hope you're doing okay."

He sighed and walked to the door. "I'll live. Just don't forget to mail the dress out."

"I won't. Will you meet us for lunch later?"

Thomas frowned. "Can't. Work."

Nora kissed him lightly on the cheek before he left. She would be sure to mention the visit, and just how sad he'd been about her, to Grace.

After Thomas left, she wore the dress into her room, closing the door on Margo who yelped her disapproval. Slipping the dress off and laying it on the bed, Nora looked at it more closely. She loved the simplicity. No fancy buttons or zippers, just a scoop neck that allowed her to slip it over her head and be done. She put it on again, this time without her nightgown underneath. Looking in the full-length mirror, she admired the way the top lay against her collarbone, and how the bodice curved and tapered below her waist, then gathered in perfect folds that settled slightly above her ankles. Most times she couldn't stand to see herself in the mirror but today she was drawn to it, twirling to get a good view from all angles.

"I'm going to call you the fish dress!" she announced.

In the mirror, Nora saw herself as she never had before. Her eyes looked more green than blue, and a tinge of gray made her think of the ocean colors the fish on this dress might have swum in. She saw how long her reddish-blonde hair was, so long her older students had recently asked if she was trying out for the role of Rapunzel in the school play. And today her hair had a golden tone she could boast as her own, not the result of some bottle concoction.

She'd been living behind a mask, hiding for so long, from the truth, from herself, from everyone in her life. The dress made her feel free from the past. She playfully proclaimed, "I'm looking through new lenses untainted by ghosts of the past," and blew a kiss to the mirror. A violet blue halo appeared around her—a band of blinding light emanating from the dress.

Nora found a puffy satin hanger and hung the dress in the closet—just for the night. Back in her nightgown, she opened the door, stepped past Margo, found her journal and started writing.

Can you believe it? I swear this dress has a magical effect on me. I feel better and look better already. I know I should send it off tomorrow, but I'd sure like to keep it—just for a little while...

Chapter 2

Nora and her sister Grace stepped inside the Lobster Claw Café. Grace rushed to the only open table.

"Damn, it's packed," Nora complained when she caught up to her sister.

"What do you expect?" snorted Grace. "You know it's Thursday, when the *Rocky Register* comes out. We don't want to lose this table. Stay here while I grab us two copies."

Nora sat on the edge of her chair, staring down at the red-and-white checkered tablecloth. When it came to mingling in the coffee shop, she didn't feel much like a local, even though she had moved to Rocky Harbor ten years earlier. Now, surrounded by patrons whose buzz sounded more like bees than humans, she guessed they were talking about births, deaths, arrests, politics, and more gossipy news that wasn't in the *Register*.

She wasn't going to mention the fish dress. All she wanted to do was talk with her sister about how she could get back in her daughter's life because Angelica was refusing to let her visit the prison.

While waiting for Grace to return, Nora felt the crowd close in on her. She took several slow, deep breaths and felt relieved when the waitress delivered two steaming mugs of coffee and set them on the table.

"Good morning, Nora," the woman chirped.

"Hi," Nora said, trying to sound cheerful.

"Haven't seen you in a while."

Nora could feel her shoulders tighten as she clutched her mug, inhaling the scent of fresh brewed beans.

"I've been busy working."

"Don't you get summers off from teaching?"

Nora nodded. "Yes, but I work at a bed-and-breakfast during tourist season."

"That's nice," the waitress said, smiling. "Enjoy the coffee. Glad you're here today," she added, dashing off to another table.

Nora reached into her purse and pulled out a pen and a notepad, the way she always did when she had a spare moment, but then Grace was back.

"No to-do lists today," she said, shoving Nora's notepad aside. Handing her the *Register,* Grace sat back and buried her face in the newspaper.

Nora soon heard loud gulps coming from behind the paper. She flipped nervously through the pages, pausing at the classifieds, where an ad caught her attention:

COME TO MYSTIQUE ON THE FOOTBRIDGE! SEE OUR NEW SHIPMENT OF CRYSTALS AND ANGELS!

It had been a long time since she'd visited the New Age shop. The last time was to buy a tourmaline crystal—a black stone with vibrant yellow and teal blue streaks—to ward off negative influences like anxiety, fear, and stress. It was for Angelica, purchased before her drug addiction and incarceration, and subsequent estrangement from Nora. For the time being the crystal sat in Nora's curio cabinet at home.

Mystique had other items to counteract negative forces—tarot decks, magic spells, and herbs—but Nora stuck to crystals, avoiding Wiccan and the occult. Maybe she would window-shop at Mystique on the way home, but for now she wanted to talk to Grace about Angelica. She reached across the table and rattled her sister's paper.

"Are you ready?"

Grace lowered the newspaper and looked at her sister with kind eyes.

"How can I get Angelica to let me visit her?" Nora asked.

Frowning, Grace answered, "I think you have to wait until she's ready."

Nora gave a huge sigh. "It's killing me. I wonder how long it will take. Or will it be never?"

Grace ran her fingers over the edge of the newspaper. "She's too ashamed to face anyone right now. That's why she hasn't called you or answered your letters or put your name on the visitor list. She doesn't want to see anyone."

"Even her mother? It's been almost six months," said Nora. "She doesn't belong in prison, she's a heroin addict, not a felon. It's a disease, and I want to get her the help she needs. I'm terrified of losing her."

Grace nodded. "I'm sorry it's been such a challenge raising Angelica. Eve was such an easy child—never got in trouble, got straight As all through school, always a self-starter."

Nora stared into her empty coffee mug. "It's all my fault. When we moved to Maine, I never realized how hard it would be for Angelica. She was happy in Connecticut—our neighborhood had a tribe of children she was friends with, and she liked school. And she had a grandmother close by. I thought moving to Maine would save my marriage—you know, like a fresh start—and it would be a safer place to raise my sweet girl. Was I *ever* wrong!"

Grace slid her chair closer. "It's only natural to blame yourself, but it's not healthy. I felt guilty after Josh died, even though I had nothing to do with it. Typical female response—always blaming ourselves."

Nora remembered the scaffolding accident that killed her brother-in-law eight years earlier. Suddenly he was gone, at forty, and Grace was a widow. Grace had mourned, then moved on and would probably be remarried by now if Thomas hadn't gotten cold feet. And now even moved on from *him* with a new boyfriend. Nora wished she could recover the way Grace did. She was still trying to get over the bad marriage she'd left shortly after they moved to Rocky Harbor.

Grace lifted her mug and the waitress came right over with the steaming coffee pot.

"Grace, I hear your daughter is teaching school in China. How's it going for her?"

"Eve? Yes, she loves it, but she misses home. Thank God, she'll be here for Thanksgiving and Christmas."

"That's good," the waitress said before moving on to another table.

"You can go back to your police blotter now," said Nora.

"How did you guess?"

"It's either that or the obituaries."

"I've read enough." Grace said, folding the newspaper.

The woman at the next table leaned over. "Morning, neighbor, did you see where Cliff got closed down for selling hot dogs out of a dirty cart?"

Nora listened to Grace make small talk as she told the woman that as far as she knew, no one had ever gotten sick off Cliff's food and that locals and tourists would miss his cart parked on the busiest corner downtown. Nora admired the way her sister made schmoozing look so easy as the words just slid out of her mouth, while Nora had to dredge her brain and filter her thoughts before saying anything, and even then, she often felt tongue-tied. In a crowded coffee shop, she might be swallowed up by her fears of insufficiency, if not for Grace.

The screen door of the Lobster Claw opened and shut with a bang, followed by a deep booming voice that drowned out Grace's chatter.

"Good morning, Miss. I'll have a lobster roll to go, please."

Nora thought she recognized the man's voice, but when she looked toward the counter and saw the back of a tall, slender man standing by the cash register, she realized she didn't know him. She couldn't help but be intrigued by his gentle rolls of near-black hair. They reminded her of what she'd read Adonis's hair looked like. If only he would turn around so she could see his face, but then she thought better of it and looked away. Not before Grace caught her staring, though, and gave Nora a knowing wink.

"I'm sorry, but this is a coffee shop, not a fish restaurant," the waitress told the stranger. "Half a block down on the left you'll find a seafood place."

"But there's a sign with a lobster out front," he said, laughing.

"That's our famous crueler. Kind of like a bear claw but it's a lobster claw."

"Thanks," he said,. "That makes perfect sense. Lobster-shaped food. No actual lobsters."

Nora felt a nudge. "FYI, now *he's* staring at *you*. Have a look," Grace said, pointing. Nora looked, noticed he was wearing creased jeans, a polo shirt, and boat shoes. His face was tanned, his eyes bright blue, and he had a dimpled chin. Nora's insides quivered, a sensation she'd not felt in years. When their eyes met, he smiled directly at her, then turned away. She watched him saunter across the room and head toward the door.

Grace stood up. "We should ask him to join us. He's probably new to the area and would appreciate a little hospitality."

Nora clutched her sister's arm, digging into the skin with her fingernails. "You do, and I'll leave right now."

Grace laughed and sat back down. "If I didn't already have a man, I'd be interested. He's almost out the door… it's not too late, Nora."

"He's all yours, Grace."

"Are you doing the thing you always do where you tell yourself you're ugly? Have you looked in the mirror lately and seen your dazzling blue eyes? How about those dentist-dream teeth, or that gorgeous mane of strawberry-blonde hair?"

Nora blushed, unable to handle compliments, none of which she believed. "I don't have time for dating. I want to focus on helping Angelica."

"Just trying to help. I thought meeting a nice, handsome man might cheer you up and take your mind off of things that you cannot control," Grace said as the door slammed.

Nora rolled her eyes. "Like when you fixed me up on that blind date last winter?"

Grace snickered. "You mean the guy from the art gallery? I thought he was a perfect match—nice-looking, artistic, and funny. What a disaster! You insisted on wearing the ugliest get-back-and-stay-away outfit you could find. No wonder he told me you were an ice queen."

Nora pictured the outfit she'd worn: a pair of faded green paisley corduroy high waders from the thrift shop, a mustard pearl-studded sweater, an olive-green coat that hung off her like a burlap sack, and Angelica's worn out UGG boots, tired sheepskin that draped in elephant folds around her ankles. A look in the mirror had confirmed she resembled an x-ray shield, perfect for deflection.

"I did it for you, Grace, to show you I was trying. "

"Life's too short, Nora. You can't let the past stop you from moving forward."

"If you're talking about sex, forget it. It's not like I'm in my twenties," Nora replied. "I don't *want* sex. I'm forty-five and I don't need *it*—or a man—to define who I am."

"What about companionship? Remember how depressed you were after you left Jim?"

"I was depressed *before* I left him."

"Your ex is a nut case. Thank God most men aren't like him. How you put up with his shit for seven long years is a mystery to me."

Too ashamed, Nora had never told her sister, or anyone, about how violent and cruel Jim could be. The thought of him still gave her the chills while her sister was able to be flippant about the whole thing.

Grace tilted her head, as if she had seen Nora shiver, and then spoke, her voice tender. "Let the past go, sis."

"Hi, again."

"Our favorite waitress," Grace said, smiling up as she squeezed Nora's hand to stop her shaking.

"Fresh coffee here," the waitress said, refilling their mugs.

Nora inhaled the aroma, savoring the way it tickled her nose.

"This is for you," the waitress said, holding out a napkin to Nora.

Nora eyed the stack on the table. "Thanks, we have plenty."

The waitress winked. "Not like this one." Setting the napkin in front of Nora, she grinned and left the table.

"I *told you* he was checking you out," Grace said, straining to see what was inside the napkin.

In her lap, out of Grace's view, Nora unfolded it and saw *HI, I'M KIRK* written in bold script handwriting with a red Sharpie. He'd drawn a little heart in one corner and a single red rose in another, and there was a phone number. She quickly folded up the napkin and looked around, not knowing what to do with it.

"Let me see," Grace said, grabbing it out of her sister's hand. She beamed when she read the message. "How romantic! You can't let him get away!"

Nora crumpled the napkin and tossed it on the table. "Nope, this is not the guy for me."

"Why the hell did you do that?" Grace asked, scooping it up and handing it back.

Nora threw it down on the table again. "I've got more important fish to fry."

"Grace!" a woman from another table called.

"You're being ridiculous. Don't let this one go." Grace glanced over in the direction from which her name had been called. She sighed at her sister and said, "You don't mind if I say hi to a few friends, do you?" She was already getting up.

"That's fine," Nora answered, rubbing her neck. She heard the wooden floor creak under heavy black work shoes as Grace walked toward a crowded table, in her white ankle socks, faded denim skirt, and wrinkled cotton blouse. She wore large gold hoop earrings. To Nora, Grace was the picture of strength with her muscular calves and solid build. She thought her younger sister beautiful and loved the way Grace's chestnut brown hair fell on her shoulders in soft layers that danced untamed. Some days she tied a large flowered bandana around her head, and when she smiled, she showed a full set of white teeth with one gold tooth covering a baby tooth that never came out. She had unusual eyes, one brown and the other hazel. What Nora loved most about Grace was her huge heart and her willingness to reach out to others, something Nora struggled to do.

Nora rubbed her hand back and forth over the folded newspaper in front of her and stared out the window. She was thankful to be sitting at a table overlooking the harbor. It was low tide, large rocks stuck up out of the mudflats, and water lines marked wooden pilings discolored from years of high tide. Sandpipers flitted across the mud, leaving their light tracks behind. Seagulls rested on top of the pilings, comforting Nora with their mournful cries, as if they were sharing in her sadness. Fishing boats stranded on flats waited for the tide to turn. Nora turned away from the window, tears in her eyes, and picked up the "Hi, I'm Kirk" napkin, twisting it to shreds.

Grace was back. "I told them about your admirer."

"Thanks, now the whole town will know."

Grace gave a sheepish grin. "They said it's a good thing you let your hair down today, compared to your usual Nora-'dos.' The way you hike it on top of your head like a rocket ready to launch, or twist it into a New York pretzel."

Even Nora had to smile because she knew it was true. "How about my clothes, do they pass inspection?"

"I'll bet that peasant blouse came from the thrift shop."

Nora nodded, tugging on a tassel. "Yes, along with this ruffled skirt, but these purple flip-flops are brand new."

Grace chuckled. "You live like a bohemian, but who am I to talk? We're both hippies. Woodstock leftovers."

"Yes, with our gypsy souls," Nora added.

Grace wanted to stay longer at the Lobster Claw chatting with friends, so the sisters said goodbye. Savoring the summer sun, Nora walked across the wooden footbridge, a weathered landmark mounted on massive barnacled posts and spanning the inner harbor, connecting the East Side with the heart of town.

She met a woman walking her dog, a jogger, a few cyclists, and a boy on a skateboard rumbling over the slats. After passing a starry-eyed couple holding hands, *HI, I'M KIRK* suddenly popped into her head. She wondered where he lived, what he did for work, and why he was in town. Lost in thought, Nora was surprised to reach Mystique so soon. She shook her head and felt the ends of her hair rustle over her shoulders as she forced thoughts of this Kirk person from her mind.

The buoy-covered fishing shack jutting out half-way across the bridge looked more like a bait and tackle store than a New Age shop, until one observed the tiny orchid tea lights that lined the front window and shone on ceramic crows, crystal wands, and stone Buddhas. The familiar tinkling of the door sounded when she opened it and stepped onto a glitter-spattered floor.

Nora inhaled the smoky curl of incense burning in a holder on the front desk, behind which Miss June stood.

"Jasmine," Nora said, smiling at the shop keeper.

"The nose always knows. Such a keen sense of smell you have," Miss June said, hugging Nora.

Nora felt the fluff of Miss June's white hair sweep across her cheek, offering comfort like a great-grandmother, the wise crone.

"Haven't seen you in a while, Nora. I trust everything's okay?"

Nora nodded, recognizing Miss June's way of asking after her daughter. Nora had never told her about Angelica's troubles, but Rocky Harbor was not known for its ability to keep secrets.

"I need a healing angel and maybe a new crystal," Nora said, eyeballing the shop's treasures hungrily. She didn't intend to actually buy something, but before she could stop herself, the words had come out.

Miss June's eyes lit up. "I've got just what you're looking for." She shuffled to the angel shelf and carefully removed a rustic stone figure, the deepest shade of blue Nora had ever seen. "Lapis lazuli. Wards off negativity, helps with creativity. Brings harmony. A powerful healing stone. "Meet Archangel Uriel. Oooo … Ree … El."

When the old woman placed the figurine in Nora's hands, a surge of heat passed through her body, and Nora felt the figurine's healing force tingle in the palm of her hand. The sensation reminded her of the fish dress and Nora felt a sudden longing for the smooth black fabric she'd worn just hours ago.

"I'll take it. What else do you know about Uriel?" Nora asked.

"He is a revealer. He sees us as we truly are and shows us what we need to work on. Sheds light on our fears. He also teaches forgiveness and releases karma."

"Exactly what I need!" Nora said. "What should I get for a crystal?"

"You won't need one because you've got an angel and a crystal in this one item—Uriel and lapis lazuli." Miss June peered over the rim of her glasses, adding, "I'm guessing this isn't just for you."

Nora nodded, wondering how she could get Archangel Uriel to Angelica. And even if Angelica weren't incarcerated, would she believe that crystals have healing power? Or that angels guide us? Did Nora believe it? In the past, Angelica had mostly rolled her eyes when she saw Nora meditating. For the time being, Nora would put the crystal angel alongside the other talismans in her curio cabinet.

While she waited for Miss June to ring up her purchase, Nora looked around and noticed a poster on the wall. She stared at the headshot of a round-faced, middle-aged woman with beady eyes that looked like they might hold secrets. Her short hair cupped her ears like raven wings. Underneath the picture read: ROSIE DEERBORN, RENOWNED PSYCHIC AND REGRESSION THERAPIST. LET ME BRING HEALING, HOPE, AND HAPPINESS INTO YOUR LIFE.

"Who is she?" Nora asked, pointing to the poster.

"A dear friend, highly intuitive, and well respected among healers. Come back this weekend. She'll be at the shop doing private readings, by appointment only."

Nora looked at the picture of the stranger who promised hope and happiness and decided to sign up for a session. She paid for the angel and said goodbye to Miss June.

Pausing on the footbridge, she leaned across the wooden railing and looked out over the open ocean. It had always been a magnet, pulling her toward it, spellbinding her with an uncanny ability to renew her spirits. She smelled the salty air and felt it seep into her skin. The sea connected her with nature in a way no other element could. Nora fantasized that she could wrap herself in its strength and let it save her from her fears. She was tired of feeling alone and afraid and needed to figure out how to get Angelica to let her back into her life.

Chapter 3

Nora counted the days until her visit with the psychic. She had experienced psychics before, both the charlatans giving superficial answers that could apply to almost anyone, and the masters of clairvoyance with their pinpoint accuracy. Nora fought nervousness as she approached Mystique, wondering what Rosie Deerborn might predict for her future with Angelica.

"Good Morning," Miss June greeted, her white hair resembling a tangle of cobwebs pinned to her head. She came over and hugged Nora, who melted into her arms in hopes of receiving some wisdom from her friend.

"Don't mind me, I'm tidying up the shop, but Rosie will be right out," Miss June said, waving her feather duster.

Nora instantly recognized the robust-looking woman who now stood in the doorway to the back room. She wore a brilliant purple muumuu covered in gigantic red roses.

"Hello, dear," the psychic said in a sugary voice. "I'm Rosie Deerborn, and I'm happy to meet you." She grabbed Nora in a hug and planted two kisses on her cheeks, and Nora immediately smelled the sweet scent of rose blossoms coming from Rosie's dress. Nora decided right away that she liked the psychic, not even minding the ruby lipstick kisses.

Rosie led the way through a lopsided inner doorway covered with hanging beads and into a tiny room with open porthole windows. Nora could smell the sea and it helped her feel safe. They sat across from each other at a small square table covered with a zodiac print cloth. A large double-pointed amethyst crystal rested between them, its purple glow reflecting the sunrays through the portholes and casting a colorful prism on the wall.

Rosie cleared her throat. "Over the next hour we will connect with my spirit guides, and they will communicate with yours—telepathically, that is."

"About what?" Nora asked, eager to follow her own agenda.

"Whatever they believe is relevant—something to learn—lessons, hidden talents, energy blocks, soul's purpose. Maybe even past lives."

Nora's heart sank. "Did Miss June mention my daughter?"

Rosie put a finger to her lips. "Shush! It's best I have a clear energy field with no background information when I do a first reading."

"But I'm not sure I need all you offer. My main concern is my daughter, Angelica," Nora said, trying to sound polite.

"If I'm to help, you must trust me. First, we talk with the guides."

Nora stared at the zodiac table and heard the dream catchers jingle in the wind.

"I'll start by building an energy link between us." Rosie leaned over and touched a spot in the middle of Nora's chest, then reached for her hands. "Oh my, they're burning up, and so dry—a sign of nerves. Long fingers—you have deep feelings and are very susceptible."

"To what?" Nora asked.

"To getting hurt by others."

A sharp pain pierced Nora's heart.

"Let's close our eyes," Rosie said. "Guides and teachers, we welcome you with love and gratitude for your commitment to Nora. We offer an irresistible invitation to join us with your energies, and we honor your perspective!"

Nora gasped when she felt a surge of electricity move to the area between her eyes—her third eye!

"You may open your eyes now. The guides wish to speak of life lessons, one of them being about your relationships with men. Passion—giving and receiving."

Nora brushed her hand across the table as if she were sweeping unpleasant memories away. "Most of my romantic pursuits have been disasters," she said.

"Your guides agree, but they want you to try again."

Nora hung her head over the zodiac table. "I don't want to go through another failed relationship."

"You're giving up, is that it?" Rosie bristled. "You'll learn nothing by hiding or punishing yourself."

"I just want my daughter back," Nora pleaded.

Rosie nodded. "We'll talk about that soon, but first we must listen to the lesson. The guides believe your present life is a recovery lifetime from your former existence, where you were a celibate."

Nora couldn't believe she was a virgin in her prior life. "I was celibate?"

"Yes, and in this life, you've picked damaged men so broken you couldn't fix them. They became your albatross. Nora, *the great rescuer.*"

Nora collapsed deep into the chair. "The only person I care about saving is my daughter."

"The guides say, 'First, the lesson.' They want you to tell them about your past relationships."

Nora winced. "I'm ashamed to admit that when I was younger, I dated a lot of different men. I was afraid to get too close to any man because he might see my inadequacies.

"But Darrell was different. From the beginning, we felt like we belonged together, and I never felt inferior to him. For the first time, love felt real. He was an Air Force Officer at Westover. We dated for seven months, which my parents didn't approve of because he was African-American. So we eloped. But our dreams shattered six months later when Darrell was killed in a mid-air refueling accident at night. He never lived to see his daughter, Angelica. She was born three months after he died."

Nora rested her hands on the crystal between them.

"It must have been hard being a young widow and a single parent," Rosie said.

Nora nodded. "I was devastated and felt like my world had shattered. I tried to raise our daughter alone, even though a huge piece of me was missing.".

Nora took a deep breath. "A year and a half later, on the way back from a teachers' conference, I met Jim Marshall on the train from D.C. to Connecticut. He was on his way to a job interview. He was a shipbuilder from Virginia."

A memory of Jim swept through Nora's mind—green eyes, a warm smile, sandy-colored hair pulled back in a little ponytail. When he stood up to go to the snack bar, she noticed how tall and muscular he was. He asked if she wanted anything, calling her *pretty lady*. Nervous and giddy, she'd replied, "Just some conversation."

Rosie leaned closer.

"He noticed I was shivering—the train was cold—so he took his jacket off and draped it over my shoulders. We sat and talked as if we'd known each other for a lifetime, and that was the start of our romance. We dated long distance for a few months and then he got the job at General Dynamics. Three months later we got married."

"That was quick," exclaimed Rosie."

"Yes, he was nice, and I was lonely. Plus, I wanted Angelica to have a father."

"The guides say the stars in your eyes blinded you."

"I didn't see his other side until our honeymoon. On the way to Maine, we got stuck in a traffic jam and he started pounding the steering wheel and cussing loudly. I went to change the radio station, when his hand ripped across my face. *Who the hell do you think you are to touch that dial without my permission?*"

Now, hesitating, Nora rubbed the spot he had branded into her skin years earlier.

"You must always hold your power and not be the victim of anyone, but I'm sure you've learned that by now."

Nora stared straight ahead.

"Your guides don't want to upset you, but they say your poor self-worth is still with you, and you believe you don't deserve happiness. They're telling me you need to find out where your brokenness comes from so we can help make you whole again."

Nora closed her eyes and saw her mother stooped over, holding her brother's limp body and wailing, "What did you do to him, Nora!"

"You've lived most of your life in fear." Rosie's voice shattered Nora's nightmare, and the vision faded. "Your low self-esteem would never have allowed genuine partnership."

You're putting your own spin on what the guides are saying, thought Nora.

Shaking her head, Rosie said, "The stories we tell ourselves will destroy us if we continue to believe them." She cupped Nora's chin, raising it until their eyes met. "You came here hoping for a quick fix for your daughter, but understand that for her to heal, *you* must heal, and the guides are here to help you."

"I'm full of regrets—not only about my daughter and the men, but the music and the writing talents I abandoned out of fear of failure."

"Or success," Rosie added. "Before moving on, let's thank them for being with us today." She recited a gracious goodbye to the guides and turned her attention back to Nora. "What's your question?"

"My daughter, Angelica—she's nineteen—and a heroin addict. She would've died of a drug overdose or been shot by a drug dealer if I hadn't gone to the police. I *had* to do it, to save her, but now she's in prison for two years and she refuses to see me or talk to me. How can I get her to let me visit her?"

The seer's eyes closed, then half-opened. "I'm getting a garbled message about a young woman cloaked in silence. When muddled messages come through, I won't share them."

Nora's head collapsed into her chest, as she shuddered and wept.

Rosie reached over and stroked Nora's hair until she calmed down. "Please understand that communicating with the spirit world can be tricky." She held Nora's hand, turning it over and pressing the palm. "Ah, yes—hardness—perseverance and energy you'll need in this lifetime. I'm going to read your aura now."

Nora sat motionless in the quiet space that settled between them. Rosie gazed off as if she were looking into another world. "I see a halo of violet blue around you. There's a journey in your future. You will travel a great distance for something needed."

Nora snorted. *Not likely.*

Rosie's eyes shone like the full moon's reflection over water. "Pink light—a man approaches—I see genuine love."

Nora froze. *She can't mean HI, I'M KIRK.*

Rosie's smile faded to a frown, and her eyes clouded over. "A patch of gray is in your aura." Rosie hesitated. "Someone will betray you."

Nora slapped the edge of the table in frustration. "Tell me something I don't know! All my life, people have betrayed me. I want to stop now."

With raised eyebrows, Rosie stretched her arms above her head and stood. "Yes, I think we've done enough work for one day."

Nora just sat there.

"I'm sorry you're disappointed but trust that everything will show in its time."

"When?" Nora asked.

Nodding, Rosie gave a half-smile. "Soon—always—soon."

Nora stood up and handed Rosie a fifty-dollar bill, which disappeared into the cavern of her cleavage. Again, the smell of roses wafted from the clairvoyant and Nora felt another surge of affection for the woman.

"When can we meet again?" Nora asked. Even though the session had been inconclusive, Nora really did hope Rosie could help heal her relationship with Angelica.

"Call me in two weeks and we'll meet at my home instead of Mystique. Here, take my card." Rosie patted Nora's shoulder gently.

Nora slipped the card into in her wallet. "Bye, Rosie. Thanks."

As Nora stepped onto the footbridge, the psychic called after her. "Next time bring a picture of your daughter."

Chapter 4

Nora couldn't stop thinking about Rosie Deerborn while she went through her morning routine the next day: Rise at 5:00 a.m., make the bed, let Margo out, drip and drink a pot of Ethiopian coffee while getting ready for work. She accomplished everything by 7:00 and wrote in her journal before heading to Heron Bay Bed & Breakfast. She loved the summer break from teaching; it sheltered her from parents and principals breathing down her neck, providing some respite from trying to close every achievement gap and fix every broken child.

At the B&B, when her shift ended, the work was complete with fresh sheets and crisp tucks, propped pillows, a shiny sink with glistening faucets, dustless bureau tops, and everything smelling like lemons. No lesson plans, paper correcting, assessments or extra duties to carry home, not to mention no students to deal with.

While she worked, Nora thought about her visit with Rosie. She mused about the travel suggestion. Maybe she and Grace could take a Caribbean cruise together. She would have to save the money. If Rosie was to be believed, a big life lesson awaited Nora. She doubted that lesson was relationships with men. Finally, the betrayal prediction. Nora had had quite enough betrayal in her life. The more she thought, the more she realized she hadn't really liked any of Rosie's predictions. The only thing she had said that Nora didn't completely *dislike* was her request that she bring a picture of Angelica to the next visit.

Betrayal was a theme in Nora's life. She wondered if she'd been the giver as well as the receiver. The therapist she saw once told her she'd made the right choice when she went to the police, which ultimately led to her daughter's incarceration. And now Angelica was punishing her mother for saving her life.

Nora still shuddered when she pictured the derelict who had shown up at the door, looking for Angelica. He resembled Charles Manson, with wiry hair, a scraggly beard, and gaps where teeth should be. His eyes were so bloodshot they looked like roadmaps. He wore a raggedy winter coat five sizes too large with giant pockets. His voice sounded like sandpaper when he demanded to know where "Angel" was. No way was Nora going to let the creep get anywhere near her daughter.

"Tell her Scab is looking for her," he'd growled, then pulled something shiny out of his pocket, just enough so Nora could see it was a gun. Her heart raced. She slammed the door in his face, and he took off. Nora had already tried so many interventions she didn't know how else to save her daughter. She drove straight to the police station and told them about the drugs and the danger Angelica was in. In so many ways she had tried to tell Angelica she loved her. Even by telling the police.

For the rest of the day, she thought about Angelica and the mistakes they'd both made, and worried. That evening, emotionally exhausted, she took out her special wine glass—hand-painted with the design of a piano keyboard. It was a birthday gift from Grace. Another unfulfilled dream of Nora's was music.

She filled the glass with cabernet and sat at the kitchen table, where she could see through the dining room and all the way to the front parlor at the other end of the house. The way the rooms hitched together like railroad cars reminded her of her ex-husband Jim and how special he made her feel when they first met on the train. And how he treated Angelica like his own child. When she was a toddler, Jim would blast the music and he and Angelica would bounce around the living room like helium balloons, filling the air with laughter. She was his *Baby Girl,* and she called him *Daddy.*

****

Nora wanted to call Rosie for help with Angelica but it hadn't been two weeks yet. Needing to talk to someone, she called Grace.

"I've been waiting to hear from you about the psychic. What happened?"

"She couldn't tell me anything about Angelica, not yet anyway, but she had other things to say."

"Like what?"

Nora shared the predictions, also mentioning the guides.

"Guides? What guides?" Grace asked.

"Never mind. She said I need to work on relationships with men."

Grace laughed. "What did I tell you? If you'd listened, I could've saved you a trip to the psychic, and fifty bucks."

"True," Nora said, nodding. "By the way, guess who came by recently?"

"Do I know this person?"

Nora chuckled. "I'll say."

Grace hesitated. "Thomas?"

"Bingo!"

"What for?"

Nora detected an undertone of jealousy in her sister's voice. "He dropped off Mrs. Carver's hand-me-downs. He's lost without you, Grace."

Nora stopped herself from mentioning the dress. She knew how Grace felt about otherworldly things like crystals, angels, and tarot cards. "Are you okay with Thomas and me still being friends?"

"Of course. The choo-choo has left the station, the boat has departed the harbor." Grace gave a low train whistle followed by a boisterous ferry horn blast, and the sisters burst out laughing. It felt good inside to laugh, and she loved how the smile felt on her face.

"Okay, good. Now, about Angelica. I don't know what to do anymore."

"There's nothing you can do other than don't give up on her."

"I won't. Maybe I'll try writing her another letter."

"It can't hurt," Grace said.

"Thanks for the talk and the laughs."

After they hung up, Nora called the prison but got a recording, part of which said, "If you're calling to schedule a visit with an inmate, please try again during normal business hours. No visits allowed without an appointment."

Her desperation to reach her daughter was growing and there didn't seem to be anything she could do to hurry the process. She poured more wine into the bowl-sized glass and carried it to the front parlor, where the piano called to her. Several months earlier she had tried to play, but her fingernails clacked over the keys, grating against her eardrums. She had banged both hands down on the ivories and slammed the cover shut.

Now, sitting on the piano bench, she lifted the dusty cover. A song she'd composed years earlier played inside her head. As her fingers glided across the keyboard, she sang:

> "*Life is full of wonder, can't quite tell what spell I'm under.*
> *Mix the good with the bad, the happy with the sad, life is full of wonder.*
> *One minute I feel like I'm in it, oh, the good times.*
> *Life lessons I thought I learned have returned, and I'm losing.*
> *I cry through the pain and get up again. Gotta love who I be, and make the changes in me, yes, life is full of wonder..."*

She sat still, feeling the joy at reconnecting with her creative side. She looked over at the crystal Archangel Uriel, who stood in the curio cabinet. She heard Miss June's words: *Helps with creativity. Sees us as we truly are. Sheds light on our fears.* Was Nora channeling his energy?

She made her way into the front hallway and up the formal staircase to the second floor. She thought about how much more house she had than she needed, but she'd gotten it for too good a price to pass up. They called it a New England Federal. It had four bedrooms: Angelica's spacious sunny room in the front, two small adjoining bedrooms in the rear, and Nora's tiny bedroom tucked in one of the angular twists of the house's odd architecture. Her room felt like a cave she could crawl into, take a sleeping pill, and lull herself to sleep.

She stood in front of her closet, looking at the fish dress. She put it on and before she was even aware what she was doing, she began twirling and spinning again, just like when she'd put it on the first time. She loved how it made her feel—like she was floating on sea foam.

Sashaying from room to room, Nora stopped in Angelica's bedroom, admiring the yellow paisley curtains, puffy white comforter and plush pillows she'd recently bought. She sat on the edge of the bed, then stretched out across it, remembering how it had looked when Angelica lived there. Before prison.

The room had been dark and dreary, with drab green curtains, black furniture, and a scratchy gray army blanket on the bed. The room had smelled dank.

Nora woke up the next morning, surprised she was still in Angelica's bed, wearing the dress. Sun poured through the blinds, casting a reflection of slats that looked like prison bars on the opposite wall. Nora was overcome with such an intense longing for her daughter that her chest ached.

She looked down at the dress and it felt heavy, oppressive. *Maybe it isn't so great after all,* she thought, heading to her bedroom to find something else to wear. She hung the dress deep in the closet, then locked the door.

FEAR NOT, MY DEAR.
I BRING BOTH SHADOW
AND LIGHT

The voice startled Nora. *Maybe it wasn't a voice,* she thought. It sounded more like the light plucking of a harp, but it couldn't be. She pressed her face against the window screen and looked outside to see if there was someone there. Other than a few birds, the yard was empty. *I must be hearing things,* she told herself. *Payback for drinking too much wine last night.*

Once she got to the B&B, her mind was back on Angelica. Nora thought about the letter she would write, hoping to find the right words to reach Angelica and reunite them. She'd make sure to keep things positive. *My darling daughter, Angelica.* Maybe she should talk about happy memories like Angelica's dance recitals when she was younger. Nora loved the way she'd arched her back like a cat stretching, her pink satin slippers tipped straight up and the crisscross of laces hugging her tiny calves. She could tell her how proud she'd been watching Angelica glide across the stage, graceful as a willow, her thin arms swaying high above her head like branches in the wind.

Perhaps Nora shouldn't sugarcoat the truth but should also talk about the burden of addiction, that monkey Angelica carried on her back, and how it had caused everyone so much pain. She'd need to include her own apologies for not being a strong enough mother, for years of cowering before James and putting up with his abuse. For seeking approval from work because she wasn't getting it in her marriage.

She had trouble keeping her mind on the B&B chores and was relieved when the clock finally read 5:00 p.m. and she could leave.

Once home, Nora sat at her desk and wrote the letter, including all the thoughts she'd had while working that day. At the end of the letter she added: *Today I reclaim my power and my daughter. I want you in my life and will stop at nothing to bring us back together. I'm ready to open up and for you to share with me your hopes, fears, disappointments, and dreams. Love Always, Mom. P.S. Call me. xxxooo.* She slid a twenty-dollar bill inside. Just as she sealed the envelope, the phone rang. Nora hopped up, hoping as always that it was Angelica.

"Hi, Nora. This is Rosie Deerborn."

"Hi, Rosie," Nora said, surprised to be hearing from her so soon.

"The guides need to see you," Rosie said, sounding serious.

"Oh, how come?" Nora asked, hoping this wasn't a scam to just get more of her money.

"We'll talk when you get here. I'm at my house, not at Mystique."

"Should I bring my daughter's picture?"

"Yes. I'll look at it after the guides have their say."

"There's something else." Nora told Rosie about the fish dress, and how it both excited and frightened her.

"Wear it when you come," Rosie said.

Nora dug out the psychic's card and stared at the blue goddess symbol with arms raised skyward, a spiral at her womb, and phases of the moon around her body. She felt a tug of war between trust and doubt inside her, but she didn't know who else she could turn to.

Nora got the dress from her closet. It slid smoothly over her head, and all traces of doubt dissolved. She grabbed a small color photo of Angelica and headed to Rosie's house.

Chapter 5

An hour later, Nora stood before a red wooden door, her hands trembling as she lifted the brass moon knocker. The door burst open and there was Rosie, wearing a fuchsia and yellow flowered muumuu.

"It's good to see you again," she said. "So that's the dress," she added, touching a sleeve.

Nora followed her down the hallway and into a candlelit parlor. She smelled the heavy scents of patchouli and sage.

"Here's my daughter's picture," Nora said, wanting to talk about Angelica right away.

Rosie fanned her face with the photo and tucked it away in her muumuu. She pointed to the pair of ladder-back chairs facing each other.

"Have a seat. I'll bring us water."

Nora scanned the walls covered with framed documents. Berkeley Psychic Institute for Completion of the Clairvoyant Program. A Past Life Regression Certificate. A Master's in Clinical Psychology from San Jose State University. Clearly, Rosie was no ordinary psychic. She seemed more like a therapist than a psychic.

Rosie returned and handed Nora a glass of water.

"Who's the Kawaiisu tribe?" Nora asked, pointing to a certificate framed in animal fur.

Smiling, Rosie answered, "A Native America tribe of the Southwest. Back in the seventies, instead of writing a thesis I took a solo journey into the Sierra Nevada Mountains in California and met up with the Kawaiisus. They taught me to conquer fear." She traced the frame with her finger. "But enough about me, let's call in the guides."

Following the opening ritual, Rosie told Nora that the guides wanted to know what traumatic event happened when she was a young child. Nora froze. Denial had served her well up to this point, and she had no desire to change that now.

"I d-d-don't know what you m-mean."

"Your spirit guides have reason to believe that something happened a long time ago that you've never dealt with, and it's at the root of your issues."

Nora bit her lower lip. "I'm not sure. When, specifically?"

"Unless you wish to remain shackled to the past forever, you must confront the ghosts in your closet. It's hard work but necessary."

Silence.

Nora finally uttered, "My baby brother."

"What about him?"

Rosie's voice drifted off and everything turned fuzzy. Nora felt her body lift and hover near the ceiling, then float out of the parlor and over the house she lived in as a child. She saw her mother inside with her little sister Grace, her older sister Diane, and her baby brother Seth. All at once, she found herself inside rather than watching from above, and strangely enough, she was five years old again.

"I love to play with my dolls. Holly's as tall as me, with yellow yarn braids and a hard-plastic face with rosy cheeks, blue eyes, and a painted-on smile. She's a rag doll. I hook her feet to mine, and we dance together."

Nora slid off Rosie's chair and sashayed around the parlor until she felt someone guide her back. She held her arms as if she were cuddling an infant.

"Cathy Coo is my baby doll. She even has arms and legs that move, and a mouth that holds a bottle. She wets her diapers, and I can take her into the tub.

"But my favorite doll is Wendy, she's the perfect size." Nora held her hands out to show how tall Wendy was. "Her skin is smooth, and she has squishy fingers and toes like real people. In doll years, I'd say she's twelve." Nora moved her hands as if she were combing Wendy's long, silky auburn hair, then pretended to dress her in a shiny dress the color of lemons, along with a crinkly petticoat. "The Christmas she came, I was so excited, but when I picked her up, one of her arms was lying in the bottom of the box." Nora frowned, then brightened. "Mommy and Daddy sent her to the doll hospital, and she came back fixed."

"Let's talk about your brother Seth," Rosie said.

"He's like one of my dolls, but he's alive! I get to hold him while my mother rests." Nora's arms swayed as if there were a baby rocking in them. Then she started to shake, and the parlor began to spin, as images of Seth swirled around her. The twitch of a curled finger, a yellow footie, his blue face.

That strange voice echoed around her again.

SUCH SADNESS AT FIVE YEARS OLD.

"The guides say you must keep going. You've got to get through this." Rosie's voice rang out, sounding like the clang of an iron bell, and the parlor blinds rustled in the background. The next thing Nora knew, she was lying on the couch and Rosie was shoving something putrid, worse than ammonia or fertilizer, under her nose.

"What's that horrid smell?" Nora asked, gagging.

"Smelling salts. You went into a trance, then fainted and fell off the chair, but I caught you just in time and carried you to the couch."

"I can't continue." Nora sucked for air, her chest tight, her throat closed.

Rosie stroked Nora's hair. "It upset you to think what happened when you were a child. It was a good start, but there's much work ahead related to shadow and light. The greater the darkness you overcome, the more the light will shine. Before we move on, let's thank the guides for communing with us for your highest good." She recited the same gracious goodbye as before.

The panic had subsided, but Nora hesitated.

"The dress," she whispered, "It spoke to me. Didn't you hear it?"

Rosie took a few deep breaths and rubbed her hands together.

"Stand up so I can take a look."

Nora watched Rosie's expression. The psychic must have thought she was crazy.

Rosie stared at the dress, circling around it like a mother dolphin protecting her young.

"Am I in danger?" Nora asked, recalling the recent morning she'd woken up in Angelica's bed, still wearing the dress, which had felt deadly upon her. Later that morning, she thought the dress might have spoken, but now she was convinced it had.

The psychic put her finger on a fish. "Jesus. Christian symbol. Most people don't know it's rooted in Pagan fertility and sexuality. Like Aphrodite, and mermaids. Womb and dolphin. Goddess of Ephesus, with a fish covering her genitals. Or the fish that swallowed the penis of Osiris. And the vulva of Isis. All fish symbols."

Nora felt as if her skin were crawling.

"Pagan? Fertility? This dress is tied to witchcraft and sex."

Rosie chortled. "Not necessarily. Paganism covers many practices, from Wicca to nature worship and much in between."

Nora made a face. "I want nothing to do with witchcraft. That's not my thing."

"You're safe but there are fertility, life force, and reincarnation connections with this dress. Certain cultures believed dead souls lived inside fish, and as part of a fertility ritual, they were eaten so the souls would be reincarnated in a newborn child. There's a lot going on with this dress, and that's just with the fish, to say nothing of the other symbols."

Nora pointed to the swirls and crisscrosses. "Do you mean these?"

Rosie touched the fabric. "Why did you take the dress?"

"Take?" Why would Rosie say that? Nora felt seasick, as if the fish had come alive and were weaving between the symbols, slapping her with their fins as punishment for deception. For the moment, she regretted having knocked on Rosie's door.

"I don't know," she whispered, staring down at her feet. "I'm just borrowing it."

Rosie emitted a deep belly laugh. "It may have chosen you, so don't worry."

Nora saw the dress shimmer and felt it cling to her body, which began to quiver. Rosie wrapped her arms around her and led her to the full-length mirror in the hallway.

"With this dress, I see shadow and light. Yin and Yang. Positive and negative energy. It will help balance you, so don't fear where it wants to take you."

Questions flooded Nora's mind. "How long do I keep it? What if...?"

"Stop scaring yourself. You'll know, sister, believe me."

They returned to the parlor and sat on the velvet loveseat. Rosie pulled out the photo from where she had tucked it in her muumuu.

"I'll look at your daughter now."

The two women stared in silence at the picture, held tight in Rosie's hand.

"How lovely!" the psychic said.

Nora gave a weak smile. "She was fourteen then. We were at Seaside Point, sitting on the rocks. She turned around, and I snapped the picture." Nora longed to hear her daughter's voice and touch her unblemished bronze skin, to brush her lips across her face framed in windblown hair, and to breathe in the once familiar scent of Angelica's essence.

"You may not see it, but there's an orange aura and a bit of blue," Rosie said.

"You can *see* that?" she asked, catching her breath. "What does it mean?"

Swaying back and forth, Rosie closed her eyes and held Angelica's picture to her heart. "Your daughter feels the emotions of others, their pain and joy. She longs for truth and clarity in relationships. But she's lost. I see it in her eyes." She handed the picture back.

Nora peered into Angelica's face. "She *is* lost."

"She'll come around. Don't dwell on her past."

Looking up through her tears, Nora whispered, "Thank you."

Rosie escorted Nora to the door. "There's a connection between that dress and your daughter, and perhaps your brother Seth. The dress will prove its power but tell no one of its influence. Call me when you're ready to confront the trauma in your childhood so you can heal."

Chapter 6

Grace was standing in the driveway when Nora arrived home from her Saturday morning shift at the B&B.

"We're kidnapping you," she said.

"Who's we?" Nora asked.

Grace winked. "You'll see."

Nora poked her head in the back seat of the car and saw their friend Katrina huddled over the *Register*.

"Hi, what's up?" Nora greeted her, trying to sound relaxed.

Katrina looked up and grinned. "You're going yard-saleing with us, right?"

"Not today; I just got out of work and need to walk Margo and clean my house and do laundry."

Katrina made a face. "Can't you ever wander through a day with no agenda?"

"Forget about your to-do list," Grace added.

Nora had to admit it might do her good to be spontaneous for once, so after checking on Margo, she slid into the front seat of Grace's ancient AMC Hornet, affectionately called the Green Hornet. As they rode along, Nora thought about Katrina and how much she liked her. Grace and Katrina worked together at a local pottery-making business.

Katrina was a sexy bleached blonde with baby-face dimples and sparkling green eyes. Men gravitated to her like bees to honey. Her pot belly was more than offset by generous breasts and toothpick legs that protruded from the denim miniskirt she lived in. Brainy, screwed up but hopeful, and able to laugh at her imperfections, she believed in taking lemons and making lemonade.

Katrina also worked part time with Nora at the bed-and-breakfast and thought nothing of indulging herself in a bubble bath, even shaving her legs in the honeymoon suite's tub when the owners stepped out.

If only Nora were half as adventurous, to lock the bathroom's old-fashioned latch and linger long enough to take a steamy bath in the antique clawfoot tub and soak up to her neck while savoring the strong scent of wildflowers that drifted through the open window. But she wouldn't dare.

They pulled into their first stop, a rambling Victorian. The girls sifted through pile after pile. Nora tried to participate but ended up just watching her friends scavenge like seagulls searching for crumbs.

Katrina picked up an ornate wooden birdcage. "This will look great on my back porch."

Grace came up to Nora with a stack of ironstone plates and an old metal toaster with sides that flapped down. "Isn't this relaxing?"

"Sure," Nora replied, as she felt the onset of a headache. Everything seemed so scattered, unlike the thrift shop, which was at least organized by color, size, or function.

Next, they stopped at an old parsonage. Katrina ran up to Nora with a box of first edition hardcover art books from the early 1900s, and a wooden wall clock in the shape of Maine.

"Hand crafted by an inmate at Thomaston Prison," Katrina read from the inside cover.

Nora's insides churned at the sound of the word *prison,* and she winced when her sister also chose a prison piece, a wishing well lamp made of driftwood.

"Eve will love this. Do you see anything, Nora?"

"Not yet." But no sooner had she spoken than she spotted a tiny metal picture frame sticking out of a box of old hymnals. She rubbed the dust off and uncovered a portrait of a young nun drawn in sepia tones, wearing a hooded bonnet and a plain dark robe, with a large crucifix around her neck. Below the picture it read "Hermana Marguerita DeRoche de la Iglesia, circa 1865." The picture frame was missing glass. The dingy water-stained parchment was glued to the cardboard backing that clung to the frame. A sudden urge to rescue the nun overtook Nora. She had seen many faces that afternoon but none as alluring as Sister Marguerita's.

"What've you got?" Grace asked, looking pleased that her sister had finally found something.

"Just an old picture."

Grace smiled, glancing at Nora's find. "You never know what treasures you'll uncover. That's the fun of it."

Nora paid the woman her dollar asking price, then slipped the portrait into her purse.

"Thanks," the woman said, pointing to a half-mangled cardboard box nearby. "You ought to take a peek. Dirt cheap and in great condition."

Pretending to be interested, Nora rummaged through the tangle of baby clothes spilling over the edges of the box. She held up a toddler-sized powder-blue corduroy jacket, soft to the touch. Her fingers moved slowly across its worn ridges, and an image of her brother popped into her mind. There he was, in the same blue corduroy jacket, his chubby fingers poking through the sleeves. The matching blue cap, the strap buckled tight under his chin. Nora, holding his hand to steady him as he took his first wobbly steps in stiff white leather shoes, his eyes round as marbles.

"Hurry up. We're leaving," Grace shouted from the Green Hornet. "We don't want to miss the good stuff."

"Be there in a minute," Nora said, hanging back. She rubbed the corduroy against her cheek, then folded the jacket and buried it deep in the pile. The fleeting memory followed her to the car.

At their final stop, a weathered farmhouse, Katrina bought a black rotary phone from the fifties, and Grace stocked up on plaid flannel shirts for winter, a wind chime mobile made from hammered forks, and Nora found nothing—that is, until she spotted a bald-headed mannequin with no arms, leaning against the barn. The lady was naked, and Nora could see how the mannequin's upper and lower halves twisted together at the waist to form a whole body. She moved closer, brushing away the cobwebs and touching the tiny cracks of plaster. She gazed at the stunning face, with a spattering of sea green eye shadow and liner around olive eyes, perfectly peaked brows, and burnt orange lips showing a hint of a smile. The mannequin resonated with Nora, and she called out to Grace, "Can we fit her in the car?"

"We can try," her sister answered, waving her over.

Several minutes later, the Green Hornet squeaked like rusty bedsprings as it drove off, loaded to the hilt with a trunk full of hand-me-downs and a naked statue twined to the roof. They dropped off Katrina and went to Nora's house. Together the sisters lugged the mannequin onto the front porch. "Where do you want her?" Grace asked.

"Let's prop her in the hallway for now. She needs clothes." Nora knew exactly how she would dress her: a vintage white muslin dress with pink baby roses, one she'd acquired years earlier from a Nova Scotia B&B that had an underground thrift shop. She loved the dress but it was too small for her body. It would be perfect for the mannequin. And Nora would drape a silk scarf of lavender daisies over the woman's bald head and cascade it down her shoulders to fill the space where her arms should be.

"Why did you get her?" Grace asked.

Nora grinned. "She reminds me of *me*—after cancer."

Grace's nose scrunched up. "Bald, and no arms?"

"Yes, battered but a survivor. She's my victory shrine." It had been awhile since Nora had thought about her breast cancer. She'd been careful to hide it from Angelica, who was almost twelve when Nora found out. "I can't believe it's been seven years."

Grace nodded, flopping on the couch. "I'd say you beat it."

"You mean *we* beat it," added Nora, standing by the mannequin. "Remember all those weeks you drove me a hundred miles a day for radiation? And Eve watched Angelica through the whole ordeal? Couldn't have done it without the two of you."

Grace smiled. "Eve loved being like a big sister to Angelica."

"And Angelica loved having a surrogate sister," Nora said, adding, "They were so close. Eve stood up for her all through school. I'm surprised she's shutting her out."

Grace got up from the couch and began to pace back and forth. "You know how it is in our family. We retreat and hide behind our problems, keeping them to ourselves. We grew up under a code of silence, for God's sake."

Nora frowned. "Don't remind me."

"Mom and Dad never spoke about 'sensitive' issues. If it wasn't all roses, they hid the truth. Like when Seth died."

Nora sat buried in silence. It was starting to come back to her.

"What's the matter?" asked Grace.

"You might not remember what happened. You were just four," Nora muttered.

"And you were only five."

"Yes, but you and Diane were sleeping when it happened, so you didn't see or hear anything.

"Did *you*?" Grace asked.

Nora hesitated. "I don't know what I saw, but Mom blamed me for his death."

Grace put her hand to her throat. "Are you serious? Why didn't you tell me before now?"

Nora looked at her sister's shocked face. "I'm not sure what the truth is, and I'd rather not talk about it anymore."

"Right," Grace said, nodding. "Why don't we pause a sec."

Nora wasn't surprised when her sister pulled out a flask. A lot of folks carried them on the peninsula.

"No whiskey for me, thanks," said Nora. She went to the kitchen and returned with two glasses and a bottle of wine, placed them side by side on the coffee table, and sat beside Grace on the couch. Before Nora realized it, she was talking about their brother's death again. "Dad was away on a business trip but he rushed home. Do you remember getting shuffled to the neighbor's house?"

"Not really," Grace muttered.

"You and Diane played with toys, but I wouldn't come out from under their kitchen table. And I wouldn't talk. I sat with my legs crossed, rocking and crying and hugging Wendy."

"Who's Wendy?"

"My favorite doll when I was little."

Grace lowered her glass to the table. "Sorry you had to go through all that, and that it never got sorted out."

"I've got to deal with it, or I'll be screwed up for the rest of my life."

"Didn't we move to New York after Seth died?" Grace asked.

"Yes, I think Dad thought Mom would get better." Nora remembered how their mother spent most of her time on the loveseat, flipping through magazines while the TV hummed in the background. She'd send the girls outside to play in the stretch of backyards until supper, but Nora rarely joined them. Instead she sat on the front steps with her dolls or looked at picture books. She continued to feel her mother's rejection, even after they moved back to Connecticut a year later. And now, decades later, Nora still felt its sting.

"I sympathize with you, Nora, but looking at it through Mom's and Dad's eyes, it must've been tough. It was hard enough when I lost Josh, and became a widow, but I think losing a child would be the hardest thing in the world to go through. It would destroy me if something happened to Eve. No wonder Mom broke down and never really recovered."

Neither have I, thought Nora. It was easier for Grace to forgive their mother for harboring secrets around their brother's death. Secrets and silences that shaped their upbringing, still molding the present. Nora wanted to forgive her mother, but how could she, feeling like her mother's scapegoat? So distant from each other, yet they seemed to share similar ways—often keeping to themselves, private with their thoughts and feelings, both unable to accept death as part of life.

Nora sighed. "I suppose we should take a ride to Connecticut one of these weekends. Maybe that would be a start."

Grace nodded. "Yes, let's do that." Then Grace's eyes brimmed with tears. "We all harbor regrets and live in denial. After I found out Josh fell from the scaffolding, I rushed to the hospital, convinced he'd pull through. But he didn't, and I regretted that we didn't have more time together."

The sisters cried into each other's arms, grieving for Seth and Josh, who had died much too young. As their tears subsided, Nora wanted to lighten the mood with happier thoughts. She suggested they make a toast in Josh's honor. In a shrill voice and with a sharp clink of glasses, she exclaimed, *"Sacré bleu!"* determined to recapture Josh's essence with words he'd often spoken when his spirits were soaring.

Grace's eyes glistened. "God, I haven't heard that in a long time."

Nora could almost see Josh sitting at the kitchen table with his chair tilted back on two legs. He'd slap his hand on his knee as the dust went flying, and he would howl, *"Sacré bleu!"* with all the gusto of Napoleon.

"What does that mean, anyway?" Nora asked.

"I can't believe you're asking after all these years."

"I assume it's a swear word, like *Holy Shit!*" Nora giggled into her wine glass.

"Originally it meant *Holy God.*"

"That's probably what the Virgin Mary said when she found out she was having a baby and hadn't had sex." More giggles and more wine.

Both sisters laughed.

"Maybe you should ask that nun you picked up earlier today."

"I almost forgot about her," Nora said, digging into her purse. She ran upstairs and propped Sister Marguerita against a perfume bottle on her dresser.

"One more for the road," Grace announced when Nora returned.

With raised glasses, they shouted another *Sacré bleu!*

"One more toast," Nora insisted. "To sisterhood. Remember when we were kids and I drew a line across the middle of our bedroom so you wouldn't cross over onto my side? How I drew blood when I scratched you and screamed in your face? I'm sorry I acted like such a jerk."

Grace nodded. "Apology accepted. I recall pinching you to tears."

"You mean the ones that hurt like bee stings?"

Grace landed a pinch on Nora's shoulder.

"Ouch!" she screeched, spilling a big blob of red wine on the couch.

Jumping up to grab a kitchen towel to sop up the wine, Grace said, "I still love you even though we've had our battles."

"I don't know what I'd do without you," said Nora, speaking softly. Bittersweet memories draped over her, as they sometimes did when she drank too much. "If it weren't for you, Angelica would be dead by now."

Grace hugged her sister. "Don't chain yourself to the past, Nora."

"I saw Rosie again, and she told me Angelica's coming back into my life soon. I need to see her."

"And she needs her mother," declared Grace.

Chapter 7

It was almost September—two months since Nora had sent the letter to Angelica. Every time the phone rang, she jumped to answer it, only to be disappointed. The same thing with the mail. Her spirits rose when she heard the mailbox creak open, then fell at finding only bills and ads. Her letter hadn't been returned unopened, though, and that comforted Nora.

Nora went to the school to get the classroom ready for the next batch of students, which helped to take her mind off Angelica. Faced with back-to-school pressures, Nora was nervous that she wouldn't do a good enough job. It was always that way.

The night before opening day, she took an extra sleeping pill. Still, she tossed and turned. The next morning, Nora opened the closet door to grab the outfit she'd chosen, a fitted blue and white polka dot blouse with a navy flared skirt. Instead, her eyes landed on the fish dress. She hadn't worn it in months but hadn't been able to send it on to Spain, either. It had been her secret, hers alone. Inexplicably drawn, she removed it from the satin hanger and slipped it over her head. When she had a minute, Nora would call Thomas and confess she still had the dress but would send it on soon.

She climbed the school steps feeling more confident than she'd felt in years. She smiled and laughed throughout the welcome back breakfast and even hugged some staff she'd worked with for years but had barely said hello to in the past.

"Nora, you're glowing," many of the teachers remarked. "Something's different," one of them said, and Nora beamed.

It didn't end there. At their first staff meeting, Nora reached out and shook the hands of administrators, who seemed surprised at the strength of her grip. Unlike her usual quiet presence, this time she spoke up about education and school issues. The principal listened to her ideas and applauded her proposals. At the end of the meeting, he rushed to Nora's side, shaking his head in disbelief. "How brilliant! I'd like you to join the Planning Committee."

Opening day, even the children seemed mesmerized. With their eyes glued and their attention hanging on her every word, they were like sponges absorbing drops of instruction. "Will you please tell us that story again, Mrs. Jenkins?" It was as if she were performing the leading role in a play, and the audience ate out of her palm. They even started calling her Mrs. Pretty Head.

Nora began to wear the dress outside of school. She stayed far away from Rocky Harbor and the eyes of Mrs. Carver. Strangers stopped Nora on the street.

Some said, "Excuse me, you look stunning in that dress," and others asked, "Haven't I seen you on television?"

Men whistled at her when she walked by, or smiled and said, "Damn, you look hot!"

As if by magic, she transformed into a different person when she wore the dress. Like Cinderella, it enchanted Nora. The dress belonged to her and now she'd shared it with school, with the public, but not yet with her sister. She had to tell Grace.

****

"Collect call from Angelica Jenkins. Will you accept the charges?"

After some clicking noises, a voice squeaked, "Mom?"

Nora shrieked through the receiver as she flounced around the living room.

"Oh, my God, it's really *you*!" Nora caught her breath. "Honey, it's so good to hear your voice! I've missed you terribly. Did you get the letter?"

"Uh-huh," Angelica answered in a tiny voice. "I'm sorry, Mom. This time I promise to stay clean." She started to sob.

Nora longed to reach out and touch her daughter, rock her in her arms, kiss her, and stroke her hair. Eight months seemed like an eternity.

"Baby, I love you. Everything will be okay."

Angelica's sobs shrank to whimpers. "I love you too, Mom."

Nora cupped her daughter's words in her hands and held them to her heart, which clouded with regret at missed opportunities to feed Angelica's emotional needs. Throughout childhood and adolescence, their links were fragile and tenuous, and now no stronger. How could Nora have let her daughter fall so far?

"I'm sorry, darling. Please forgive me for all the mistakes I've made."

"What about the mistakes I've made?"

"Honey, you have your whole life ahead of you."

"My whole life? I'm almost twenty. Mom, can you come?"

"I'll be up this weekend."

Nora thought about their phone call as she stood at the kitchen sink washing dishes. She wanted her upcoming visit with Angelica to be happy and hopeful, instead of filled with heartbreak, mistrust, and doubt. Yet she couldn't stop thinking about the past. When Angelica was almost seventeen, Nora found a pile of DVD cases lying on the living room rug. She picked them up, and a syringe fell out. She shrieked and shook as she scooped up the needle with a paper towel.

Angelica insisted the needle was her friend's, a diabetic. Nora apologized for accusing her, and Angelica stormed out of the house, slamming the door, yelling, "You think I'm a scumbag drug addict!"

Two months later, Nora received an overdraft notice and called the bank and found out her checking account was overdrawn by $2,000. It hit Nora like a detonated bomb: *My daughter is a heroin addict and a thief.* She called a hotline counselor who told her eighty percent of addicts end up dead or in prison within one year of becoming addicted. That was not going to happen to her daughter. Nora confronted Angelica with the evidence. This time she couldn't deny using and agreed to go for sessions at the Addiction Center. At last Nora felt a wave of calm, telling herself that treatment would work. And for a while, it did.

But Nora's suspicion grew when Angelica's habits began to change—little things that in and of themselves meant nothing—but worried Nora. Her daughter started spending long blocks of time in the bathroom. When Nora knocked on the door, Angelica snapped, "God, I can't even take a dump in private."

She was spending more time in the basement. Spoons went missing from the silverware drawer and reappeared in the dishwasher with bent handles.

Nora called the Addiction Center and spoke with Angelica's counselor, telling him she worried her daughter had relapsed. He told her that since Angelica had just turned eighteen, he couldn't share any information and that her daughter would have to go to a program voluntarily, and that in all honesty, she needed more help than they could give her.

Now, with Angelica in prison, it felt as if demons were bombarding Nora with bad memories, threatening to undermine their chances of truly reconciling. How could she look at her daughter without seeing her shadow side? But how much of it had been Nora's shadow side? She wrestled with the child she adored, versus the addict she abhorred, and knew she must face the truth: *She*—a mother in denial until too late—was to blame for Angelica's fractured life.

She ran to her bedroom, flung open the closet door and grabbed the dress. She wrapped it around her trembling body until a wave of calm washed over her. Then the voice. Clear. Warm.

BE STRONG AGAINST THE DEMON OF FEAR.
THOU MUST FORGIVE AND HAVE HOPE.

Maine State Penitentiary for Women was a cold block of buildings in the middle of nowhere, a wasteland surrounded by barbed wire. As Nora waited outside the gate, pleasant thoughts streamed through her, having to do with the dress and the ease with which it had slipped over her head that morning, banishing all traces of negativity. She'd styled her hair in a French braid and applied more makeup than usual, adding eye shadow and mascara that in an instant grew her lashes to full bloom.

Now, standing in a long line of visitors, she studied the motley crew around her: women bursting through polyester pants, chain-smoking men. And there she was, flaunting the fancy fish dress and black patent leather heels because this was a day so special it warranted dressing to the nines.

Inside, they squeezed shoulder to shoulder on seats that lined the wait-ing room walls. When it was her turn to pass through the metal detector, she handed her purse to the grumpy guard who stuffed it in a locker.

"Take your shoes off and step on the machine," he grunted, a minute later ordering her to put them back on and move along.

A guard ushered Nora into a cubicle where she sat alone on the only piece of furniture, a perforated metal bench that faced a glass wall, covered with finger smudges and etchings of *FUCK IT, I LOVE YOU,* and *THIS SUCKS.* Then, she saw a flash of orange on the other side of the glass.

There Angelica stood, her thick black curls draped over bird-wing shoul-ders. Unblemished skin, almost robust again, instead of grey, greasy, and pim-ply, as Nora had last seen it. Angelica's hazel eyes shone bright, unlike the pinpricks Nora remembered. The lunar eclipses that once settled around her eyes were now gone.

Nora couldn't stop looking at her daughter, strikingly beautiful. But how difficult it had been for her when they moved to Rocky Harbor. She looked more black than white, and her schoolmates, most who had only seen pasty-skinned people like themselves, ganged up against Angelica for the color of her skin, killing her confidence. No wonder things had gone so poorly for her.

Nora spread her fingers against the thick window that separated them, and Angelica placed her hands opposite her mother's. The glass turned warm, then hot as if the fish dress were melting the barrier.

Nora wanted more, to wrap her arms around her daughter the way she had when Angelica, then a child, had hidden under her bed covers and screamed, "*I hate myself!*" Over and over, Nora told her daughter she loved her more than anything, and she should love herself. Angelica finally told her mother that the kids in school were mean to her and called her "Chocolate Girl." Nora had had enough of the bullying and demanded the school do something to stop it. It wasn't enough for the guidance counselor to hold a few classes, when much of the ignorance had racist roots well beyond the classroom. It was like putting out a sea of flames with an eye dropper.

Now, with a glass barrier between them, words of comfort would have to suffice. Nora approached the round wire speaker grate, groping for conversa-tion, but at first all that came through were gasps of air.

"Are you okay in there?" Nora uttered, though those weren't the words she wanted to use.

Angelica's eyes shifted. "I'm all right—kind of. Not crazy about my cell-mate, and I hate living in a fishbowl. I can't even use the toilet in peace."

"I'm sorry, I wouldn't like that either. I hope you're sleeping and that the food's decent."

Angelica made a face. "If you like to eat crap."

"I'm sorry, honey."

"Why do you keep apologizing, Mom? It's my own fault I'm locked up."

Nora gave a nervous laugh, not meaning to. It had been easier talking over the phone than gawking through glass.

Her daughter slowly looked up from staring at her knuckles and eyeballed her mother instead of side-glancing.

"I've missed you, Mom, and I love you, otherwise I wouldn't have opened the letter." Her lips quivered as the words crackled through the grate.

Nora searched for words but found none.

"I feel so alone and ashamed, Mom."

"I'm to blame. I wasn't there for you in ways I should've been. I was a nervous wreck all the time, never knowing when your stepfather would blow up. And I worked too much, when I wanted to spend time with you instead, but I couldn't count on him to help support us. I'll never forget you asking, 'How come when you're with me, you're not really with me?' It broke my heart because you were right."

Through the glass, Angelica sat like a statue, her eyes vacant. Nora wondered what her daughter was thinking. There had been many grueling times, so many bad memories. Nora's throat turned dry and prickly.

"Honey, I'm sorry I didn't do better."

Angelica stayed silent, her eyes pointing downward, her head in her hands. The visit wasn't going the way Nora had hoped.

The speaker gave a harsh blast. "Five minutes."

Angelica looked like a waning rose petal about to fall from its blossom. There were tears in her eyes. She looked so weary for her young age. Nora wished she could restore her daughter to innocence and wholeness, shield her from fears and regrets, and instill her with hope.

"You're more lovely than ever," Nora said to lift Angelica's spirits.

Angelica managed a weak smile. "In this bright orange monkey suit? Speaking of clothes, what are you wearing, Mom?"

Nora stroked the sleeves of the fish dress. "Just something I picked up." She looked at her daughter and said, "If it's okay, I'd like to come back next weekend."

Angelica's smile even reached her eyes. "Sure." She kissed her fingers and pressed them to the glass, like her mother had done earlier. Nora reciprocated and gave a wobbly smile as her daughter turned around, vanishing through the doorway.

Nora lingered in the visitor's cubicle, hoping to catch another glimpse.

WELL DONE, MY DEAR, LIVING THY TRUTH.

"Tell me how to help her," Nora whispered, a tear escaping and dripping down her cheek.

SHOW THY STRENGTH, AND SHE WILL FOLLOW.

Now, driving back, the earlier buoyancy of the dress transformed into something ponderous as more negative thoughts flooded Nora's mind. All the signs of Angelica's addiction she had missed. The years she had put up with Jim, hiding at work, leaving Angelica to weather the man's moods on her own. The fights. The tension. The failures. So many failures. But the voice wouldn't hear anymore:

LET GO OF WHAT NO LONGER SERVES THEE.

By the time she reached home, the dress felt airy and light again, and Nora's spirits soared at having seen Angelica for the first time in eight months. She called Grace to go for a walk downtown and was still in the fish dress when her sister arrived.

"Did you wear that rag to see Angelica?" Grace asked.

"Yes, and I'm going to wear it downtown," Nora replied. "You don't like it?"

Grace chuckled. "If I were a mermaid, maybe. What are those bones and crap?"

"Not sure, but I know one thing—it's changing my life, mostly for the good."

"I suppose you got it from your psychic."

Nora shook her head. "It came from Mrs. Carver." Nora pressed a finger to her lips. "Shh."

Grace rolled her eyes. "If it came from her, it's got to be weird. How did you end up with it?"

"You know, the stuff Thomas brings us." Nora wanted to add, *and that you used to get before you left him.*

Grace made a face. "It's almost dark so at least no one will see it."

On their way downtown, Nora talked about her visit with Angelica. "I'm going back next weekend."

"That's great," exclaimed Grace. "I'd love to see her, but I'll wait until you two have had more time together."

"Yes, maybe when Eve's home, the three of us will go."

"Eve would love that," Grace said.

After passing the fudge and taffy factory, with its goo no longer churning in the window, they passed by downtown's ritziest restaurants, now ghost quiet. During tourist season, college-bound waiters ushered wealthy tourists to linen-covered tables, while Caribbean natives prepped salads and rattled dishes in back kitchens.

They walked by the "Bar-mu-da" Triangle. The Wharf. The Gull. And the Buoy, epicenter of summer nightlife that had earned the nickname for engulfing thirsty patrons and not releasing them until after closing. Now the structures sat silent, kitty-corner on elephantine algae-encased pilings, awaiting next season's influx of the Navy, when jaunty-capped sailors would rush the docks like shoppers at a Filene's basement sale.

Nora found the stillness therapeutic, it reminded her of the ocean's ebb.

As they neared the footbridge, Grace said, "I hope Cliff will be back in business next season."

"You'd eat his hot dogs after what the *Register* wrote?"

Grace replied, "I like the guy. He's a Rocky Harbor tradition, and besides, nobody's ever died from his food."

Nora pictured eighty-five-year-old Cliff standing with his cart in the middle of downtown, dressed in black-and-white checked chef pants covered with mustard and ketchup stains.

"Have you ever looked in the barrel on his cart?" Grace asked.

"Should I?"

"There's a sign on the cover." Grace started to laugh. "*Biggest Crab in the World!*"

"What's so funny about that?"

"When you lift the lid and look inside, you see yourself in a huge mirror." Nora chuckled.

"He's a riot. Tells the funniest jokes. One time he asked me, 'Did you hear they won't have the footbridge any longer?' and I answered, 'No, really? Then he said, 'Yeah, it's long enough.'"

"That's hilarious," Nora said, rolling her eyes.

Grace stopped suddenly and pointed toward two silhouettes huddled in the dark at the other end of the footbridge. "Who's that?"

"Can't tell from here," Nora said.

As they moved closer, the strangers called out, "Can you help us?"

The two women stood under a lamp light, which allowed Nora a better look. They reminded her of gypsies, with their long billowy skirts and tasseled shawls. One was tall with thick black braids piled on top of her head, and the other was short with red hair. Their jewelry glittered.

"Do you know where the Crow's Nest B&B is?" the taller one asked in broken English, her accent heavy.

"It's closed for the season," Nora answered. "The motel on 78 is open, a mile up the road. She raised her arm and pointed in the direction they should go.

The strangers gushed in a foreign dialect as they reached out and stroked the sleeve of Nora's dress, which made her skin crawl.

"Where did you get this?" the shorter one asked.

The taller woman held out her hand and waved a fancy ruby-looking ring in Nora's face. "You like? You want to trade for dress?"

Grace stepped between her sister and the foreigners. "We've got to run along now. Good luck."

The gypsies drifted off, their heels clicking on the bridge's wooden slats, their voices muffled and growing fainter as they disappeared into the night.

"Maybe there's a gypsy convention in town," Grace speculated.

"What language was that?" Nora asked.

"Something Eastern European, I imagine. I wonder what they were saying."

"I caught a couple words—Marguerita—Sacromonte, whatever that means."

"Isn't Marguerita the name of the nun you bought at the yard sale?" Grace asked.

"The picture? You're right. How odd."

"Those gypsies had their hearts set on that dress. I didn't like their vibes. I warned you to watch it with Mrs. Carver. The whole thing is bizarre."

"Might be time to meet with Rosie again," Nora said.

Chapter 8

Nora was working at home when the phone rang.

"What're you doing?"

"Lesson plans."

"On a Friday night?"

"Thomas, you know I don't lead an exciting life."

He laughed. "Katrina and I are at the Ark. How about joining us for a glass of wine?"

"Sure," replied Nora, surprising herself.

"Katrina wants you to bring someone."

"Who?"

"The nun."

Now Katrina was on the phone. "The picture of the nun you bought at the yard sale."

"Why?"

"I'll tell you when you get here. Just bring her."

"I'll be down in a few minutes."

Nora took the fifteen-minute walk along the harbor to the East Side, glad to breathe the crisp fall air. She wondered why Katrina wanted the nun picture so badly. The closer she got to The Ark, the more nervous she felt about having to walk alone into a crowded Friday night bar and restaurant scene. She took several deep breaths, convincing herself how much she liked the feel of the Ark, with its rich history of being built by a ship's sea captain in 1861 and showing all the signs of his sea legs.

On her way inside she paused to look up at the Coast Guard oar, signed and dated 1861, hanging above the door. The bar was right inside the door, and she spotted Katrina and Thomas sitting on captain stools. They had saved her a seat between them, where a glass of red wine held the spot.

"Thanks, guys," she said, looking up at the antique whale harpoon above the bar.

"It's about time you got here," Thomas said.

"Did you bring her?" Katrina asked.

"Here," Nora said, propping the nun against Katrina's glass. "What's this about?"

The corners of Katrina's lips turned upward. "It's my Catholic upbringing—confession time. I feel guilty dating a married man, but I can't stop seeing him because I'm crazy about him. And he's rich."

Nora pointed to Sister Marguerita. "Tell *her*, not me.

Katrina scooped up the picture, turned her back to Thomas and Nora, and spoke in a low voice. When she was done, she placed the nun back on the bar and thanked Nora.

"I feel so much better now," she said, fanning herself with a Shipyard Brewing coaster.

"You're a nut," Nora said.

Thomas grabbed the picture. "It's too late anyway. You're already going to Hell. No way is she a nun. See that smirk and those sneaky eyes? That's the face of someone who's hiding something, not a holy woman."

Katrina snatched the picture back. "I see forgiveness and peace in her eyes. What do you think, Nora?"

"Definitely a Bride of Christ."

Thomas stood up. "Now that I don't smoke anymore, I'm going outside for a puff of fresh air. I'll be back when confession's over." He headed toward the door, and Nora slipped the picture back in her bag.

"Don't mention Grace in front of him, or he'll cry in his beer," Katrina said. She dabbed her eyes with a napkin and made boohoo noises.

"He needs to cheer up," agreed Nora. "He didn't even hold his annual cookout this summer."

Katrina sighed. "He's so kind-hearted, even inviting the barflies to his parties."

Nora smiled. "Remember last year when a drunk passed out in the doghouse?"

"Yes, with his dog still in it," Katrina said, slapping the bar with her hand as she howled.

"He guzzled his way through his parties with a vodka tonic and lime in one hand, and a Marlboro in the other—that was before he quit smoking. He shuffled around like a silver-haired energizer bunny."

Katrina stood up and imitated Thomas, circling around the bar. "Isn't this fun?" Returning to her stool, she added, "And each year it's a new cooking tool. Last year it was a rotisserie grill."

"With a side skillet and an oven attachment. He always has to have the best."

Katrina nodded. "The Carvers have rubbed off on him."

"Speaking of the Carvers, you should see the dress I found in Mrs. C's castoffs." Nora bit her lip and looked toward the door through which Thomas had disappeared.

"Is it a straitjacket?" Katrina leaned in conspiratorially.

"No, it's black and white with weird fish bones and tribal symbols."

"You should've worn it tonight."

"Thomas would've killed me. He thinks I sent it to Spain, where Mrs. Carver wanted it to go. I've got to tell him I still have it. He could lose his job if she finds out."

"Why?"

"It's a long story." Nora couldn't stop herself from describing the dress and telling Katrina how it both enhanced her mood and depressed her, but mostly it was positive. She tried to explain the symbols on the dress and their ties to Christianity, Pagan fertility, and sexuality."

Katrina asked, "Can I borrow it? I could use more sex."

"I doubt that," Nora said. She went on to tell the tale of the fish that swallowed the penis of Osiris, and Katrina grabbed a napkin and drew a lewd sketch.

When Thomas returned, Katrina said, "Did you know Nora's been walking around in a dress with a fish on it that's swallowing a penis?"

He gave a blank look. "What the hell are you talking about?"

"The dress from Mrs. Carver."

He raised a finger to his mouth and shushed her, looking like his eyeballs might burst. Then he glared at Nora. "What the hell is going on? I thought you sent that to Spain."

Nora winced. "I've been meaning to tell you. I promise I'll send it. Just give me a little more time with it."

Thomas grunted. "Whatever you do, don't wear it anywhere near Rocky Harbor."

"Don't worry, I won't tell anyone," Katrina said. "Rosie Deerborn told Nora what the symbols mean."

"Who the hell is Rosie Deerborn?"

"Nora's new psychic."

Nora glared at Katrina, wanting to hook her with the whale harpoon.

"Not another word about a psychic *or* the dress," Thomas ordered. "Let's have another round. Wait till I tell you what happened to me today. No wonder I drink. Mrs. Carver insisted on getting behind the wheel of the Mercedes. Her husband tried to stop her, and when he couldn't, he begged me to."

"What did you do?" asked Nora.

"What power do I have over an obstinate pill-popping blue-blood red-hat who's determined to do whatever she damn well pleases? She thinks she's a spring chicken. I got in the passenger seat and went with her." Thomas took a long drink from his pint, finishing the beer. "All the way from the tip of West-gate Island, through the center of town. By some miracle, we survived, and so did everyone else. She almost flattened a pedestrian. I tell you, drinking is my therapy from this job."

As Nora listened, she raised her long-stemmed crystal wine goblet with both hands, adoring the way the bartender filled its oversized bowl to the rim. Raising it to her lips, she inhaled strong smells of violet, black currant, oak, pepper, and earth. The wine tasted fleshy yet noble. She savored its flavor with the ritual swishing of each sip in the folds of her mouth before surrendering it to her throat. She rubbed her hand across the smooth wood of the bar, made from an old dory that had sailed the waters of Rocky Harbor. Was she enjoying the fruits of Dionysus too much?

"Anything new, Nora?" Thomas asked, reeling her thoughts back into the room.

"Angelica called, and I visited her," she exclaimed.

"That's great!" said Thomas, and Katrina hugged her.

"I'm going back this weekend."

"You're there for her now," said Thomas, "Your daughter's lucky."

Nora looked away, not sure "lucky" was the way she and Angelica would describe their reconciliation.

"Let's celebrate," he said in a cheerful voice. "Dinner, my treat."

Katrina gave Thomas a cutesy smile, and they all moved to the dining room. A tall young waiter strolled over to their table, his shirt tails untucked and his hair settling over his left eye. He grinned at them and then back at Katrina.

"Hi, I'm Peter. We're offering a special tonight—whole Mediterranean fish with aged sherry-tarragon vinaigrette."

Katrina looked at the young man with glassy eyes and a dimpled smile, as if she'd just chosen her next conquest.

"Excuse me, Peter, is this the fish that's served with a penis in its mouth?" Her voice sounded serious and helplessly feminine. She held up the lewd dia-grammed napkin for the waiter to see.

Nora couldn't believe it, coughed, snorted, and managed a spit-take, spat-tering red wine all over the white linen tablecloth.

The waiter shook the hair away from his eye to catch a closer look. "No, we're fresh out of that variety. I'll see what I can do later." Then he winked.

"Oh, my God, now I've seen everything," Thomas snapped, grabbing the napkin out of Katrina's hand.

After studying the menu, everyone chose fresh lobster. Nora watched Katrina's eyes track Peter's movement around the dining room. She flirted throughout the meal with requests for oysters, more lemon, and extra butter. He even helped her put on her lobster bib.

Over Thomas's objection, Nora brought up the fish dress one more time during dinner. "Katrina needs to hear that the symbols aren't just about sex—"

"I resent that. Do you think I'm obsessed with sex? Wait, don't answer that."

"They also have to do with reincarnation and the life force," Nora said.

Thomas rolled his eyes. "I should've known. Next you'll be telling us that Sister Marguerita wore the damn dress."

Nora smiled at Thomas. "I hadn't considered that."

"Good God, what have I done?" he asked, swiping his forehead with the palm of his hand.

During the rest of dinner, the dress floated back and forth through Nora's mind. She kept to herself what she was thinking, that perhaps there was a sliver of truth to what Thomas suggested.

"Time for a nightcap," he announced after paying the bill.

They followed the sound of a guitar and vocals coming from the bar. Nora heard a familiar song, *You Were Always on My Mind*. She froze in the doorway. "My God, it's *him*!"

"Who?" Katrina asked.

"*HI I'M KIRK*. The napkin guy." The last half she hissed, ducking her head into Katrina's shoulder and turning to leave.

"At the Lobster Claw, right? Grace told me. Come on; let's find a seat."

Nora felt a nudge from behind and moved to a table in the corner, where the lights were dim. Hopefully *HI I'M KIRK* wouldn't recognize her in the crowd. Thomas ordered a round of drinks. Nora welcomed another wine to clutch as she dared to look.

He looked so masculine in faded jeans and a plaid flannel shirt. Straddling a bar stool onstage, he held an electric guitar in his arms. She watched his fingers glide across the strings and heard him sing with a tenderness that surprised her. If only she could feel as much at ease as he seemed to. For a moment, under the spotlight, Kirk looked in her direction. She quickly looked away, hoping he hadn't seen her.

Slurring her words, Katrina said, "God, he's hot. If you don't talk to him on his break, I will. Wait a minute, I'm supposed to hook up with the waiter. What's his name?"

"Peter?" Nora asked.

When Kirk announced he was taking a short break, Katrina asked Thomas to go outside for some air. Nora stood up.

"You're staying here," Katrina insisted. "He's headed this way."

Nora cringed and sat back down.

"Hello, there. I thought I recognized you. Do you remember me?"

"The Lobster Claw, right?" she answered, trembling. "*HI I'M KIRK.*" The nickname she'd given him tumbled out of her wine-warmed lips.

The lighting was dim, but she saw him smile. "No, I'm Kirk. And you are?"

"I like your music."

"You're very kind. Mind if I sit for a minute?"

Nora waved at the chair. "Nora," she said.

"The chair is named Nora? Or that's you?" Kirk grinned and Nora laughed, too.

He sat down across from her and cleared his throat. "First, I apologize for coming on so strong at the Lobster Claw. I've never done that before." He gave a nervous laugh.

"Apology accepted," Nora replied, focusing on her wine glass between them.

Kirk cleared his throat again. "Nora's a pretty name. So. Um. Now that we've officially met, maybe I can take you to lunch sometime?" He leaned across the table, his face closer to Nora's, and she knew she was blushing. "Maybe next Saturday?"

Nora hesitated. "Maybe."

"I'm being pushy again." He sat back, putting some space between them.

Nora lifted the wine glass to her lips and took a sip. "No, you're fine. I'm a little nervous. You're a little gorgeous."

Kirk smiled that beautiful grin. "Believe it or not, I am, too. Nervous, that is."

"And gorgeous," Nora said again. At that moment, Nora did not know what to believe. Was the dress, tucked deep in her closet, making her bolder even if she wasn't wearing it?

Kirk stood up. "I've got to get back onstage. Do you still have my number?"

"I left it there," she said, feeling her cheeks blush. "But I didn't forget you. I hoped we would. You know." Then she flushed again. Had she just suggested they … what? exactly?

"Meet again?"

Nora nodded.

Kirk asked a passing waiter for a pen and wrote his first name and phone number on a coaster. Nora took the pen, wrote, "HI, I'M" in front of "KIRK" and then smiled up at him.

"You're funny, Nora. I'll see you after the next set." He winked and gave a little wave.

She watched him walk onstage and pick up his guitar. Nora's hand shook when she placed the coaster in her purse alongside Sister Marguerita. Then Thomas and Katrina were back.

"Did you talk to him?" Katrina asked.

"I feel like I'm in a daze. He invited me to lunch next Saturday, but I doubt I'll go."

Katrina reached for the purse and pulled out the Sister Marguerita picture, pressing it to her ear before holding it out facing Nora. "She orders you to accept his invitation."

"Give me that." Nora snatched the frame and stuffed it back in her purse.

"This next song is by one of my favorite artists, Eric Clapton, *Wonderful Tonight*." This time, Kirk's voice sounded strong and deep, sending chills through Nora's body. Seconds later, Nora couldn't believe her ears. "I'd like to dedicate it to a lovely lady in the audience."

"Ooh-la-la!" Katrina burst out.

Nora felt the eyes of the bar upon her and wanted to disappear—until he sang about the love light in her eyes. When the song ended, she told Katrina and Thomas she was leaving.

"I've got to be up early to visit Angelica."

"Have fun tomorrow," Thomas said. "Need a ride home?"

"No, I want to walk. Thanks for dinner and drinks, and your company. If Kirk comes over, tell him I had to leave."

Nora slipped out of the Ark and into October's cool air. After seeing Kirk again, she felt as if she were coming alive. But self-doubt was creeping in, and the thought of a romantic renaissance terrorized her. Should she trust her feelings? Would she overcome her fears? Did she deserve to be happy?

Nora took the long way home across the footbridge. The boats rocked like metronomes keeping time with the low wail of foghorns, while waves tapped at wooden pier posts. She stared at the full harvest moon, wishing that answers to her questions would appear across the night sky.

As soon as Nora got home, she collapsed on her bed. She heard a rustling sound and turned toward the wall.

FEELING SORRY FOR THYSELF?

She was in no mood to hear from the dress. "Leave me alone."

I OFFER HELP. HAST THOU FORGOTTEN THAT SELF-WORTH COMES FROM WITHIN?

"I have no self-worth."

THOU HAST CLOGGED THE HEART WITH SHAME, GUILT, AND FAILURES OF THE PAST WHICH MUST BE INCINERATED TO REVEAL THY TRUE WORTH. A PAINFUL BUT NECESSARY PROCESS.

"It's too late," Nora said, her voice dwindling. "I've fallen too far from goodness."

FORGET NOT THAT GOD'S MERCIES ARE NEW EVERY MORNING.

Chapter 9

The last thing Nora remembered was walking home from the Ark and collapsing under her covers, wishing she could disappear. The next morning, she awoke feeling refreshed and ready to take on the new day. She sat straight up in bed and swung her legs over the side, stretching her arms overhead. She was convinced that something cathartic had happened while she slept. Today her mood shone bright as the sunlight beaming through her bedroom window.

After coffee and a shower, she ruffled through her closet for something to wear to the prison. It wouldn't be the fish dress because Angelica would probably ask more questions about it. Instead, she wore a pair of raggedy jeans, a turtleneck, and worn sneakers.

Nora paced back and forth in the visitors' booth, which felt cold and barren until Angelica appeared, grinning and waving on the other side of the glass. Nora sat on the metal bench and leaned into the speaker grate. "I missed you, honey."

"I missed you too, Mom."

"How are you? Keeping busy?" Nora asked.

"I'm okay. We have jobs to do, like cooking, cleaning, and working in the laundry. I mostly keep to myself. Otherwise I'd probably get into trouble."

"Like what kind of trouble?" Nora asked, trying not to put her daughter on the defensive.

"Like fighting. I can't stand most of the women here with their attitudes."

Nora sighed. "I'm sure prison's hard but try not to let your emotions get the better of you." Nora knew Angelica could act like a storm.

"So, what's new in Rocky Harbor?" Angelica asked.

"It's pretty quiet in town now," Nora said, relieved that Angelica had changed the topic.

"It's that time of year," Angelica remarked, with a faraway look in her eyes.

"What're you thinking?" her mother asked.

"How I missed the whole summer."

"You didn't miss much," Nora said, only half-truthful, remembering their moonlight walks at Ocean Point and midnight visits to the only sandy beach in town. How, in their younger days, Nora, her daughter, Grace, and Eve dragged their bare feet through the damp, cool sand and collected driftwood to carve glowing paths of phosphorescence. Those days were gone, and it made Nora sad.

"You probably don't know that Eve has been in China since February. She teaches at an American School."

Angelica's eyes lowered, and her head drooped.

"She's coming home for Thanksgiving and Christmas and wants to see you."

Angelica looked up, and Nora could almost feel the lump in her daughter's throat as she struggled to say, "I'm going to write her a letter."

At the end of their visit, Angelica and her mother again pressed their fingertips together against the glass.

****

Whether it was Grace who convinced Nora to call Kirk, the influence of the fish dress, or a few glasses of wine, Nora couldn't say. Chills ran up her spine when he answered the phone, his voice deep and sexy. She was relieved that he sounded excited to hear from her. She thought she heard Hendrix playing in the background and told him she was a Hendrix fan.

"That's not him," he said. "It's me riffing on my electric guitar."

Nora melted.

Kirk told her he worked at Miracle Ear in Rocky Harbor, and that when he saw her in the Lobster Claw, he'd just been transferred from Portland, which meant he lived about an hour away. He mentioned his dogs, two Rottweilers named Chiller and Mondo. "They're huge but they're wusses." Nora told him about Margo. She learned he had two daughters and Nora told him she had one. Nora agreed to meet for lunch on Saturday at noon in front of the Golden Pagoda, a few doors from Kirk's workplace.

On the morning of their date, she chose a long-sleeved tunic embroidered at the V-neckline, black velveteen pants, and red ballet slipper flats. She draped a fringed shawl around her shoulders. She wanted to wear the fish dress but didn't dare risk being seen by either Thomas or Mrs. Carver.

Nora arrived at the parking lot a few minutes early and sat in the car, thinking about their phone conversation. A few minutes later, she saw Kirk walking toward the restaurant. He wore jeans, a brown leather jacket over his shirt, and penny loafers without socks, she guessed. With his aviator shades, Kirk looked even more handsome than she remembered.

Nora slowly emerged from her car. The closer she got, the more frentic the butterflies inside her swirled.

"Hi, Nora, it's good to see you," he greeted her. "Thanks for coming."

She looked at him and smiled. Like the rudder of a ship, his strong hand on the small of her back guided her through the entrance of the Golden Pagoda. No aquarium in the alcove, but a four-foot cloth fish with bells hung in the doorway, its tail jangling.

Inside, red and gold paper lanterns swayed from the ceiling. Nora gawked at the giant Chinese dragon on the wall. Low lighting cast a warm, soft glow over the dining room. A wrinkled Asian gentleman seated them at a booth in the back.

"Enjoy your meal," he said, stepping away before they could thank him.

In an awkward silence, Nora fumbled with her shawl. She ran her hand along the booth's bamboo stalks, smooth and contoured, simple like the lines of the fish dress. Ah, yes, the fish dress. Didn't Rosie say it was in her life to bring her true love? Suddenly her imagination went wild. She pictured drapes that could be drawn for privacy. Cushions that felt more like mattresses. What was the dress doing?

Kirk opened the menu, so Nora did the same. "Did you ever get your lobster roll?"

"Oh, yes, and it was delicious. I should've asked if you like Chinese food."

"I eat most anything except raw fish."

Nora stared at the menu—Moo Goo Gai Pan, Crab Meat Chop Suey, Moo Shu Pork, General Tso's Shrimp—but she had a hard time focusing. Was she imagining her attraction to this man, and his to her? She tried to turn her attention back to the menu, but seconds later she pictured Kirk's lips on hers. The fantasy had the same rosy glow of the pillow image from moments before. She suspected both were the work of the dress.

The waiter delivered a steaming pot of tea, then stood by the booth with pen and pad in hand. Pointing to the menu, Kirk said, "We'll have this, this, and that, and two orders of spring rolls, thank you." The waiter retreated and Kirk turned his attention to Nora.

"You really have beautiful hair."

Never able to accept a compliment, she started to apologize for her split ends, but then ran her fingers through her hair and gave it a light toss as she looked into his eyes.

"Thank you."

"I didn't expect to hear from you after Friday, the way you disappeared."

Just then, the miso soup arrived, giving Nora time to compose herself.

"I told you, I'm shy. I don't date much."

Kirk nodded. "I'm new to this dating thing, too." Frowning, he added, "I lost my wife three years ago to cancer."

"I'm sorry." She looked away, not knowing what to say next. Her eyes landed on a wall-hanging of a wood block print of a young lady seated at a vanity, beautifying herself before a mirror. Ruby lips like petals, black-lined eyelids, and tiny new moon brows on ivory skin. Puffed up ebony hair, strands held in place by a pair of jeweled sticks. The lady's neck, a spindle extending up from her silk tapestry robe. In her hands, a fan, its folds spread to show a handsome peacock, feathers unfurled. The studied naiveté of a courtesan.

"So, tell me about you, Nora."

She didn't have the right words to tell her story and why she was single, and she was frustrated she even felt the need to have to explain. She didn't know how to describe her past, how even though she felt used by most of the men she chose to get involved with, she'd stayed, come back for more, let them repeatedly use her body and fill her mind with ugliness. About her first husband, and about her bad marriage to her second.

Kirk sensed her frustration. "Did I say something to offend you?"

"Not really," she replied, silently comparing Kirk with her sister, for Grace's belief that a woman can't survive without a man by her side. "You're wondering why I don't have a boyfriend or a husband?"

"Could be," he smiled.

"Actually, I was happily married to my daughter's father, but he died in a freak accident before she was born.

"So, we share that agony. I'm sorry you lost your husband."

"My second marriage was a disaster."

"If you don't mind my asking, why was it so bad?"

Nora drew her shawl tight around her shoulders.

At that moment, the main course arrived. Nora felt spared from having to explain herself, and Kirk turned his attention to the food on the table. They shared their dishes. Kirk handled his chopsticks easily, while Nora dropped half her food on the tablecloth. The old Nora would have felt like crawling under the table, yet this time she laughed, put her chopsticks down and picked up the fork.

"What do you do at Miracle Ear?" she asked.

"I'm an audiologist. You want the textbook definition?"

"Sure."

"I test, diagnose, treat, and manage hearing loss," he smiled. "And you?"

"I'm a schoolteacher, and during the summer I help manage a bed-and-breakfast."

He pulled out his wallet. "These are my kids. That's Paulette, the older one. She's twenty-two and an accountant with Barkley Bank in Portland. Here's the younger one, Lizzy. She's a sophomore at Lesley University, studying to be a Special Ed teacher. How about your daughter?"

Nora rubbed her neck. "My daughter's name is Angelica and she's almost twenty. She's smart but taking a break from college."

"I didn't go right out of high school either. What's she doing?"

Nora wanted to sink into the floor. Her eyes turned watery, and her lips began to quiver.

He reached for her hand and held it as if it were a china teacup. "I'm sorry if I upset you, Nora. You don't have to tell me."

"My daughter's in prison for drug possession and sale of narcotics. She's a heroin addict."

Nora expected him to gasp but he didn't. "God, you're living a parent's worst nightmare, and I can't imagine what your daughter's been through." He stood up from his seat and moved to Nora's side, draping his left arm over the back of the booth.

"Thank you for understanding," she whispered, resting her head on his shoulder. For the first time, she didn't feel the need to fill the silence with conversation.

"Have you ever been to Misty Island?" Kirk asked.

"I've heard of it, but I've never been there."

"It's off the coast of Portland. I have a cottage out there. I was lucky to buy it at the right price twenty years ago. It's a perfect place to visit at this time of year, the weather's crisp and the crowd thins out." He moved his face closer to Nora's. "I'd love to take you there."

Nora rubbed her hands together, not sure about accepting such an invitation so soon. But then a second thought took over—something the dress had said—*BE STRONG AGAINST THE DEMON OF FEAR.*

"I'd love to go," she said, hiding any doubt.

The owner came over and placed a small tray containing the bill and two fortune cookies. "I hope you had good meal, and may you have good fortune." The lines of his face resembled a roadmap to wisdom.

"Thank you." They nodded their heads in his direction.

"You first," Kirk insisted, offering Nora the cookies and picking up the bill. "Did you know China stole the idea of fortune cookies from Japan and brought it to the U.S?"

"How do we know the Japanese didn't steal it from the Chinese?" Nora laughed.

"I did the research. Americans credited China because at the time they were our allies, and Japan was the enemy."

"So, it's all about politics?"

"The way of the world." Kirk raised his eyebrows. "What does your fortune say?"

She opened the slip of paper. *"Fortune favors the brave. Be steady and strong with your emotions."*

"In bed," Kirk quipped.

Nora's jaw dropped. "What?"

"You've never heard that?"

"Heard what?"

"You're supposed to say, 'in bed' at the end of every fortune."

Nora's body tingled. "But I wasn't finished. *And be certain in your choices.*"

"In bed."

Nora felt herself blush.

Kirk cracked open his cookie. "Wow, two fortunes. Double luck." He cleared his throat. *"Thorns protect a rose, but withhold them from your lover..."*

"In bed," Nora said, chuckling. "What about the second one?"

"Be gentle, fiercely defending what you believe is right..."

"In bed," Nora repeated, quite enjoying herself.

"Especially in bed," Kirk added.

She felt his hand on her thigh. Did the dress, now tucked in her closet, have the power to provoke sensual pleasure?

"I'm sorry, I can't resist," he said. "Excuse me, I'm going to the men's room. Be right back."

As Nora watched him walk away, the "in bed" phrase bubbled inside her, awakening her curiosity and arousing her libido. She wondered just what he might be like in bed while considering the dress's influence on her questionable behavior. She scooped up Kirk's fortunes, folding them together with hers, and carefully placed them deep in her purse.

They held hands as they left the restaurant and strolled to her car. Their lips brushed with the promise of meeting again, and she gave him her phone number. With his eyes on her, he walked backward toward his office, waving the entire time.

"I don't even know your last name," Nora called out.

"Kloppenheimer!" he shouted.

Nora laughed to herself. She couldn't wait to tell Grace, knowing her sister would appreciate a name that sounded like a brand of thick-soled shoes.

Chapter 10

Nora felt like she was floating on air when she reached home. She'd meant to call Rosie earlier about the strange encounter with the gypsy women, but time had gotten away from her. She took out the card from her wallet.

"Hi, Nora. It's good to hear from you."

"I need to see you." Nora shared the mysterious run-in she and Grace had with the gypsies.

"Come over now and wear the dress."

The gypsies had left her feeling leery about wearing it. How could she feel so elated one minute and miserable the next? She approached the closet with halting steps and trembling hands, then reached in with her eyes closed and grabbed the dress. As soon as she slid it over her head, strength pulsed through her body. She felt like she was wearing a suit of armor.

A delicate whisper brushed against her ear. *HERMANA MARGUERITA.* Nora grabbed the small framed picture off the bureau and slipped it into the dress's side pocket.

Rosie greeted Nora in a bright orange muumuu intertwined with pink blossoms and white roses. By now, Nora was accustomed to the routine of heading into the parlor, clearing their energy fields, and paying homage to the guides.

"Before we start," Nora said, "I have some great news: my daughter and I have reconciled!"

Rosie clasped her hands together. "How marvelous!"

"I know we have a long way to go, but it's a start," Nora said, grinning.

"And now the guides want to know how you're doing with your relationship lesson."

Nora blushed. "I met a nice man—it's all happening so fast my head's spinning."

Rosie laughed. "That's because you're in Divine Time."

"What's that?"

"It's the way things move when you're aligned with the Universe and tapped into your intuition. You must act, otherwise you're sending the message you don't believe it will happen. Very different from ordinary time, when we plod through life counting seconds, minutes, hours, days, and years, doubting ourselves and fearing our futures."

"I *think* I'm ready for a relationship," said Nora.

Rosie tilted her head to the side and nodded. "Our guides say these developments are fine but prepare for obstacles."

Nora frowned.

Rosie waved the guides off, casting a solemn look in the distance. "I must be honest with you, Nora. We come into this life alone, and we must leave our legacies behind for others." She looked at Nora with tender eyes. "Let's move on. What's happening with the dress?"

Nora related the unpleasant run-in she and Grace had with the gypsies, who obsessed over the dress and tried to trade it for a ring. "We can't figure out why they were so insistent. It was creepy, and I'm not that comfortable wearing it now."

"Are you sure they were gypsies?"

Nora nodded. "With the clothes they wore, and their heavy accents? I'm positive. They talked in a foreign language, but I only caught a couple words. Sacromonte. Marguerita."

"I can tell you about the Sacromontes. By the way, they are gypsies but more respectfully, you should call them Romanies, or Roma.

"Who *are* they?"

"A tribe that originally came from India and settled in the mountains of Spain. They've been there for centuries, and many still live in caves near Granada. The women you met might be descendants."

"Why would they want the dress?"

"My dear, the key to the dress and the answer to your questions can best be found by taking a past life journey."

Nora glanced at the certificates on the wall. "Where are we going with this? Past life regression?"

Rosie nodded.

"I've never done it before, and I'm not sure I want to."

"It might save lifetimes."

She's trying to hook me, Nora thought. *If she were a true psychic, she'd also tell me more about the picture of the nun in my pocket.*

As if Rosie were reading Nora's mind, she said, "In your previous life, you were part of a religious order whose members took a vow of silence. The vow was huge, and you made it in a solemn and devotional way."

Nora's jaw dropped. "Me, a nun?"

Rosie pointed to the dress. "Well, yeessss, black-and-white dress? Habit, convent? Fish symbols, Christ figure? You could help others, but you couldn't speak. Silence allowed you to observe and reflect. The problem is that the vow of silence is still in your energy field."

Nora heard a sudden buzzing and felt a strong vibration coming from inside the dress. Rosie stared at the pocket. Nora pulled out the picture of the nun, squirming as she handed it over. "I was going to show you."

Rosie's eyes narrowed as she read aloud, "Hermana Marguerita DeRoche de la Iglesia, circa 1865."

Made mute by questions she wanted Rosie to answer, Nora wondered if she, herself, was Sister Marguerita in her previous life. Were the nun and the Romani people connected, and what about the fish dress?

And now Rosie was spewing words about Nora's soul's purpose this lifetime being quite the opposite of last lifetime.

Nora swallowed hard. "Soul's purpose?"

Rosie touched Nora's throat, turning it hot with her hand. "Fifth chakra, your soul's purpose in this lifetime. It's about creativity and communication, expressing what you know, feeling entitled to say what you believe. To speak out about what you're questioning most, to write songs and sing them, to write books, and encourage others to be in touch with their voices."

Nora's eyes glazed over.

Rosie continued. "Let's talk about it in terms of colors. You soul's purpose is green light, and you have this leftover vow in your energy field that's a red light. You go here and slam the brakes, then over there, and the brakes go on again." The chair rocked from side to side, and for a moment Nora worried that Rosie would topple over. "Sound is your service and keeps you grounded in this lifetime. Silence was your service last lifetime. Do you see how it's all switched around?"

Nora's insides churned. "No wonder I feel so screwed up. My life has been one big letdown after another, and most of the time I've sabotaged myself." She remembered her passion for writing in sixth grade when she won the short story contest for *Maya the Cat Girl*. The teacher shook her hand and presented her with a box overflowing with large black-and-white photos of scenes from movies and TV shows. She'd coveted that prize as if it were gold. "But whenever I tried to do something with writing or music, I fell apart, and everything around me did, too."

Nora felt an ache in her heart that dug deep into the past, to the summer she insisted on carting the heavy Royal typewriter on a family vacation to Lake Pocosaki. Her older sister Diane had chided her, telling her she was acting fifty instead of twelve and that she was a weirdo.

Rather than hanging out with the gang, she stayed in the screened porch, glued to the typewriter, feeding its carriage with paper—thin, soft, onionskin that rustled to the touch. The plucky sound of the keys as they struck the onion skin and the pull of the carriage as it zinged from line to line mesmerized and excited her. She discovered a world she could create and control, moving rapidly from chapter to chapter, escaping the real world.

Grace had sneaked some pages from Nora's secret folder and shared them with friends. They marched to the cottage and found Nora on the porch, sitting at the metal typing table rolled up to a wicker chair. One boy taunted her with the missing pile of papers, and the others snickered. She lunged at the boy, snatching the papers out of his hands while the kids teased her. She ran out the back door in tears, abandoning her novel as if it were a deserted island. Despite apologies from Diane, Grace had maintained that she got what she deserved. Nora retreated from her dream of becoming a writer.

Now, as they sat in Rosie's parlor, Nora asked, "Why is the nun's vow of silence in my energy field, and why do I have to break it?"

Rosie shrugged. "Call it what you will—destiny? Fate? Karma? Remember, you were once in her shoes. Perhaps you're being called to finish a life lesson and heal from the pain of your previous life."

Nora rested her chin in her hands, with her elbows on the table. "Great. Just what I wanted, more pain."

"The fish dress is in your life to help you break the vow of silence, and you must return to your previous life to do so. Otherwise, you'll find neither fulfillment nor happiness in this life."

Nora felt nauseous. "I'm not sure I can do it."

"It's karmic justice. Do you want to rediscover your creative self? Do you want to have open communication with your daughter? And won't life be empty without a mate? Don't forget that you experienced something traumatic when you were a young girl. The guides tried to unlock the memory to free you, but it's tied to your previous life and you can only release it by going back in time."

"And what do you propose I do once I get there?" Nora snapped.

Rosie's eyes looked like crescent moons when she grinned. "You'll know."

"You mean, once I do whatever I'm supposed to do with this dress, my life will change for the better?"

Rosie squinted. "I wouldn't tell you if it were not so. Do you think the fish dress and Marguerita appeared randomly in your life? No, they came to free you from the bondage of your previous life and the shipwreck of your present one. We can now move forward, or shall I say—backward. We're going on a past life journey."

Nora tried to smile, feigning courage. Knowing the answer, she asked, "Who was I in my last life?"

Rosie gave a joyful chuckle and placed the picture back in Nora's sweaty palms. "Sister Marguerita, of course!" Rosie patted the top of Nora's head. "I have something that will help you. I'll be right back."

Two minutes later she returned with a cassette tape in her hand. "Practice this meditation at home to prepare for your past life regression."

"How prepared do I have to be?"

"Enough to fall into a hypnotic state at the proper time. A past life regression is much more intense than a psychic reading."

Nora shuddered.

Rosie handed the tape over, touching Nora's arms with the care of an arborist tending to a sapling. "Don't worry, my dear, I'll be guiding you. Call me when you're ready."

The words Rosie had spoken months earlier now rippled through Nora's mind. *You will travel a great distance for something needed.* She hadn't had past life regression in mind.

"It's a lot to take in at one time. Make sure you treat yourself to something utterly delicious and relaxing in the next few days. Honor yourself, dear."

On the drive home, Nora thought about her connection with Sister Marguerita and their link across time. Should she scrutinize this stranger for clues about what she might expect on the other side? And why was she suddenly clinging to the dress, as if it could protect her from the unknown?

Once inside the house, Nora gathered the courage to prop the beguiling nun in her usual spot on the dresser, as if nothing about their relationship had changed. That evening, she observed something mystifying: Marguerita's eyes were following her across the room, rather than showing their usual gazing-off-into-the distance glance. Also, the eyes seemed to smile instead of casting a mysterious glow.

Nora took it as a positive sign and got ready to meditate. She had listened to plenty of meditations before—light harp music, synthesizers, and breathy sounds guiding her to create a sanctuary on a beach or in a lush meadow. But she had never considered meditation a form of hypnosis. To her, it had seemed more like a prayer. Determined to try, she moved Marguerita to the nightstand and laid down on the bed, with Margo nestled at her feet, and the cassette recorder by her side. She pushed the play button and closed her eyes.

Rosie's voice drifted pleasantly into Nora's head, guiding her to take full, deep breaths and exhale completely. "Ahhhhhhhhhhhhhhhhhhh," they breathed in tandem. "Release the breath." Nora felt the rise and fall of her chest. It was as if the dress and Marguerita were breathing along with her. The ins and the outs of life force continued for several minutes. Nora expected soft music but heard none. Only breath, then Rosie saying, "If random thoughts enter your mind, simply acknowledge them and send them away."

Ocean sounds flooded her mind, along with cosmic primeval timbre and swish of sea tide rising. The cry of ocean surf. Above all other sounds, Rosie chanted, "Listen to my voice," as she slowly counted down from ten to one, droning through the numbers. All at once, Nora experienced the whole of creation as one. She entered a world that connected with the sea, and she swam through a myriad of levels of the subconscious, losing all track of time.

A clicking sound brought her back into the room. The tape had ended. The ocean receded. She felt the protectiveness of the dress, as if it were a new covering of skin over her body, mermaid-like, a motif of her life. Matron of enchantment, elusive, she held the combs made of fish bones—an ancient nautical symbol of power over storms at sea.

She woke up bubbling with excitement about what she might face in her previous life as Sister Marguerita.

Chapter 11

Nora followed Rosie's advice to do something relaxing. She decided on a massage. She'd only had one in her life. Saturday morning, she showered then covered her body with honeysuckle lotion. Honeysuckle—a living symbol of love, with its yellow blossoms resembling two lovers intertwined. Its essence wafted up her nostrils, triggering memories of honeysuckle vines spilling through an open window of the house she and her ex-husband James once shared. Now, sitting on the edge of the bed, she thought *how ironic* that something so delicate as a flower's fragrance had such power to pull up the negative past.

HOLD ON TO WHAT SERVES THEE, LEAVING BEHIND
WHAT DOESN'T.

Nora vowed to stay in the present, where gratitude for a new day could bloom.

She looked at herself in the full-length mirror. "Not bad," she said aloud, viewing the curves no man had seen for years, and picturing Kirk's hand on her thigh. She stepped into her underwear and sweatpants and threw on a T-shirt, then headed to the massage parlor.

"Your name?" the receptionist politely asked.

"Nora Jenkins. I called earlier."

"Yes, thank you." After paying, Nora followed the woman down the hallway to a cubicle. "You may undress and wrap yourself in this," she said, handing Nora a sheet. "Romar will be with you soon."

Nora stood still, and the receptionist asked, "Is something wrong?"

"I thought it would be a masseuse."

"He is the masseur on duty today. If you'd like to reschedule, you may, but Romar is the best."

"No, that's okay. Should I wear something under the sheet?"

The receptionist smiled. "Your choice. Many people wear nothing, others leave their underwear on."

There she was, with only her lace panties, wrapped in an orchid cotton sheet, waiting. She paced from one end of the tiny dressing room to the other, trying to remember how many years it had been since a man had touched her, other than Kirk with his thigh swipe. *I hope I survive this,* she thought, her heart racing.

"Good morning." He gave her hand a warm quick shake and introduced himself. An attractive olive-skinned middle-aged man with creased black hair, he wore what looked like a karate instructor's white belted uniform. "Follow me, please."

She walked gingerly behind him, passing one, two, three square windows overlooking a row of Japanese cherry trees and stone Buddhas. She followed him into a small but airy room, and he pointed to the massage table, decorated with plush green blankets. Nora couldn't wait to cover herself with them. *This is so awkward,* she told herself, slipping off the sheet, scooting under the covers, and closing her eyes.

"Why don't you lie on your stomach first," he suggested.

Nora imagined that she was lying in a Zen garden and that Romar was her meditation master. The scent of coconut lime candles and the sound of harp music playing in the background relaxed her. She sank into the table and lost track of everything except his fingers, which skittered like daddy longlegs across her backside. He bore into the tiniest muscles as if he were searching for a hidden piece of her.

"You're very tense." Pushing and prodding, he didn't ease up. Romar turned Nora over and her body heat rose. She pictured herself singeing his skin, igniting the tips of his fingers as he worked on her toes, one by one fondling them as if they were Chihuly glass sculptures. Next, he smoothed out the wrinkles on her sandpaper soles.

Her mind drifted to a place it had never been: She's in Romar's kitchen, or is it Kirk's? They're fixing dinner—rack of lamb with coconut sauce. Standing at the stove, her back to him, she stirs the gravy. Her breasts are full, and his hot breath is at the nape of her neck. He nudges her from behind, as if by accident at first, then with intention. She turns to face him, and he drinks the milk of her swollen breasts, his lips on her nipples keeping perfect time with his fingers at her toes. She turns to reach for the fresh mint to mince into the coconut sauce, and her fantasy crumbles.

She was back in the Zen garden and Romar was still at her feet, working each toe with the precision of a maestro working his baton. An invisible cord vibrated inside Nora's body, and she felt a stirring she hadn't felt in a long while. He moved up her front side and she started to recoil when he touched near her scarred left breast.

A gentle breeze brushed by, and Romar was gone.

Nora continued to lie on the table, remembering what it felt like to feel alive.

The candle scent grew faint, and the harp music stopped playing. Wrapped in the sheet, now damp, Nora made her way back to the dressing room in a daze. *What is the fish dress doing to me?*

****

Nora had promised to meet the girls at the Lobster Claw after her massage.

"You look so starry-eyed. Must be that new boyfriend," Katrina greeted her.

If only you knew what just happened, thought Nora. "I don't even get to sit down before the rumors fly?" she quipped, eyeing Grace.

"I didn't think you'd mind if I told her about your date with Kirk."

"Why didn't you wear the fish dress on your lunch date?" Katrina asked.

"He might've seduced me in the booth," replied Nora, still thinking about her massage experience.

"I would wear it. Sex on the first date, in the restaurant, sounds perfect."

"You're so full of shit, Katrina."

"I'm not kidding. It reminds me of when I used to give blow jobs to my high school boyfriends in the back of the bus."

"Sex freak," Grace said, pointing to Katrina before turning to Nora. "Has he called you since your lunch date?"

Nora nodded. "I might as well tell you, seeing as you will find out one way or another. Kirk asked me to spend next weekend with him at Misty Island."

"I hope you said yes," Katrina said.

"You'd be a fool not to," Grace added.

"I'm going." She spoke in a wimpy voice, as if she didn't trust her own words.

"You'd better go before the snow flies. It's already the middle of November," Katrina said. "Wear the dress and come back with a juicy story. *Somebody* might as well have sex."

"There's another side I haven't mentioned," Nora said softly. The girls pulled their chairs closer to the table and leaned in. "Rosie told me I was Sister Marguerita in my last life."

"The picture of the nun from the yard sale?" Katrina asked.

Nora nodded.

"Sure, and I was Cleopatra in my last life," said Grace.

"And I was Lady Godiva," Katrina added, galloping in her chair. "Tell me more."

"Marguerita took a vow of silence in her lifetime, and it's carried over into mine."

"So?"

"The vow is blocking communication between Angelica and me. It's keeping me from living the life I should be living. She says my soul's purpose is sound, not silence. I should be writing or doing music and helping others to use their talents."

Katrina paused. "You're doing that teaching, but what does the dress have to do with it?"

"Good question. I have to break the vow to straighten out my life, and the fish dress plays a part."

"How do you break a vow of silence?" Grace asked.

Nora hesitated. "Rosie will take me into my previous life."

"In her time machine," Katrina said, pulling imaginary levers and making missile sounds.

Nora heard Grace chuckle.

"It's called past life regression. She hypnotizes me, and I go back."

"Make sure you *come* back," Grace pleaded.

"Maybe the dress is a ransom you have to pay to break the vow," suggested Katrina.

"How so?" Nora asked, recalling that Katrina had been churched growing up.

"If you believe the Bible, God ransomed His Son to pay for human sin after Adam screwed up in the Garden of Eden."

Nora was not quite sure about that but said nothing.

"Leave it to a man to fuck up a good thing," Katrina said.

"Don't overlook free will," Grace reminded them.

"And the influence of Satan and temptation," Katrina added.

Nora asked, "So the ransom is what you have to pay to get something back, right?"

Katrina nodded. "Or it can be the price that covers the cost, like the crucifixion of Christ."

"Okay, so if Sister Marguerita caused something bad to happen, I might have to repay it my whole life?"

"It's the cross you bear," Katrina answered.

"I've been living a vow of silence and sacrifice most of my life," Nora stated.

"When you sacrifice to pay a ransom, you're supposed to do it out of love," said Grace.

Nora bristled. "What are you saying?"

"That you've acted out of guilt and fear, which is self-destructive."

Nora glared at her sister. "When did you become an *expert* on religion?"

"You don't have to be a Christian to use common sense. I'm sorry, Nora, I'm just trying to help you, out of love."

Nora felt the touch of her sister's hand, and the awkward moment passed.

"I'm sorry, Grace. It's my nerves."

Katrina looked at Grace. "Too bad you and Thomas aren't together. You could charm him into getting Mrs. C. to talk. She must know plenty about the dress. Speak of the devil, he's standing inside the door, pretending not to notice us."

"He needs to get used to seeing Grace around town. Hey, Thomas, come join us," Nora said, waving him over. "How's it going?"

He searched the table for a vacant seat, one faraway from Grace. "Don't ask. They've got me doing a hundred things at once, and I'm only one person."

Nora stared at his half-closed eyelids. "Why don't you get a double espresso?"

"What I need is a vacation. I'm thinking about Florida. Katrina, are you game?"

"Sure."

Nora expected Grace to flinch, but she didn't. Nora felt a chill in the air that wasn't the room temperature. Was it Thomas's remorse at letting Grace walk away, and his pride insisting he save face? Or was the chill Grace's regret over forcing the marriage question, entangled with her deep love, and the security he could provide?

It all confirmed how complicated relationships can be. *What am I getting myself into?* she asked herself, thinking of Kirk.

Back home, Nora received a collect call. "I can only talk for a minute, Mom, but I want to tell you I miss you."

"And I miss *you*, darling. It's great to hear your voice."

"Thank you for the card. It lifted my spirits, especially the part where you wrote how proud you are of me."

"Well, I *am*." Nora said.

"I love you," Angelica said.

"Before our time's up, I want to tell you I'm going away for the weekend."

"With Grace?"

Nora paused. "No, with a nice man I recently met. He has a cottage on Misty Island."

"You should go. You deserve to have fun and be happy."

"So do you, Angelica, and we'll make up for lost time."

"Come see me when you get back," Angelica said, her voice cracking.

Chapter 12

Nora daydreamed of Kirk while she dressed for their getaway. She looked in the full-length mirror, admiring the dress's primitive yet complex crisscrosses and swirly symbols, which gave her a flair of mystery she hoped Kirk might find intriguing. The fish skeletons glowed in the black sea cloth, and its tribal symbols spiraled upward to a scoop neck, offset by a silver necklace with a black onyx stone. She styled her hair in herring-bone braids to give the look of a mermaid.

"All I need is fins," she joked, looking down at her shiny black heels.

Some of the dress's fish designs looked crude and masculine, while others looked feminine and delicate. The dress made her look younger, shaving at least ten years off her age. A final turn in the mirror convinced Nora she could deal with whatever the dress might bring, until it struck her that he might want more than a kiss or a hug. What if he touched her left breast? She couldn't allow that to happen. Then she would have to confess her cancer, and he might not want to be with her after all he'd been through with his wife.

The sun was barely up when she heard a knock on the door, took a deep breath, then opened it. Kirk looked like he'd just stepped out of a catalogue, with his wide-corduroy green pants, tan turtleneck, fishnet sweater, and brown leather boots. She sensed he liked how *she* looked, too, the way he ogled her with a gaze that made her insides quiver.

Kirk insisted on carrying Nora's overnight bag to the car. "Where's Margo?"

"She's with my sister Grace."

"I should've told you to bring your pup. My guys love company."

Nora looked inside the car. "Where are they?"

"Out on the island with my daughter. You'll meet them. And her."

He'd mentioned the overgrown Rottweilers but Nora wanted to see for herself just how wimpy these brutes were before bringing Margo along.

On the way to the ferry, they made small talk. Kirk asked a lot of questions about work and family. "Besides Grace, any brothers or sisters?"

"Just Diane, two years older than me. She's married, but no children. She says she's around enough kids, with her job as a librarian. She lives in Connecticut, near my parents. What about you? Any siblings?"

"A bunch, but we're not related, although I think of them as family. I grew up in an orphanage."

Nora flashed back to psychology lectures of long-term deprivation effects on kids raised in institutions. "I'm sorry," she said, reaching over to touch his arm.

He sighed. "Please don't pity me."

"I don't. You're smart, handsome, and rugged. It's like you're carved of rough stone and won't crumble when life throws you a curve. But you also have a smooth, sensitive side."

He broke into a broad smile. "You learned all that in one lunch date?"

Nora didn't know what to say because she had no idea where the words had come from, so she simply smiled.

"Didn't do too badly for an institution kid, did I? Raised by a flock of nuns and turned out okay."

Nora cringed at the mention of nuns. She had hoped to leave Sister Marguerita behind and wanted to let the day unfold without worrying about the past or the future, or even the present. She liked the way the dress was teaching her to accept a new way of thinking.

"Do you believe in love at first sight?" Kirk suddenly asked.

"Maybe in movies and romance novels," she replied. "As for real life, I haven't experienced it. Why, do you?"

"I'm beginning to," he said softly and squeezed Nora's hand.

She looked down at the dress and saw the fish glowing. She quickly turned toward the window before Kirk noticed.

They pulled into the loading dock at 7:15 a.m. and drove into the bowels of the boat. The horn blasted, and the ferry pulled out of the harbor.

"Let's go up on deck," Kirk said.

He led her by the hand as they wove through rows of cars and up two flights of iron-grated steps, with Nora wobbling in her high heels. They reached a crowded deck and found a seat on one of the metal benches. Nora tilted her head back to catch the sun's brilliant rays.

"I feel so alive," she exclaimed, with an ocean breeze blowing her hair and sea spray spilling over them.

"Me, too," Kirk said, his curls waving in the wind.

Nora looked down at her shoes. "I don't know what possessed me to wear these." She started to undo the thin black strap that dug into her ankle. "What a relief," she said.

"Excuse me, madam, allow me." Kirk knelt on one knee and lifted her foot, tugging at the strap. Nora knew he was pretending to fumble with the strap so he could stroke her ankle. He removed the shoe in slow motion, heel first, then he unbuckled the other shoe, dangling it from her toes. His fingers spidered up her leg and under the dress, pausing at her kneecaps, then moving back down to her feet. In her mind, without warning, Nora was back in Romar's Zen garden feeling pure desire, which stayed with her until they reached land.

After disembarking, they drove past the *Welcome to Misty Harbor, Prettiest Little Island in Maine* sign. "And I've got the prettiest little woman in all of Maine with me," Kirk said, grinning.

Nora blushed, quickly changing the subject. "How big is the island?"

"Seven miles by ten."

She tried to keep the conversation flowing like Grace would have. "Many year-rounders?"

"Under a thousand."

They drove through the village, passing a bank, a general store, a doughnut shop, and a gas station. Then they headed inland where lush smears of green caught the corner of Nora's eye, and trees unfolded along the winding road. The car made a hairpin turn onto a narrow dirt road, and Nora's body slid into Kirk's.

With his face close to hers, he raised his eyebrows and in a thick accent, said, "Come with me to the casbah." It sounded so corny, but she laughed anyway.

A short time later, the ocean returned, its whitecaps unfurling and rocks jutting out as the forest disappeared, along with the rest of civilization. They pulled up to a cozy-looking cottage with weathered clapboards and a grey shingled roof. A white Range Rover was parked in front.

"My daughter." Kirk leaned over and nuzzled Nora's neck. "How do you like this place?"

Nora nuzzled him back. "It's paradise."

They raced each other from the car to the front pillared porch, with its slatted, robin-egg blue floor, lazy rockers, and green canvas glider. A glass jar overflowing with seashells sat on the driftwood table, and a hand-painted ceramic seagull perched on the steps. Nora pointed to the rustic wooden sign above the door: *Simple Pleasures.*

"I love it!"

Kirk smiled. "They say simplicity's the key to a successful life."

"The way I'd like to live," Nora said softly. "Wait, where are the dogs?"

"Must be out with my daughter." He led her inside to the living room which burst with color: red daybeds piled high with green and yellow throw pillows, royal blue wicker armchairs with navy tack-upholstered backs, and built-in bookcases that bore the weight of first edition classics covered with a thick layer of dust. Kirk went straight to the stereo.

"What kind of music do you like?"

"Most everything except hard rock."

A minute later Prince's *Diamonds and Pearls* filled the room, and Nora's head filled with lyrics promising a love meant for two. They sank into a daybed, and the song played softy in the background. Kirk moved closer and put his arms around her. She surrendered to his touch, her heart pounding. When their kissing was over, Nora's head was spinning.

FEAR NOT, MY DEAR, THY TRUE BEAUTY, BOTH INNER AND OUTER, SHINETH THROUGH, murmured a voice that resonated like the light plucking of a harp.

As they held each other in the silence that followed, Nora's fears retreated like the changing tide. A wave of loving energy passed between them.

"Maybe we should get a cold drink," Kirk said, sounding breathy. He led them to the kitchen. Nora sat down at the indoor picnic table while Kirk poured two glasses of ice water. She looked at the cast iron frying pans hanging from hooks by the stove, and a dartboard on the wall. He sat at the opposite bench, smiling while they sipped their water.

She stared at the stack of white ironware dishes. "I love open shelving."

"Uncomplicated," Kirk said. "No doors to open and shut and hide things in."

Nora felt the dress nudge her, as if to warn her that Kirk's words had a double meaning.

Just then, she heard a commotion of dog paws on the porch.

"Hel-*lo*," a voice called out, the door opened, the dogs—huge!—rushed in and jumped on Kirk.

Nora hid behind him.

"Meet Chiller and Mondo. They're gentle giants who love tummy rubs," he said, laughing.

Nora slowly stepped out from behind Kirk and stood beside him.

"You're right, they're not the monsters I imagined them to be. They look like they're smiling." She moved closer and reached out her hand. Soon it was covered with drool, but she didn't mind.

"Hi, I'm Paulette, and you must be Nora." Kirk's daughter reached out and shook Nora's hand. The bold grasp of this stunning woman surprised Nora.

She told Paulette about Margo, describing her as a barky ball of fur.

"I'm not sure what she'd do if she saw these big boys."

"Nora's going to bring her next time. You'll like that, won't you, guys?" Kirk said, stroking their backs.

"Guess what, Dad? I'm getting a promotion. You're looking at the next assistant manager of Barkley Bank."

"My baby's upgrading to an executive's office with fancy furniture. Hot damn!"

"Something like that," Paulette said. She glanced at her watch. "Yikes! I've got to catch the ten o'clock ferry."

She disappeared and returned with an overnight bag. Her shoulder-length auburn hair was now tucked in a Red Sox cap.

"I'm taking the dogs back with me, okay, Dad?"

"That's fine, honey. We'll connect after the weekend." He gave Chiller and Mondo final rubs before kissing his daughter goodbye.

"I enjoyed meeting you," Nora said, hugging Paulette lightly. "Congratulations on your new position."

"Thanks, Nora. I see why my father's crazy about you. By the way, I love your dress. I've never seen anything like it, with those runes and fish bones. I hope you don't mind my asking where you got it."

"It came from a friend, but that's a long story. Remind me to tell you next time."

"Promise?" Paulette asked.

"Pinky promise," Nora replied, wrapping her baby finger around Paulette's.

After seeing his daughter and the dogs off, Kirk suggested he and Nora take a walk on the beach. "Let's bring a blanket and a bottle of wine and some snacks."

The November sun cast a dusky glow over the late morning sky. The temperature was unusually warm for the time of year, warm enough for Nora to go barefoot. The cool sand between her toes refreshed her feet, and the salty air hydrated her skin. She felt alive.

Kirk, wearing sandals, spread out the blanket near the water, where they could watch the birds dive-bomb for food and the waves brush tiny rocks and shells ashore while they ate cheese and crackers and sipped wine.

"My wife loved it here," Kirk said, sounding far away.

Nora nodded, sensing his need to talk. "It must have been difficult to lose her."

He gave a wistful look. "Yes, Janine was the perfect wife, mother, friend, artist, you name it. She was diagnosed with breast cancer thirteen years ago, and we dealt with that. Five years later, cancer came back. The second time we got more aggressive; she had both breasts removed. Five years after that, it was cancer of the liver. She died three years ago, after twenty-three years of marriage." He bit his quivering lower lip.

Nora touched his hand. Cancer. Nora knew all about it, but she hesitated to tell him she was a survivor.

"You mentioned you had a bad marriage. Do you want to talk about it?"

Nora shrugged her shoulders. "There's not much to say except he was abusive."

"Verbal? Physical?"

"Both," Nora uttered. "I stayed with James for almost eight years, and I haven't seen him since, but the scars never completely fade."

"So, it's more than just shyness that keeps you from getting involved."

Out of Nora's mouth came words she never intended to speak. "Relationships frighten me, but what I feel right now, I haven't felt in years."

He looked into her eyes as if he were searching for truth. "What *do* you feel?"

Her throat turned dry and she felt her vocal cords tighten.

"Like I'm falling in love," she whispered, sifting a handful of sand through her fingers. She let out a nervous laugh. "It makes no sense, does it?"

Kirk gently turned her face toward his. "Love doesn't have to make sense. There are no rules about how long it takes to love someone or for two people to fall in love. I told you, for me it was love at first sight, but for you, it may take longer. Sometimes it's the baggage we carry. Don't worry, I've got the patience of Job." He touched her cheek and kissed her lips. "Let's go back to the cottage."

Inside, he showed Nora the rest of the rooms, starting with the bathroom. Nora admired the buttery walls and black-and-white checkerboard tile floor, the ironstone sink with separate hot and cold faucets, and a drain plug on a chain; and the antique clawfoot tub. She felt the touches of his wife, Janine.

Next came his daughters' bedroom. It was cozy with periwinkle bunk beds and matching oak dressers, with a wingback chair by the window, its sill filled with midnight blue glass bottles of all shapes and sizes. Nora noticed a framed photo on one of the dressers—an attractive woman in her fifties with green eyes and long auburn hair.

"She's beautiful. Is that Janine?"

Kirk held up the picture. "Nora, meet Janine. Janine, meet Nora."

Nora felt his wife's energy in every detail of the cottage décor. It was warm and inviting. When they stepped inside the next room, Nora knew it was Kirk's bedroom because it felt so masculine. With its mossy-green bead board walls, king-size bed with a rustic walnut headboard, and a burgundy comforter with matching pillow shams, Nora thought maybe he had redecorated the room after his wife died.

They moved to the guest room, which instantly became Nora's favorite. *Pure and simple*, she thought when they crossed the threshold. Creamy white pine panels covered the walls. She stood by the antique double bed, admiring its scalloped headboard inlaid with bone in the shape of a trident—the symbol of power held by Poseidon, God of the Oceans. She looked around at the only other pieces of furniture in the room—side tables and candle lamps with beaded shades she imagined would cast dreamy shadows on the walls at night.

Kirk sat on the edge of the bed with Nora alongside him. The simplicity and purity of the room were suddenly swept up in the sexual tension Nora felt between their bodies, those high frequency vibrations that might lead to making love.

FEAR NOT, NORA. THOU ART MUCH MORE
THAN A PHYSICAL BODY.
THE BEAUTY HE ALSO SEES IS THY INNER BEING.

There was something magic about the room. *Oceanic energies,* she thought, suddenly on the verge of falling into a trance.

Kirk gently stroked her hair and wrapped his arms around her before pulling back the creamy white comforter to reveal a soft layer of sheets. He lifted the dress over her head and carefully hung it on the door hook as if he knew to respect its power.

RELEASE THE PAST AND LIBERATE THE SPIRIT.

"Kirk, wait, I need to tell you something."
"I'm all ears, baby." He flapped his hands to imitate an elephant.
"Be serious for a minute. Remember when you told me Janine had cancer?"
"Yes."

"I should've told you that I've had cancer, but I was afraid it would scare you away." Nora shut her eyes, sensing Kirk's mood shift as he bombarded her with questions. *What kind of cancer? How long ago? Invasive or confined in the ducts? The prognosis and treatment?*

She answered truthfully, stressing that her breast cancer happened over seven years ago.

"Let me see that left breast," he said playfully.

She reluctantly lowered the sheets and looked away.

His tender fingers touched what to her felt like shoe leather, but it didn't stop him from caressing and kissing the breast.

Speech no longer became necessary. Perhaps there were no words to describe what they experienced when they sank into the featherbed. Afterward, with her finger, she gently touched the dimple in the middle of his chin, and they softly stroked each other's faces, smiling deeply into each other's eyes.

Only Nora heard the wind harp.

MY DEAR, THOU DESERVETH TO EXPERIENCE SUCH PLEASURE.

Late that afternoon, a deep voice floated through the restaurant at the Lighthouse Inn. "Mr. and Mrs. Kloppenheimer, your table is ready,"

Nora looked at Kirk. "I can't believe he just said that."

Kirk grinned. "You'd better get used to it, hon."

She remembered what Rosie had said about Divine Time—how things move quickly when the universe is in charge.

The host seated them by a window overlooking the ocean. "Thank you. It's lovely here," Nora said. She gazed at the grey-green water and listened to the waves crash like cymbals against the rocks below.

"The Lighthouse Inn is one of my favorite restaurants," Kirk said. "Fabulous food and great scenery. Wait until you see the sunset."

A tailored waiter brought a bottle of cabernet sauvignon to the table. Kirk sampled it, nodded his approval, and they lifted their glasses to everlasting love.

While they waited for the appetizers, Nora showed Kirk a photo of Angelica at fourteen, standing in the backyard, her eyes bright, her hair in a loose bun on top of her head. She held Margo like a baby, and she was smiling.

"What a natural beauty!" exclaimed Kirk.

"She is," Nora said, nodding. "She loves animals, and they love her."

A platter piled high with plump shrimp and cocktail sauce arrived. Together they devoured the shrimp, nibbling each morsel down to the tail as they watched the sun turn into a fireball, its rays piercing the water like samurai swords. It slipped through a layer of pinkening clouds, peering like a tiger's eye, hurling purples and yellows across the sky. Nora sighed, happily. "I feel like part of a vast universe that makes perfect sense at this moment."

Kirk nodded. "It's like my heart is on fire," he said, leaning across the table. Their lips touched when the last bit of the tiger's eye plunged into the sea.

Suddenly the dress began to shine, its scales and symbols casting a luminous glow. Nora saw it shimmer before Kirk's eyes. This time, she secretly thanked the dress, and she heard it say,

*THOU ART THE ESSENCE OF BEAUTY AND
EVOCATIVENESS.*

"You're sparkling," he said.

Nora touched his cheeks. "So are you."

Kirk smiled. "Must be the afterglow."

*THOU MUST NEVER UNDERESTIMATE THE
POWER OF THE DRESS.*

"To be sure," Nora whispered, patting the dress, hoping to silence it.

Kirk pointed to a lighthouse offshore. "It's haunted."

Through the dusk, she saw the tall granite tower with its iron, dome-shaped roof and the keeper's quarters with its crumbling balcony. "Really?"

"In 1916, during a hurricane, the lighthouse keeper drowned when his boat capsized. Later he showed up as a ghost. The logs are full of sightings."

"Like what?"

"He glides down the tower stairs, and the beacon blinks on and off when it's not supposed to."

"Do you believe it?"

"I don't know about ghosts," Kirk winked, "but there might be a case for the supernatural when it comes to our future together. What do you think?"

Nora gave a tentative nod but said nothing about the fish dress or her alleged past life as Sister Marguerita. He'd think she was a weirdo and have second thoughts about her, so she changed the subject.

"Do you go to the cottage a lot?"

"As often as I can."

The waiter arrived, balancing a steaming tray above his head. He set down several platters: fresh broiled sea scallops, blackened salmon, twice-baked potatoes, and asparagus tips. Cayenne pepper welled up in Nora's nose.

"Nice presentation!" Kirk remarked.

They took their time eating dinner, with Nora savoring every bite.

"This is melt-in-your-mouth," she said, making *mmmm* noises as she ate. "Jumbo scallops baked with buttery breadcrumbs are my favorite."

He stared at her near empty plate. "Didn't you eat today?"

Nora laughed. "You'll get to know my habits. My sisters say I'm like a car. I fill up, then go until I'm on empty, then fill up again."

"I guess you were just about out of gas," he said, chuckling. "Coffee? Or more wine?"

"Both."

"Excuse me, miss."

Nora looked up to see an attractive woman wearing a bright red knitted dress with block-printed lobsters all over it.

"Hi," Nora said, smiling a little nervously, hoping this wasn't a friend of Mrs. Carver's. "Do I know you?"

"Sorry to interrupt, but I simply must ask you a question," she said, extending her hand. "I'm sitting a few tables down, and I've been admiring your dress throughout dinner. When you stood up, I got a good look. Please forgive me if I'm being too forward but wherever did you get it?"

Nora could hardly breathe. "I'm not sure where it came from." *Did the dress just squeeze her body?*

"Would you like to join us for a nightcap?" Kirk asked.

The woman pointed to a table where a man appeared to be dozing, his head tilted on the table. "That's kind, but my husband's ready to go home. We've both had enough liquor to sink a ship, but I couldn't leave without asking about your dress. I swear the fish skeletons were moving. I'd love to have a dress that *looks* alive. You must know what those symbols mean."

"I'm afraid I can't help you."

She rested her hand on Nora's shoulder, stroking the sleeve. "I'm a buyer of women's clothing for Nordstrom's. If you learn more about the dress, I'd love to know." She handed Nora her business card and walked away.

Kirk's eyebrows arched. "Do you see how she's weaving back to her table? No wonder she thought the fish were moving. But your dress *is* getting a lot of attention—first my daughter, now this total stranger—what's up with it?"

Nora's eyes shifted. "No idea."

TELL HIM.

Nora felt the sharp swish of a tail against her hand and began spewing details of the dress—how she acquired it, that it freed her to feel good about herself and gave her charisma, most of the time—but she kept to herself its ability to speak.

"Sounds good to me. Who wouldn't want such a powerful dress?" Kirk remarked.

As if under the dress's spell, Nora shared secrets she never intended to tell him—about symbolic meanings and the shadow side of the dress, and the story of the gypsy encounter.

"I might have been a nun in my previous life," she confessed.

Confusion spread across his face.

"What's wrong?" she asked.

Kirk stood up. "I'm trying to understand, but I've heard enough for one night. A magic dress? Reincarnation? A fella can only take so much." He flagged down the waiter and ordered a martini before heading to the patio.

It was a rustle loud enough for only Nora to hear.

FORGIVE ME, I WAS JUST TRYING TO HELP.

Nora fought the urge to yank off the dress and tear it into tiny pieces.

"How could you do this to me? I might lose him," she hissed. A tearful Nora followed Kirk outside and plopped down next to him on the stone bench, throwing her arms around him. "I'm sorry. I'll explain everything, at least as much as I know," she pleaded. The night air had turned chilly, she could see dragon breath shoot boldly from her mouth.

"Kirk, please listen to what I have to say." She stood up and paced back and forth in front of him. He glued his eyes to the fishy swirls, as if the dress were mesmerizing him. She told him about Rosie Deerborn and Sister Marguerita and the vow of silence.

He placed his hands in prayer position and shocked her with a deep kiss. "You're the freakiest nun I've ever met, and I've known plenty of penguins in my life."

"I'm serious, Kirk."

"Nora, I think you're a bit of a fruitcake but I adore you. I'm just not sure I can wrap my brain around what you're telling me."

She shushed his lips with her fingers. "Sound, not silence, is my purpose this lifetime. I'm supposed to speak out about what I know, believe, and feel. It's about creativity and communication—composing music and singing songs, writing books, and showing others how to get in touch with their voices." The dress turned heavy upon Nora, and she paused to catch her breath. "Silence in my last life has caused huge problems this lifetime, including not standing up to an abusive husband, and not being as strong a mother to my daughter as I should've been."

Kirk's eyes were watering. "I'm sorry, Nora."

"The vow is still with me." Her body shuddered and her teeth chattered. The stone bench turned cold as a coffin, and the dress felt like bricks upon her.

Kirk wrapped his arms around her. "No wonder you're shaking. You're not even wearing a coat."

"That has nothing to do with it. I've made such a mess of my life."

"Stop being so hard on yourself. Most people go through life not knowing what they're missing and not missing what they could know. You're a little out there but I can't help myself. I'm love struck."

"You're totally in touch with your creative side while I struggle to connect with mine." She buried her face in his chest.

"You mean the music?"

"Yes. I don't mean to envy you but you're using your talents while I'm barred from mine, still haunted by the dead."

He gently pulled her face to his, tracing her cheekbone with his finger. "Look at me and listen. The dead will always be with us. I'd be lying if I said I never think about my wife, but I know she'd want me to get on with my life. Just the way you need to bury your past and make your dreams happen."

"Excuse me, folks," said the waiter. "We'll be closing in twenty minutes. Would you like anything else?"

"We're all set," Kirk replied. "We'll be in to settle the tab. Thanks for a wonderful evening." The waiter nodded, smiled, and back-pedaled his way inside.

"Believe me, sweetheart, I'll do anything to help you break this vow, or whatever you call it." He knelt on one knee in front of Nora. "I'm the knight in shining armor who will rescue you." Then he jumped to his feet and grabbed the plastic toothpick sword that had held the olives in his martini, waving it in the air as if to ward off evil.

Nora laughed at the unlikely hero who stood before her, looking a bit buzzed. "Oh, dear gilded knight, if only you could do the work for me, but I fear it is only I who can break this vow." She offered Kirk her hand as if it were bone china.

He kissed it gently up one side of her arm, on to her neck, and then to her ear before whispering, "This is only the beginning for us, Nora. Let's go home now."

Back at Simple Pleasures, Nora and Kirk ended up in the guest bedroom again. They lay in each other's arms against the trident-etched headboard and watched a kaleidoscope of colors dance on the walls. They romanced each other over and over like they'd been together for lifetimes. Each lovemaking was as fresh as if it were the first time. By dawn, Nora's insides ached with both pain and pleasure, and she felt satisfied.

* * * * *

They lay on their backs, side by side, and Nora talked of the past like she never had before, telling Kirk as much as she could remember about her brother—their time together, his death, and her mother's blame. She shared how, deep down, she felt out of sync with the rest of the world, and how worthless she regarded herself, how most relationships with men had been empty, how she'd been a failure as a mother, and how she regretted suppressing her creativity. As Nora's confessional mounted, she began to understand why, for most of her life, she so desperately tried to numb her inner pain.

"Now that you know me, don't leave me."

"Nora, I'm in this. Rocket-fast and no turning back."

He gently drew her into his arms, and they were back in *Simple Pleasures*.

****

Nora stopped at Grace's house late Sunday night to pick up Margo. She knocked several times before her sister, rubbing her eyes, opened the door.

"I'm sorry it's so late, Grace."

Grace yawned while handing over the dog. "Did you have a good time with Kirk?"

"Fabulous, but I'll spare you the details tonight so you can go back to bed."

Grace hesitated. "I don't want to spoil your weekend, but Diane called yesterday about Mom. She hasn't been feeling well. Stomach pains and nausea, but she refuses to see a doctor."

Nora sighed. "Let's go down for Thanksgiving. It's only a week away."

Nodding, Grace said, "I'll tell Diane."

"Thanks for watching Margo."

Chapter 13

Nora wore the fish dress to the penitentiary. Angelica insisted on hearing the details of her mother's weekend with Kirk. Nora painted a blissful picture of their time on the island, his cozy cottage, walks on the beach, and dinner at an elegant restaurant overlooking the ocean.

"I'm glad you had a good time. It sounds like you like him."

"I do," Nora said with a nod.

"What else is new, Mom?"

At first, Nora thought she would hold off telling her daughter about her grandmother. But Angelica wanted to know the truth about things, so Nora talked.

"Grammy's not feeling well."

"What's wrong?" Angelica asked, her worry lines showing.

"She has stomach pains, nausea, and isn't eating, so Grace and I are going down for Thanksgiving to check on her."

Angelica stared at the floor. "I'm stuck here for another year, and she might be gone by then."

"I'm sure Grammy will be fine," Nora said, trying to sound optimistic for her daughter's sake. She knew their bond was strong. When they had lived in Connecticut, Nora's mother often cared for Angelica.

"Do they know the truth about me?"

"No, it would only hurt them." As soon as the words left Nora's mouth, she regretted having said them.

Angelica's shoulders drooped. "They can't be told what a loser their granddaughter turned out to be, right."

Nora wanted to cry. "You made mistakes. You *aren't* a loser."

"Then why can't you tell them?"

Nora hesitated. "They've been through a lot."

"What do you mean?" Angelica asked, lifting her head.

"When we were young, something horrible happened." She explained how their brother's sudden death fractured the family, how her mother blamed Nora, and how nothing could ever be spoken of, leaving Nora to silently harbor blame and shame for his death.

Angelica glared at her mother. "Why have you kept it from me all these years?"

Nora shrugged. "Maybe because I couldn't accept it. And I don't remember how it happened. I was only five."

In the silence that followed, they looked into each other's eyes, and Nora said, "I'm thankful you and I are finally opening up with each other. We should have had this conversation years ago."

"Remember when I did three months in juvenile detention?"

What can of worms had Nora opened? Her mind filled with convictions for underage drinking and pot possession, breaking and entering, and stealing prescription drugs. That was before her daughter turned to heroin.

"I promised you I'd never do time again. Here we are, five years later, and I'm sitting in prison. I really am such a loser, Mom." Angelica's body seemed to cave in on itself.

Nora clenched her jaw. "Don't *ever* say that about yourself again. Your past has brought you here, but it's no longer part of you. Learn the lessons and leave the heartache behind." As an afterthought, she added, "But don't throw away the good stuff."

"What good stuff?" There was no defiance in Angelica's voice, only deflation and distance, as if she were observing every mistake she'd ever made. She lowered her head. Nora's heart cracked open.

She searched for words of encouragement to lift her daughter's drowning spirits, something tangible Angelica could use as a life jacket.

"You were a talented dancer, and you still can be."

"Sure," Angelica muttered, then looked at her mother. "What's with the dress? It's the second time you've worn it, and it's only your third visit."

Seeing a chance to redirect the focus of the conversation, Nora stood up and struck a modeling pose. "This dress? A castoff. You know, one person's trash is another's treasure."

"You got it at the thrift shop?"

Nora grinned. "Not exactly."

"Who gave it to you?"

"You wouldn't know her."

Angelica stared at the dress. "What's so special about it?"

Nora smiled, twirling and flaring out the skirt. "It lifts my spirits."

"How the heck do you wash it?"

"I haven't washed it yet, but I would hand-wash it very carefully, and then I'd hang it out in the moonlight to dry."

Angelica grinned. "You're too much, Mom," she said, blowing a kiss through the glass. "I love you."

"I love you, too."

****

Holidays stressed Nora, and Thanksgiving was no exception, especially with Angelica in prison. Nora was running out of excuses to tell her parents why their granddaughter couldn't visit or call.

At least one granddaughter, Eve, would be with them. Grace was thrilled that her daughter had just arrived home from Hong Kong.

Nora's stomach churned like a rough sea as they headed to Connecticut for the first time in many months. Each visit felt like she was entering a compression chamber where emotions were crushed into a short space of time. Instead of relaxation and pleasant reminiscences, shadows of the past and secrets of the present ignited. Why did they have to wear masks and pretend to be perfect to cover the family's dysfunction? Yet Nora sensed unspoken words and emotions just under the surface, filling the air with angst.

When they arrived, Nora was relieved to see her sister Diane standing in the breezeway. They all hugged, and Grace asked, "How's Mom?"

"Worse than she's letting on," Diane said, pointing toward the entryway leading to the kitchen. "I ordered a cooked turkey from the grocery store, but she insisted on making the side dishes."

Through the window, Nora saw steam rise from the stove. Her mother was stirring a pot, her back to them. She looked pencil-thin in a Pendleton plaid skirt and satin blouse, apron strings tied at her waist.

"Has she seen a doctor?" Grace whispered.

Diane shook her head. "She might as well be a Christian Scientist."

Their mother turned around, her cheeks bloomed with rouge, resembling roses against the pallor of her skin and her faded blue eyes. Nora wished she could ask her mother why she blamed her for Seth's death, and why a code of silence like an untreated malignancy had festered in the family and still remained. But this was not the time.

Now, standing in the kitchen, though she felt the sting of rejection, Nora reached out and embraced her mother, just as she had done with Angelica. "Hello, Mom, Happy Thanksgiving!" She kissed her mother's cheek, something she hadn't done in a great while. The softening of her own heart surprised Nora. Did her mother feel it, too?

Their mother turned to her granddaughter and they hugged.

"It's so good to see you, Eve." After hugging the others, she asked, "Where's Angelica?"

"I'm sorry, Mom, she had to work a holiday banquet."

Frowning, her mother said, "She works so hard, with school and her job."

Before Nora could say more, their father entered the kitchen, his arms outstretched. When he spotted Eve, he closed his arms around her, then hugged his daughters.

"How was the drive? Was there much traffic?"

"Not bad," Grace answered.

"I'm sure the girls are hungry, Martha. Is it time to eat?"

She looked at him with tired eyes. "It'll be a while before dinner."

"What can we do to help, Mom?" Nora asked.

"You could set the table. Everything's on the sideboard in the dining room."

Their father took the bottle of Canadian Club from the top shelf of the cupboard. "I'm fixing your mother a drink. Do you girls want whiskey or wine?"

"Wine, please," they answered.

Their dad poured the drinks. "Time to get out of the women's way and go watch football."

While their mother stayed in the kitchen, cooking, they transformed the dining room into a festive sight, covering the table with an ivory laced table-cloth, candles, and a fruit-filled cornucopia. They removed the good china and the silverware from the corner cupboard.

Thanksgiving unfolded like the Macy's Day Parade as they marched one dish after another into the dining room: a platter heaped with carved turkey, bowls of dressing, mashed potatoes, gravy, cranberry sauce, green bean casse-role, and creamed onions, a basket of warm rolls covered with a cloth napkin, and a dish of celery and olives.

Nora gazed at her mother across the table. She'd forgotten how stunning she was, with her golden rust-streaked crown of hair, buoyant and stylish, and her glowing face. But her eyes were ice blue, so distant. Nora reached out.

"Thanks for fixing this feast, Mom. You shouldn't have."

"It's what I do—tradition."

Her mother's voice sounded disconnected from the family. But had Nora treated Angelica any different than her mother had treated her? Both were shadow mothers, at times emotionally abandoning their children.

"Tell Angelica we miss her and how proud we are she takes her work so seriously," their father said.

"It means a lot coming from you, Dad," Nora said. "You've always set the bar high."

"And Eve, our world traveler," he remarked, winking at her. "How do you like teaching in China?"

"Very different from Maine, but I love it."

"Who wants a refill?" Diane asked, picking up the bottle and pouring more wine into her sisters' uplifted glasses before filling her own.

"May I please have more stuffing?" Eve asked.

"Dressing, not stuffing, right Mom?" Grace said, smiling as she passed the bowl.

"Don't forget to mention slice of turkey instead of hunk of meat," Diane joked.

"Or powder room instead of bathroom," Nora added.

Their mom sipped her white wine as she pushed her food around the plate with her fork. At dinner's end, plates dotted with last bites sat, while their mother's plate lay heaped with food.

Diane served dessert, warm apple pie with vanilla ice cream, their father's favorite. Their mother, who'd been quiet throughout dinner, finally spoke.

"I'm going up to rest for a few minutes."

"Are you okay, Mom?" Grace asked.

"Yes, just queasy." Her voice sounded slight as she raised herself up from the table, clutching the arms of the chair. "I'll be fine."

Nora stood up to help but her mother pulled away. "I can make it," she said.

After their mother left the dining room, their father headed to the den while the girls cleared the table and cleaned up the kitchen.

"Mom seems so weak," Grace said, her eyebrows knitting.

Nora frowned. "She hardly ate anything."

Nodding, Grace suggested, "Maybe Dad can convince her to go for tests. After we finish the dishes, let's talk to him."

"Good luck, Diane said. "How's Angelica?"

"Up and down," replied Nora. "Do you think Dad and Mom are wondering what's going on?"

Diane shook her head. "We'd know it. They'd be pumping me for information."

"Why are there so many secrets in our family?" Eve asked her mother.

"It goes back to our childhood," Grace answered, sighing.

"What happened?"

"You've heard me mention Seth. Well, when we were young, our baby brother died unexpectedly, and it was never talked about."

"Why not?"

"It was never allowed," Grace answered, "plus Mom had a nervous breakdown."

"I bet that's why Grammy seems so distant sometimes," Eve remarked. "How old was he when he died?"

"Almost two."

Suddenly Nora spoke up. "We don't know what he died of, but Mom blamed me for his death."

It got quiet.

Diane stared at Nora. "*What?* All these years you've kept it inside? How can it be true?"

"Are you sure?" Grace echoed. "Maybe we should talk to Mom and Dad about it."

"It would upset them too much," Nora said, "and I'm not sure we'd hear the truth."

"And Grampy?" Eve asked.

"Forget it. He's in denial," answered Diane.

"I'm trying to resolve it in my own way. Eventually I hope I'll find out what happened," Nora said.

Grace rolled her eyes. "You're not involving that psychic, are you?"

"Perhaps," Nora murmured.

Eve and Diane looked at each other in surprise. "Tell us more," said Eve.

"Another time. Let's go find Dad."

In the den, the football game aired softly. Their father hunched over a *New York Times* crossword puzzle, a pair of tortoise-shell glasses perched on the tip of his nose.

"How's the puzzle going?" Nora asked.

He looked up and grinned, his dimples showing. "Great, except for those damn foreign words. At least I know what *ague* means."

"Dad, can we talk?" Diane asked.

"Sure." He laid his pencil on the table and looked at his daughters.

"Something's not right with Mom," Diane said.

A cloudy look came over his face. "What do you mean?"

"She's been feeling nauseous," said Grace.

"And she hasn't been eating right. Today she ate like a bird," Nora added.

"She doesn't trust doctors, but she needs to see one," said Diane.

"It's probably a bug, hon. She'll be fine," her father replied, returning to his puzzle.

The next morning, Nora was relieved to find her mother buzzing around the kitchen, fixing bacon and scrambled eggs while humming to herself. She wore a long terrycloth robe over her nightgown. Her father sat at the breakfast table in his velour bathrobe and matching slippers, sipping coffee and reading the newspaper.

"Good Morning, Mom," Nora greeted. "How are you today?"

"Much better. I think I just needed a good night's sleep."

"It always helps me," Nora said, pouring a cup of coffee. Then, determined to show her mother affection, she hugged and kissed her on the way to the table. "Morning, Dad."

He looked up from the paper and smiled. "Good morning, honey."

"Would you like breakfast?" her mother asked.

"No thanks, just coffee, but you need to eat."

Her mother half-smiled before fixing herself a plate of bacon and eggs. *Maybe Dad's right. She seems better this morning,* Nora thought.

When Grace and Eve joined the family for breakfast, they talked about the upcoming Early Bird sale that would be happening in downtown Rocky Harbor to kick off the Christmas season.

"It's a tradition," Eve shared. "It starts at five in the morning and everyone wears their pajamas."

Then talk turned to the weather—a storm was heading northeast toward the coast of Maine. "I think we should try to beat the snow by leaving this morning," Grace said.

A short time later, Diane arrived. They all sat around the table, eating coffee cake and drinking coffee. Nora looked at her mother's plate, still untouched, and worry returned.

When they said their goodbyes, Nora held onto Diane for an extra minute. She'd always looked up to her older sister and could still picture the college calendar photo pose—*Miss July,* with Marilyn Monroe-esque hair, and a tall, twig-thin body, Diane perched on a boulder in the middle of a wildflower field, that determined look and smile broadcasting, *I know who I am,* while Nora, the middle child, floundered trying to find herself.

Now, preparing to leave, she struggled to find the perfect parting words for her parents. Hugs and kisses felt stiff, and unexpressed emotions hung heavy in the air. Shame, never-ending, stalked Nora wherever she went, even at Thanksgiving. She wondered if it was the same for her mother.

Nora asked herself why she hadn't taken the dress to Connecticut. It might have deflected the underlying tension she felt at her parents' house. But maybe it was best that the dress stayed behind. It was too unpredictable. Who knows what might have come to light?

On the drive home, they made plans to visit Angelica. Nora was going the next morning, but Eve couldn't, so they decided to go after the Early Bird sale.

"Let's surprise her," Eve said in a cheery voice, lifting the mood.

Ahead of the snowstorm, they stopped to pick up Margo from Kirk's house. When he opened the door, Nora collapsed into his arms.

"I missed you so much," she said, welcoming his lips upon hers. "I need some levity. Will you go with me to the Early Bird sale next weekend?"

"Anything for you, honey," he replied, planting another kiss on her lips.

Chapter 14

Nora slipped the fish dress over her head to get ready for her visit with Angelica. She knew her daughter would ask about her grandmother's health, and with no clear answers to give, Nora counted on the dress to provide clarity.

Angelica giggled when she saw her mother. "It's that weird dress again," she said, making a cross with her fingers and pointing it at the dress.

"It's a charming dress," Nora said, smiling and twirling before landing on the metal bench. "How was your Thanksgiving?"

"The turkey meat had a rainbow film over it, and the mashed potatoes were instant," Angelica said, gagging. "The only good part was dessert. Apple pie and vanilla ice cream, like Grampy's favorite. How's Grammy?"

Nora hesitated. "We're not sure. Dad says it's nothing, and Mom seemed better the day we left, but we still think she's covering up something. Still not eating much."

"That's not good," Angelica muttered.

"Diane's keeping a close eye on her, and she'll let us know."

Angelica frowned "I can't even send her a letter. She'd see it came from prison."

"You're right," Nora said, nodding. She felt the dress flinch. "Grammy and Grampy miss you and are proud you're such a hard worker."

Clenching her fists, Angelica groaned, "I can't take it."

"Don't be so hard on yourself," Nora said in a comforting voice.

Angelica sighed. "Well, I do have some good news. I've made a few friends and started a dance group."

Nora beamed at the shimmer in Angelica's eyes, thankful she acted on her mother's suggestion. "How exciting!"

"That's not all. I'm taking classes. Psychology. It's interesting."

Nora pressed her hands against the glass barrier and exclaimed, "I'm so proud of you!"

Angelica smiled and pressed her hands against her mother's, and Nora felt their warmth between the glass wall that separated them. "Mom, I need to ask you something. I know it's a touchy subject. We've been talking about domestic abuse, and I'm thinking of working in a battered women's shelter when I get out. How did you get the courage to leave Dad?"

Nora felt a knot in her stomach. "To be honest… well, it's a long story." Rosie's words flew into Nora's mind, *She longs for truth and clarity in relationships.* She could tell by the faraway look in Angelica's eyes that she was thinking about an old memory.

"Mom, remember when we lived in Connecticut and Dad would take us crabbing at the shore? He'd put me on his shoulders, and we'd walk through the woods to the water, and he taught me how to bait the traps and throw them in. When we pulled them out and put the crabs in a bucket, he would chase me with them and I'd hide behind you. I loved those times because you and Daddy weren't fighting."

Nora nodded. "We had some happy times," she said, recalling a kind, sensitive side of James, how he treated Angelica like his own kid, and how they both loved nature and the outdoors, especially the ocean. Nora had a vivid image of him carrying the traps, buckets, and long-handled net, a sheathed knife at his hip. At times he showed such strength and confidence. She clung to his words when he told her she was the perfect wife, and his beautiful stepdaughter was just like her mother.

Now, through the glass, Nora watched Angelica's face cloud over. "I remember he threw you against the wall and pounded you like you were a piece of dough. You could hardly walk, but you made it to the door and got away. I think that's my first memory. What happened?"

Nora's heart ached. She'd hoped her daughter had been spared the memory, at three years old. It had been cruel and vicious and for the first time, Nora had fought back. And now her daughter wanted to know more.

"The truth? It started when he came home and saw a sink full of dirty dishes. You and I were in the living room looking at books. He grabbed me by the arm and pulled me into the kitchen, yelling that I was a lazy bitch. Then he knocked me around the room and shoved me against the wall, pinning me in the corner and screaming that he was going to kill me. His eyes didn't look human. I was scared, and I could hear you crying in the next room.

"I waited for him to let his guard down, then I slipped through his hold and grabbed the closest weapon I could find—a heavy metal bar stool. My adrenalin kicked in, and I flung the stool at him full force. Then I grabbed the car keys and ran."

Nora saw Angelica's questioning eyes and thought she might ask, *Why did you abandon me that day?* But she didn't, instead asking, "Did you go to the police?"

Nora took a deep breath. "I wanted to, but I was scared of what he would do to me if they arrested him. I should've pressed charges. I drove to your babysitter's house and begged her to check on you. I couldn't go back; he would've killed me, so she went. We both knew he wouldn't dare lay a hand on her. When she came back, she told me you were playing dolls in the living room and your father was watching football on TV, calm as could be, like nothing had happened."

"So, what did happen?" Angelica asked, picking at her fingernails.

"I went home the next morning." Nora never forgot the babysitter's parting words but kept them to herself: *If it were me, I'd have grabbed my kid, gotten the hell out and divorced him. Then I would've gone back one more time and cut off his balls.*

"I should have left him for good that night and taken you with me, but I tried to make it work for your sake, and I was scared to leave him. I'm sorry, honey."

"So why did you leave?"

Nora took several deep breaths. "He started acting really strange. One night he came home from work with a pamphlet. It had a picture of a man chained to his bed, cringing with pain. Under the picture it said, 'It's too late to overcome the power of Satan.' He kept waving it in my face and growling that the devil is here, and I'd better watch it."

Angelica's eyes grew wider. "What drugs was *he* on?"

"Not sure he was on any drugs at that point. The next morning, I went to take a shower and there wasn't any water. Your father had shut the main off." Imitating Jim's gruff voice, she said. "I decide when you take a shower. I'll turn the water on when I'm damn good and ready. I'm the master, and you do what I say. Do you understand?"

Angelica made a face. "That's sick! Did he turn it back on?"

"Only after I got on my hands and knees and *begged*. But just the cold water, and he had the nerve to say, 'Enjoy your shower.'"

Angelica stared through the glass. "Pure evil." The five-minute warning buzzer sounded. "Hurry, Mom, I want to hear the rest."

"The next morning, our new neighbor knocked on the door after Jim left for work. He said he couldn't help overhearing our fights. That's when he said, 'Take your daughter and get out *now!* I don't want to be the one calling the police to report a murder. Or two.' That's when I made my big mistake. I waited for James to come home from work and I told him I was leaving him for good. Do you remember that day, when you ran to that neighbor's house for help?"

Angelica nodded. A glint of fear shone in her eyes.

"You saved my life," Nora said in a half-whisper.

"So that's why we went to live with Aunt Grace?" Angelica rubbed her eyes. "Mom, I need to ask you a question. I know he's not my real dad but he's the only dad I've ever known. What made him turn his back on me?"

"I don't have a good answer, but that doesn't mean he didn't love you."

"If he loved me… forget it. What ever happened to him anyway?"

"He disappeared and I didn't try to find him. Better safe than sorry."

"Fucking loser." She bit her lip. "No wonder I drown myself in drugs."

Nora felt powerless to stop the pain from boiling up inside her daughter, while she, herself, raged against Jim for breaking Angelica's heart, and even her spirit. But Nora knew she was complicit.

A few seconds passed in silence. "I wish I could have met my real father," Angelica said. "He would have loved me."

Nora's heart jumped. "He does love you—he'll always be in your heart, just as he's in mine."

Angelica placed her hand on her heart. "Thanks, Mom."

Nora stroked the sleeve of the fish dress. "I'm glad we're finally opening up and speaking the truth with each other."

"And within ourselves," Angelica added.

They kissed their fingers and touched them to the glass. Although divided by a thick wall, Nora believed they penetrated it with their love.

"Someday I'll make you and my real father proud. Promise."

With a wave and a blown kiss, Nora said, "You already have."

As she walked to the car, she thought about something Rosie had said to her—*While you may reconcile as mother and daughter, she's on her own journey.* Nora felt a glimmer of healing in herself that she hoped would ultimately set her daughter free.

Chapter 15

"**D**o you have your pajamas?" Nora asked Kirk over the phone. They were going to spend the night at her place and walk to the Early Bird sale in the morning.

"Sure do."

"We could stop for coffee at the Lobster Claw tomorrow morning before the Early Bird Sale."

"We can do that. I'll be over in an hour."

While she waited, Nora decided to practice meditating. She lay on her bed and played Rosie's tape, trying to catch the rhythm of the rise and fall from her stomach to her chest, with each breath in and out. She hadn't practiced as often as she'd meant to, what with work, visits to Angelica, and the trip to Connecticut.

She tried to relax but her mind filled with questions about her brother's death and how it might be linked to her past life. And what did she need to do to break a leftover vow? She was getting nowhere with meditating, so she stopped the tape and got up. She stood before her dresser and stared at the picture of Marguerita.

"And what secrets are *you* keeping?"

She called Grace. "Are you going to the Early Bird sale tomorrow?"

"Of course."

"Who are you going with?"

"Eve and Katrina. You want to come with us?"

"Kirk and I will meet you there. He's never been before."

Grace chuckled. "I hope he wears his pjs, otherwise he won't get the discounts."

"I told him. Why don't you meet us at the Lobster Claw at 4:30 tomorrow morning?"

Nora melted when she saw Kirk standing in her doorway holding a bouquet of long-stemmed red roses. "You shouldn't have," she exclaimed.

"Why not?" he said, his eyes gleaming. "Is it wrong for a guy to show his woman how much he loves her?"

This must be what Rosie meant by Divine Time, the way the relationship was progressing so quickly, Nora thought. She took the bouquet in her arms and inhaled the sweet fragrance of romance and passion that had been dead for so long. Kirk followed her into the kitchen and watched her trim the stems.

When she reached into the cupboard to get a vase, she felt his hands around her waist. Before she knew it, the roses lay on the counter, and she and Kirk were on the couch in the living room. They pleasured each other into the night, then drifted off to sleep in each other's arms, while Margo nested in the clothes which lay in a pile on the oriental rug.

Nora woke to the bells of downtown's clock tower, counting four tolls. "Rise and shine," she announced as she shook Kirk.

He yawned like a bear near hibernation. "Already?"

Nora hopped off the couch and ran to the bathroom where she showered and dressed in her flannel pajamas, the lavender ones imprinted with angels. "Hurry, get your pajamas on."

Kirk groaned. "I'm coming."

Several minutes later he emerged from the bathroom, stark naked.

"What on earth are you doing? You're supposed to be wearing pajamas."

"I am. This is what I wear to bed. You should know that by now."

"Wait a minute." Nora returned with a one-size-fits-all fluffy pink bathrobe. "There you go, tough guy."

Light snow had fallen through the night and continued as Nora and Kirk stepped out into the crisp, black morning. The sky hung over them like a dark canopy. Nora watched the flakes float down, glistening through the soft glow of streetlights. Their arms entwined like vines, and their boots crunched on the deserted snow-covered road leading to the East Side and the promise of strong coffee.

When they stepped inside the Lobster Claw, Kirk leaned Nora back in his arms and smothered her with a juicy kiss.

"Wow!" she said, savoring the sweet taste of his lips on hers. "What did I do to deserve that?"

"This is where we met." He grinned widely, pointing to the mistletoe above them.

"Good morning. I see it worked out well," the waitress shouted from behind the counter. "I'm the matchmaker who delivered the napkin."

Nora and Kirk laughed, and he shouted back, "You have a good memory. That was six months ago."

"Did you ever get the lobster you were hunting for?"

He patted his stomach. "Oh yes."

The waitress raised her eyebrows. "That's quite a robe you're wearing. Grab a table, and I'll be right over."

"I love the reindeer tablecloths," Nora said when the waitress brought two jumbo mugs of steaming coffee. "Do I smell cinnamon?"

"Yes. Freshly made doughnuts. You've got to have at least one. They're free."

"In that case, we'll take a dozen," Kirk said, winking.

There was a commotion at the door, and in walked Katrina wearing a black peekaboo negligee trimmed with fur, and a shawl draped over her shoulders. She clicked across the wooden floor in red kitten heels.

"Meow," Kirk said in a whispery voice, prompting Nora to give him the stink eye.

Grace, in a red plaid flannel granny gown, and Eve, in a stunning scarlet embroidered kimono, followed.

After everyone sat, Nora introduced Kirk, reminding him that Katrina had been at the Ark the night he played. "And this beautiful woman," Nora continued while pointing to Eve, "is Grace's daughter—my niece."

"Enjoyed your music," Katrina said with a smile, her dimples showing.

"Aren't you cold? asked Eve, eying her skimpy outfit.

"Of course," she laughed.

The door slammed. A figure stood inside the entrance, brushing the snow off his coat and stomping his feet on the door mat.

"Thomas!" Katrina shouted. "Take your coat off so we can see what you're wearing and come join us."

He scowled as he lumbered to the table, then froze when he saw Grace.

"There's a seat here," she offered, pointing to the only vacant spot, which happened to be beside her.

Surprised at the offer, Nora glanced at her sister.

"No thanks," he replied in a chilly voice, dragging an empty chair from another table and wedging it in the aisle, close to Katrina.

"A onesie!" Nora exclaimed. She admired the crimson color and shiny metal snaps that trailed down the front of Thomas's pajamas. "I haven't seen one of those since my daughter was a child. Does it have footies and a butt flap?

He nodded.

Katrina said, "It would look better if you wore it backwards."

Everyone laughed except Thomas. Nora reached over and rested her hand on his wrist. "Thomas, meet Kirk. And Kirk, meet my good friend Thomas. He was also at the Ark the night you performed."

They shook hands and Kirk said, "Just getting in the holiday spirit." He stroked the collar of his robe. "Are you out to do Early Bird shopping?"

Thomas groaned. "Orders from my boss to pick up a present for his wife."

"What are you getting her?" Eve asked.

"Not a clue."

Katrina smirked. "How about a fancy fish dress?"

"How would you like a harpoon up your ass?" Thomas said in a half-joking voice.

"Ouch," she yelped, squishing up her nose.

"Does this have to do with Nora's dress?" asked Kirk.

Nora patted Kirk's fuzzy thigh. "I'll explain later."

"Be right back," Thomas said as he headed toward the counter.

Katrina looked at Grace. "I don't know what he's getting Mrs. Carver, but you should give him a hatchet for Christmas."

"Why?" Grace asked.

"So he can bury it."

Eve looked at her mother. "Mom, I didn't realize it was that bad between the two of you."

Nora spoke up. "I don't think he means to be nasty, his heart's broken."

"I suppose," Grace said.

Thomas returned with a full coffee pot and a dozen doughnuts, as if he were making a peace offering. He seemed to have emerged from the cloud he'd been in a few minutes earlier, now acting jovial and even glancing in Grace's direction. When they got ready to leave, Thomas insisted on giving a generous tip.

As they exited the coffee shop, Kirk swooped Nora under the mistletoe again and they kissed.

"Oh my God," Katrina screeched. "How did I miss that before?" She grabbed Grace and planted a kiss on her lips.

"Yuck," shrieked Grace, wiping her mouth with her hand.

Katrina turned to Thomas and Grace. "C'mon, you two. Don't you know it's bad luck not to kiss under the mistletoe?"

Thomas fumbled as he took Grace's hand and brushed his lips across her cheek. Nora was surprised Grace didn't pull away. Afterwards, Grace took Eve by the hand and stood under the mistletoe, kissing her daughter's forehead.

They crossed the footbridge, which was decorated with rainbow colors of Christmas tree lights casting a ghostly glow through twilight fog. In the harbor, the low wail of a foghorn orchestrated a syncopated sea chant that Nora imagined once filled the air with songs of sailors. Early Bird shoppers passed one another like apparitions. Half-way across the footbridge, Nora and Kirk stepped into Mystique, tinkling the bells on the way in, while the rest of the group continued downtown to help Thomas find a gift.

Inside the shop, a magical wonderland unfolded, with crystals, angels, witches, and snow babies strung from the ceiling, and a strobe light that made Nora feel as if she might enter a vortex. Mystic sounds chanted in the background, while the strong scent of Siberian fir incense swirled around them.

Miss June burst forth from the back room, dressed in a winter white cape over a granny gown. She threw her arms around Nora.

"Hello, dear. Good to see you, and who might this handsome man be?"

"Kirk, this is Miss June."

"Nice to meet you. Quite an unusual shop you have here."

She smiled and gave him a hug. "Thank you. Help yourselves to free coffee and doughnuts, and don't forget about the raffle."

Nora puffed out her cheeks. "Thanks, I'm stuffed. We just came from the Lobster Claw. But I'll fill out a raffle ticket."

It pleased Nora that Kirk accepted June's hospitality by making room for one more glazed doughnut and another cup of coffee.

The door swung open. A hooded figure in a long crimson cloak crossed the threshold and stamped the snow off shiny black patent leather laced boots, revealing red and white striped stockings.

"Hello, Nora," a familiar voice rang out as the woman pulled back her hood.

"Rosie!" exclaimed Nora. "I've been meaning to call you."

Rosie gave a hearty laugh. "I've been wondering what happened." She turned her attention to Kirk. "Perhaps this gentleman knows."

Kirk extended his hand toward Rosie. "Hi, I'm Kirk, and yes, I'm responsible for monopolizing Nora's spare time."

"I'm happy for both of you," Rosie said, encircling them with a bear hug. "I see the love aura around you. Don't you, June?"

"Absolutely." June's eyes shimmered, and silver wisps of hair danced around her cherub face. "Young man, come with me." She led him by the hand to the other side of the shop. Nora heard them whisper and saw them point at something in the glass case.

Rosie pulled Nora aside. "I'm glad we bumped into each other. Are you ready to take the journey?"

Caught by surprise, she muttered, "I've been practicing."

"That's good. How about tomorrow at noon?"

"Sorry, I'm going to see Angelica."

"Then Monday?" Rosie persisted.

Nora heard the exuberance in Rosie's voice and didn't want to disappoint her, despite a nagging fear of the unknown. "Um—sure. I'll come after work at four."

"Perfect! Now, why don't I help you pick out a Christmas present for Kirk while he's busy with Miss June. Does he wear jewelry? Maybe a pendant."

"He might think it's too feminine."

"Well, he *is* wearing a furry pink robe."

Nora laughed. "Don't ask."

"Miss June has lovely wooden vintage valet boxes. That's jewelry boxes for men."

"Come to think of it, he wears a watch and has two rings." She remembered seeing a wedding band and an old high school ring in a dish on his dresser.

Nora spotted a box inlaid with orange-red nuggets that emitted an irresistible translucence. She ran her fingers over the smooth dark wood, touching the gems, which reminded her of the setting sun. "Is this carnelian?"

"Yes. A stabilizing stone of truth, love, and faith."

Nora hesitated, not because she didn't want the box, but it was out of her price range. Perhaps she could work out a payment plan with Miss June.

"It's precious, and the perfect gift for him," Rosie said.

"Then that's the one I'll take."

"We don't want him to see it. I'll hide it under the counter, and you can settle up with Miss June later. Not a second too soon. Here they come."

"What's that?" Nora asked, eyeing a small bag in Kirk's hand.

He tucked the package in his bathrobe and cast a secretive glance her way. "No peeking."

Nora turned to the women and thanked them. After final embraces and well wishes, they exited the shop and greeted sunrise and the lifting fog, where passersby now looked more like the living than the walking dead.

Carolers serenaded Kirk and Nora off the footbridge. A Salvation Army bell ringer stood on the corner, grinning when Kirk tossed a twenty-dollar bill in the bucket.

"You are so kind," Nora said, squeezing his hand.

"I can't help it. It's contagious." He kissed her on the lips.

Hand in hand, they walked along Main Street, popping in and out of shops and observing pajama-clad patrons, many overloaded with bags and boxes. "I wonder where Grace and the others are," Nora said.

"I'm sure we'll bump into them."

They approached a crowd blocking the sidewalk, with a television station van parked nearby. "Probably Santa," Kirk remarked.

"Is that Katrina?" asked Nora.

Kirk strained his neck to get a better look. "Yep. I'd recognize that skimpy outfit anywhere."

"No wonder she's being interviewed," Nora said.

The camera lens zoomed in on Katrina, perched on a stool and giggling into a microphone. She waved to Kirk and Nora, now with Grace, Eve, and Thomas. Pointing to Kirk, Katrina told the announcer it was his first time at the Early Bird event.

They immediately summoned him to the makeshift stage.

"Whom do we have the pleasure of speaking with?" the announcer asked.

He cleared his throat. "Kirk Kloppenheimer."

"So, what's your opinion of the Early Bird sale?"

"Great bargains, and I'm having a fantastic time."

"What brings you here?"

"My girlfriend, she lives in town and does the Early Bird every year."

"You're in a holiday spirit. You look tremendous in your fuzzy pink robe," the announcer said, winking.

Smiling, Kirk replied, "Remember, I'm not available—already taken."

Just then, Cliff, dressed in a ketchup-red Santa suit, passed by with his wiener wagon, decorated with miniature light-up plastic hot dog ornaments. The crowd heard he was giving away breakfast sausages in buns. After shaking the announcer's hand, Kirk hopped offstage, grabbed Nora's hand, and joined the parade of shoppers chasing the cart.

While waiting in line, Nora and Kirk met up with Grace and the others. They chatted about Thomas purchasing an elephant-shaped teapot, certainly Third World enough for Mrs. Carver, and Eve winning the gas grill door prize from the hardware store. Kirk and Nora were sorry to hear they'd missed Katrina falling off the stool.

"The announcer caught me in his arms," she said, her dimples still glowing. "I gave him my number to call and make sure I'm okay. What have you two been up to?"

Kirk's eyebrows twitched. "I met the psychic. She's a cross between Red Riding Hood and the Wicked Witch of the West."

Everyone laughed except Nora.

By early afternoon, all were ready for a nap, so they said their goodbyes. When Nora and Eve hugged, Eve whispered, "I miss Angelica. She would have enjoyed this. I can't wait to see her when we visit her later."

****

"Surprise!" the trio shouted, jumping up and down in the booth when Angelica entered the prison cubicle. Nora watched helplessly as Angelica's face turned red and her eyes looked down at the floor, her head slumping. Nora regretted not preparing Angelica for the visit. She should have known that seeing Eve might trigger feelings of shame.

Angelica cried, and soon Eve was crying, too. And Grace. And Nora. They huddled together against the glass barrier and Angelica joined them on her side. They pressed their fingers together on the glass, and all sorrow melted into recollections of carefree childhood memories.

"Remember the old camper?" asked Eve, grinning.

Angelica giggled. "Of course. It never left your driveway, but we had some great adventures in it. Like sleepovers, even though it was full of spiders."

"And it smelled like dirty socks," Eve added, pinching her nose.

"How about catching fireflies?" Grace remarked. "I think you used them as lights in the camper."

"Auntie Grace, I remember you used to make paper mache piñatas stuffed with candy for our birthdays."

Nora smiled. "Grace, you're so artistic. I remember we would all go to the beach and collect shells and beach glass. Then you'd help us make jewelry out of them."

"Eve, when you watched me after school, we used to make fairy houses. I think there's still one in Mom's attic."

"And then there was the time we took the whale watch cruise," Eve proclaimed.

Angelica burst out laughing. "And I threw one of my new sneakers overboard, and it disappeared into the ocean."

"You've always been curious," Nora said lightly, thinking that *impulsive* would be a better description.

They continued reminiscing until the five-minute warning sounded. Nora, mesmerized by her daughter's beauty, stared longingly at Angelica's shimmery hazel eyes, radiant skin, the rich mane of fluffy black hair that danced around her face, and a broad smile that filled the room. Nora could not remember the last time she had seen Angelica so happy.

At the end of the visit, Angelica raised her hands to the glass again, and one by one, each visitor touched the glass and blew her a kiss. When it was Eve's turn, she and Angelica fought back tears. "Have fun in China. I can't wait to see you again. Thanks for always having my back, Eve," Angelica told her cousin.

Chapter 16

Nora slept restlessly on the eve of her past life regression with Rosie. She dozed alongside Margo until the sun rose, then got up and brewed a pot of Sumatran coffee. She drank it until her body shook like a tree branch in a windstorm. To calm her nerves down, she slipped the dress on and practiced the meditation tape before heading to the school.

Most of the day she kept her attention on the students, but by the time she lifted the moon-shaped door knocker, her jitters had returned.

Rosie greeted her with flickering eyes, a hug, and a lipstick kiss. Something looked different about her. Perhaps it was the muumuu, not the floral design she usually wore but lacy layers of cream-colored muslin cascading down her body, with thorny stems woven into the fabric. Flared sleeves trimmed with fringe extended to her fingertips. One of the oddest features was the dress's length, which had no distinct hemline but jagged edges lapping at her legs. Nora preferred the cheery flower patterns, not these jagged layers of cloth, and hoped they weren't premonitory.

Rosie looked at Nora's feet and grinned. "Take your shoes off. You won't need them where you're going."

As they walked toward the parlor, Nora asked, "Will it be like watching a movie, or will I be *in* the movie? Will I levitate? How do you know I'll come back?"

"Not to worry," Rosie assured her, wrapping her arm around Nora's shoulders. "Your body will stay on the couch, but your mind and spirit will enter another world—Marguerita's—and she won't even know you're there. I'll be guiding you back and forth between both worlds. I promise you won't get stuck. Trust me."

"Have you done this before?" Nora asked, her voice quivering.

"Time travel? Of course. Most people don't think it's plausible but that's because they put limitations on life, and themselves." She pointed to Nora's wristwatch. "Take the whole notion of time: a device invented by humans to stay in a single dimension, where they never evolve into what they could become."

"You're talking about me, right?" Nora asked, blushing.

Rosie nodded. "And others. People would be better off viewing themselves from different perspectives. When you step outside of time, you'll be able to see things from both your perspective and Marguerita's. You want to keep going, right?"

"I-I think so. I was quite sure when I walked in here, but now I've got doubts."

Rosie waved a hand in the air. "Oh, how the demon of fear loves to rear its ugly head. You *do* want to break the vow so you can get on with the life you deserve, right?"

"Yes, but I wonder about the dress."

Rosie's eyes penetrated like darts. "What about it?"

Nora gave her a side glance and looked down at the black sea cloth. "I thought it would help me."

The psychic leaned over and touched a crisscross symbol. "Have faith in the dress, for if it did *all* the work, what would you gain? I promise it will point you in the right direction. Hasn't it served you well so far?"

Nora was silent.

"Come, lie down," Rosie said, patting the recliner.

Nora hesitated, first clinging to the edge of the recliner, then easing her way down and sank into a plush velvet mound of fluff.

"Just like the meditation tape, I will count slowly from ten to one. When you fall into a trance, I'll call you by the name of Marguerita DeRoche, living near Granada, Spain, in the mid-1800's. Oh, I almost forgot to give you this."

Rosie handed over the picture of the nun. Nora clasped it between her hands while her eyes batted open and shut like window shades until she could no longer fight the urge to close them. Inhaling through her nose and exhaling out her mouth, she drifted off into a pleasant, hypnotic state, with Rosie's calming voice and ocean sounds splashing over her.

"Focus on the rhythm of your breath, and let your whole body go limp as we count. Ten, nine, eight, seven, six…"

Nora's eyelids grew heavy as stone, and her mind turned fuzzy. Unsure if the nun and Rosie were still with her, she floated in a vast sea, bobbing up and down in waves of time, until she slipped through one of its cracks.

****

My eyes open. I'm standing on a plateau tucked in a mountain ridge and surrounded by caves offering torchlight and warmth from the chill that runs through my bones. In the distance, I hear the clattering of hooves and wagon wheels over rocky turf, as well as packs of barking dogs. All familiar—along with blazing furnaces, iron pounding, and sparks flying. Suddenly it dawns on me: *I'm in Marguerita's world!*

A young girl stands near one of the caves, wearing a bright red skirt and a white blouse with puffy sleeves. She's draped with scarves and beads of every color. *I'm a gypsy? I expected a nun.*

I slip into Marguerita's body as seamlessly as putting on stockings. Twirling and whirling my scarves in the breeze makes me feel wild and free, as if I could soar like a raptor above the snow-capped mountains.

The wind whispers, "Mountains?"

Yes, I live in the mountains, hidden in the hills of Spain with my Sacromonte gypsy family. Hark! I hear dogs barking and see children playing tag near the wagons, but before I step closer, I want to make sure I can slip out of Marguerita as smoothly as I entered her.

Slip out? Now I will slip back in—but where is Marguerita? A patch of red disappears into the woods. I'm certain it is her. I follow the girl down a winding path and discover she is not alone but with a girl she calls Heathera. They gallop like wild horses, their manes flying in the wind—Marguerita's coal black locks and her friend's blazing red hair—as their hooves clatter along the stony turf. They are having fun pretending to be horses, so I catch up with them and shift back inside my former self.

"You seem to be a happy child."

Is it the wind?

"How old are you?"

Again, a voice.

"Nine, I believe. Who are you?"

A hearty laugh tumbles from the sky. I recognize it as Rosie's, though her voice sounds wobbly, like she's talking under water.

"I told you I wouldn't abandon you. Remember, we can speak to each other but no one else can hear or see us. The thoughts you have, and the words you use, may not be those of a nine-year-old, for you are also Nora."

"I know, it's all very strange and exciting, but I don't feel her age."

"That's because you're much older in spirit, and when you are with her, you think and speak like Nora."

"Rosie, I must tell you something."

"What is it?"

"I'm a gypsy!"

"But you're Sister Marguerita—a far cry from a Romani."

"Ouch!"

"What happened?"

"Heathera and I just pricked our fingers and rubbed our blood together. We stole a needle from the beldames. Blood sisters forever!"

From where we are hiding behind our special rock, we hear the shouts of Sacromonte men and women and watch them pass. The mules and horses trudge along in slow-motion with their bellies sagging under the weight of saddlebags stuffed with gold coins, silver candelabras, and musical instruments inlaid with ivory. The gypsies have done well in their trip to the city of Malaga.

Still inside Marguerita, I race to camp with Heathera, and we sit around the bonfire, listening to tales of good fortune—how the men traded their iron-ware for livestock and precious gifts, and how the beldames—those ancient turbaned women with fiery eyes and a thousand wrinkles—read palms and told fortunes, interpreted dreams and sold potions, promising fulfillment of hearts' desires for the exchange of gold pieces.

Through the smoky hiss of fire and crackling branches, I hear Rosie ask if the Romanies have such good luck every time, so I step outside Marguerita and tell Rosie, "Some nights there is weeping, but they have an old saying, *We croon like violins through our tears, and cinders send secrets into the sky. Still, we feast, dance, and sing into the half-light."*

Still standing apart from Marguerita, I watch the women move around the fire, its fingers scorching my skin while smoke clouds my vision and transforms the gypsies into orbs of color as they twirl to strumming guitars. Women lower their veils to just below their eyes, and then their halters; thousands of coins jangle furiously from belted scarves tied around the skirts swirling before my eyes.

The men edge closer, and the sharp voice of a crone cries out, "Restrain yourselves. Romani women may look desirable, but they are not to be touched."

I relish the night air, a concoction of burning cedar, incense, and fatted swine sizzling on the spit. My mouth waters at fresh bread baking in the embers. Eager to eat, I move back inside Marguerita.

What's happening? I was inside Marguerita a moment ago, but suddenly I'm being pulled up by a gale, tossed around like a rag doll. Another crack in time? *Rosie, where the hell are you? ...* I'm free-falling ... dying? ... crashing ... a bed of ice ... my head.

Nora drifted back and forth between sleep and wakefulness. She heard faint chanting sounds and thought she saw a shadowy figure hover over her in the dim light. Much later, she returned to full awareness of the present, lying on the recliner in the parlor. Rosie was sitting beside her, stroking her hand.

"Welcome back. I didn't mean to smother you with blankets, but your body was ice cold and turning blue, and your teeth were chattering as loud as a flock of magpies."

A hazy memory of gaiety-turned-to-doom filled Nora. She rubbed her eyes.

"I was celebrating with my gypsy family. What happened? Did you try to bring me back?"

"Of course not. However, glitches occur once in a blue moon."

The disappointment was overwhelming. "If my body stayed on the recliner, why am I freezing to death, and why is my head killing me?" Nora snapped.

"My dear, when the emotions are strong, it can fool the physical body into thinking it's actually experiencing physical pain."

Caught between trust and mistrust, Nora didn't know whether to believe Rosie. Contrary to what she said, it was possible Nora's body, mind, and spirit had *all* left the room. She placed her hand on the crown of her head and moaned. What little strength she had evaporated like water in a dry summer heat.

"I just want to go home," she murmured.

****

Nora tucked the dress and the picture in a trunk in the attic, rather than keeping them in her bedroom. Out of sight, it might help her forget how her past life regression ended with that dreadful experience, almost freezing to death.

She'd barely recovered when Thomas showed up with more hand-me-downs. "You're welcome to come in, but leave the bag outside," she told him. "After what I've been through with the dress, I don't wish to touch another thing from Mrs. Carver."

"You were supposed to return the dress. I warned you." A slight smirk appeared on his face as he dropped the bag. He looked at his watch. "Got to go, duty calls. I enjoyed meeting Kirk yesterday. Seems like a nice guy."

Nora blushed. "I never thought I'd be in a relationship again."

A foggy look rolled over his eyes.

"I'm sorry. But, hey, at least you and Grace were civil to each other at the Early Bird."

"It never would have worked," Thomas muttered, shaking his head. "I love your sister, but I can't give her what she wants."

"Someone who'll spend more time with her and make her feel appreciated? Is that asking too much?"

He shook his head. "You don't understand, it's not that simple."

"I do understand. Until I met Kirk, I was afraid to commit to a relationship. I think you've got the same problem."

"She's got a boyfriend now, so it doesn't matter."

"She loves you, *dummy*. You're both too stubborn to admit it."

That night, Rosie called to check on Nora, who thanked her for showing concern, adding that it would be awhile before she would consider returning to her past life.

"Nora, you must expect trials and tribulations. Remember our first session, when I touched your palms, and they were hard as rocks? Symbolic of the perseverance you'll need for this quest. You've got to deal with the past, otherwise, it will steal your future."

Nora groaned. "I'll call you when I'm ready."

Chapter 17

Nora usually avoided Happy Hour, especially on a Monday. It seemed like such a desperate way to start the week, but she needed to talk. She stepped inside the Ark and felt instant relief at seeing the girls at the bar, Katrina's dancer legs dangling to one side and Grace wearing the usual—a denim skirt, clay-stained tee, ankle socks, and scuffed black work shoes, which she planted on the bottom rung of the stool as if they were in it for the long haul.

"I can't believe you made it," Katrina called out.

"I told you she'd come," Grace chirped, patting the empty stool next to her. "She's a changed woman since she met Kirk."

Nora waved a twenty-dollar bill at the bartender. "This round's on me."

They toasted to Grace's new man Jon, Katrina's sex romp with a plumber, and Nora's deepening feelings for Kirk. She navigated through the conversation like a boat slipping into the harbor at night as she changed the subject from the men in their lives to her past life regression misadventure.

"It started out okay but turned into a disaster. I nearly froze to death. Plus, I thought I was going back as a nun, but I turned out to be a gypsy."

"You're kidding," Grace said.

"How do you explain the picture of Sister Marguerita?" Katrina asked.

"I was too upset to ask."

"What about the dress?" Grace asked.

"I never even saw it."

Grace said, "Wasn't it supposed to help you?"

Nora shrugged.

"How much does Kirk know?" asked Katrina.

"Probably more than I should've told him," Nora answered, looking down at the table.

Katrina frowned. "I'm surprised he didn't walk away."

Grace grimaced. "We don't want that to happen. Nora, do you remember—"

"Wait," Nora said, holding up her hand. She'd noticed the bartender hovering, with his ear tilted like a satellite in their direction. They moved to a table in the corner, set down their drinks, and like magnets, drew closer.

"As I was about to say," Grace continued, "Your bed was shaking, and it levitated three feet off the ground, with you in it."

Katrina looked at Nora, her eyes round as full moons.

"That was a long time ago. I threw that thing in the trash and haven't looked at a Ouija board since."

"You need to do the same thing with the fish dress," Grace said. "Get rid of it!"

"Burn it!" insisted Katrina.

Grace added, "You and I have had many conversations about yin and yang, shadow and light. We agree that the Universe has negative and positive forces. Maybe the karma connected with Marguerita and the dress is too dark for you to keep. If it were me, I'd toss it in the ocean where some poor mermaid's searching for it."

Nora pictured the fish dress sloshing around, tangled and twisted, gasping for air, much the way she, herself, often felt.

"If you must know, I packed away Marguerita and the dress in the attic, and that's where they will stay until I talk to Rosie again. I'm not ready to give it up, not yet anyway."

"You're going back after what happened?" Katrina asked.

"I'm not saying I would, but if I did, I'd need the dress."

"What makes you so sure Rosie's right about the nun and the dress holding the key to a fulfilled life?" Grace asked. "Look at you—things couldn't be better—Angelica's recovering, you're with the man of your dreams, and you're happy for the first time in years."

"And you're having great sex. I should borrow the dress," Katrina said in a dreamy voice. "Don't get rid of it yet. But Grace is right. Your life is improving."

Nora looked around the table. "It's true, I *am* doing much better." Turning to her sister, she said, "Let's talk about you. Thomas stopped by again. He still loves you, Grace."

Grace made a face. "He's got a weird way of showing it."

Katrina said, "As long as you're with Jon he won't try to win you back."

Grace sighed. "It wouldn't have worked anyway. I couldn't be the Stepford wife he wants."

"If you ask me, you're both stubborn. Admit it, you still love him," Katrina said.

Grace ignored her and looked at Nora. "How are things going with Angelica?"

Nora lit up. "Great! She started a dance group, and she's taking psychology classes. Wants to be a counselor in a battered women's shelter."

"Wow!" Katrina said.

Grace beamed. "I knew she would come around."

"Yes, she's finally beginning to feel worthy about herself," Nora said, breathing a sigh of relief.

Grace chuckled. "Like somebody else we know?"

"True, just like her mother," Nora agreed. Then in a serious voice, she said, "I need to ask you all a question. Do you think it's a good idea if I take Kirk to meet Angelica this weekend?"

"What have you told her about him?" asked Grace.

Nora blushed. "That he's smart, handsome, and treats me like a princess. She's happy I'm dating."

"In that case, it would be fine to bring him with you," Grace said.

Katrina nodded. "Do it, Nora. Speaking of Kirk, did he have a good time at the Early Bird sale?"

"He loved it, especially visiting Mystique. Did I tell you I won their hundred-dollar raffle?" Nora asked, thankful to fund Kirk's Christmas gift, the valet jewelry box embedded with Carnelian, a stabilizing stone of truth, love, and faith.

Grace cheered. "He brought you good luck."

"I'm sure you'd rather believe the angels stepped in," Katrina teased, "but he's a keeper."

****

"I hope your daughter's okay with me coming along," Kirk said on the way to the prison.

"She'll be fine, just be yourself," Nora said, sliding over closer and resting her hand on his thigh. She admired him for caring about Angelica, despite having never met her. "Have you been to a prison before?"

"As an inmate or a visitor?"

"Either."

"Can't say as I have." He glanced at Nora. "Why?"

"The first time I visited, it overwhelmed me to see concrete blocks in a wasteland, barbed wire fences, and people lined up outside looking like they were waiting in a food line."

"Humbling, wasn't it?"

Nora nodded. "There I was, dressed to the hilt in the fish dress and my high heels, while everyone else looked like they were wearing regular work clothes. I was so embarrassed."

He gave her a funny look. "Why did you wear the dress?"

"Don't ask," she replied. "I kept thinking *my daughter deserves better than this.*"

They parked the car and joined the long line of visitors waiting to enter. When the floodgates opened, a guard herded them into a large room, made them stuff their belongings in lockers and ordered them to sit on folding metal chairs lined up against the walls. One by one they passed through the metal detector, handing over their shoes for a contraband check.

"What a friendly place," Kirk commented with raised eyebrows.

They returned to their seats and waited. From where they sat, they could see the inmates standing in line, down a long glass corridor leading to the visiting cubicles. Dressed in bright orange suits, the women reminded Nora of fire ants tunneling through a plastic ant farm Angelica once had. As they filed through, she spotted her daughter.

"There she is," Nora said, pointing and jumping up and down.

"She's gorgeous!" Kirk said, his eyes planted on Angelica.

"I can't believe she's wearing a plastic cross around her neck. That's new," Nora whispered.

"Looks like she's having a 'Come to Jesus' moment."

"What's that?"

"Sometimes prisoners find religion in a moment of despair. That's probably how she's coping."

"Oh," Nora said, recalling when, years earlier, she had sought solace in secretly visiting her brother's cemetery plot and adorning it with tiny metal toy trucks that he would have loved.

"At last," Kirk said under his breath as they were ushered into a small room. He stared at the *FUCK YOU* graffiti on the glass wall overlooking the empty cubicle.

"That's nothing," Nora whispered, "I'm used to it by now."

The cubicle door opened, and Angelica entered. There she stood, looking somberly peaceful, her eyes doe-like. She sat down opposite Nora and Kirk, the glass barrier and the grated microphone between them.

"Hi, Mom." Her eyes were watering.

"Hi, sweetie. I'm so happy to see you. I've missed you terribly. Are you okay?

"Happy tears." Angelica smiled and gave a thumbs up.

"This is the man I was telling you about." She rested her arm on his shoulder and announced, "Kirk, meet my daughter, Angelica."

He stood up and bowed to her. "I'm honored. How are you doing?"

"Okay, thanks. Nice to meet you." She fingered the cross as she spoke.

"I hear you're doing amazing things."

Angelica beamed. "I'm trying… to redeem the time."

Nora nodded, vaguely recalling an old Bible quote. "I like your pink cross."

Angelica blushed and lifted the plastic crucifix in the air. "This? I got it in a Bible study group from the chaplain."

"That's wonderful," Nora said, trying to disguise her guilt at not having laid a building block of a religious foundation in her daughter's life, one that might have saved her from temptation.

"Thanks, Mom. I found a Bible passage that's been helping me. Do you want to hear it?"

Without waiting for a response, she recited,

"To everything there is a season, and a time to every purpose under the heaven: A time to be born, and a time to die; A time to weep, and a time to laugh; A time to keep silent, and a time to speak; all are of the dust, and all turn to dust again."

"Ecclesiastes 3," Kirk nodded.

Angelica's eyes widened. "You know that?"

"It's a Byrd's song I play. Guitar. Besides, I was raised in an orphanage. Up at dawn for prayers and a Hail Mary or two. The nuns didn't think twice about paddling me with a ruler, hanging me by my ears, or sending me to solitary without supper."

"Sounds like prison," Angelica quipped.

"All things considered, I turned out okay, and you will, too."

Angelica crossed her arms. "I've decided to make the best of my time here—it's half over, so I'll be out next December, a year from now."

Nora sighed. It had been one year already, but another year of incarceration seemed inconceivable.

"Mom, how's Grammy?"

"She's doing okay. Grace and I might go down during Christmas break, which is only two weeks away."

A momentary faraway look spread over Angelica's face. "I wish I could go."

"I wish you could, too," Nora said, as sadness filled her insides like air inflating a balloon. Kirk held her hand, and the five-minute warning bell blasted the silence.

"I enjoyed meeting you, Angelica. You have to come out to the island sometime," Kirk offered, his voice resonating with kindness.

Angelica nodded. "I'd like that. My mom says it's beautiful."

He gave her a thumbs-up, and she reciprocated. "Plan on it," he said.

"Will I see you before Christmas, Mom?"

"Yes, darling, I promise," Nora answered, wiping away the shred of a tear. Nora felt Kirk's arm around her shoulders. It comforted her, that human touch, yet it triggered a yearning to embrace her daughter. Their fingers mirrored on the glass. They exchanged smiles, but both understood that beneath those smiles, melancholy hearts hid.

On the way to the car, Kirk asked, "How do you think it went?"

"She seemed in better spirits than I expected."

"That's encouraging, but don't be shocked if the Jesus jacket comes off."

"What do you mean?"

"I doubt she understands the commitment. Has she gone to church much?"

Nora gave him a nervous smile. "No, not really." *I never even had her baptized,* she admitted to herself.

"Beware of religiosity. Superficial, extreme worshipping rules and rituals instead of having a genuine relationship with Jesus—someone to talk to like a friend. Believe me, I know from personal experience."

"Have you made a real connection?"

A peaceful glow came over his face. "Yes, in my own way."

"I hope she'll do the same." Then Nora frowned, regretting her failure as a role model. How could she, so filled with anger against God for taking away her brother and casting her in the depths of despair? Over time, she'd softened but still questioned her faith in God.

"There's strength inside her, just like her mom." He pulled Nora into his arms and kissed her forehead, squeezed her once, then let go and opened the passenger door.

"Let's go home and partake of some bedroom communion."

Chapter 18

Three days later, Nora received a call from her sister Diane, who told her that their mother had been rushed to the hospital in the middle of the night and admitted. " We're meeting with the doctor today, we should know more soon."

"Do you think Grace and I should come home?"

Diane sighed. "It would be a good idea. Dad's not much help. He's still convinced it's just a stomach bug."

"I'll talk with Grace. You shouldn't have to handle this alone."

The next night, Nora and Grace headed for Connecticut, stopping at Dunkin' Donuts on their way off the peninsula. With Nora at the wheel, they plowed through the dense fog and heavy rain pounding the windshield. At first, the sisters chattered like magpies, talking about Katrina's torrid love affairs and the latest arrests in town.

After a rare moment of silence, Grace said, "Listen to us, you know this isn't what's really on our minds."

Nora nodded. "You're right. I keep thinking about all the years I've wedged Mom between deadlines and obligations—not calling her or hopping in the car to visit, and now she might be dying." Nora choked on her words as her eyes watered.

Grace leaned over and touched Nora's arm. "We know nothing yet. Hopefully we'll find out more when we get to the hospital."

"You want to hear something ridiculous?" Nora said. "I feel guilty taking time off from work to see Mom."

"It's an emergency, Nora. For God's sake, if something were to happen to you tonight, they'd have someone doing your job tomorrow."

Nora's chest heaved. "You're right."

In the wee hours, wrapped in a blanket of silence, the sisters drifted along the interstate, lost in private thoughts. Regret loomed large over Nora. If only she had tried harder to reach out to her mother, even though they rarely had a meaningful conversation. If only they could talk about Seth. Now she feared it might be too late, a missed opportunity to make amends. Nora wondered if Grace had her own regrets and fears.

"I wonder if Mom will be awake," Grace said.

"It'll be early," said Nora, "but who sleeps in the hospital, anyway?

"I hope the gift store is open so we can pick up flowers," Grace said.

On the last leg of the trip, Nora tuned the radio to her sister's favorite country music station.

Even though it was dawn when they reached Connecticut, a thick fog enshrouded the hospital and blanketed the parking lot. Near the main entrance, they spotted a flower shop but it was closed, so they continued on to the Information Desk and were directed to the fourth floor.

"This elevator couldn't move any slower," muttered Grace. "I hope it doesn't break down."

Nora's heart was in her throat. "It probably senses our dread of what might lie ahead."

The corridors were eerily quiet except for the crisp squeak of their sneakers against the shiny floor tiles. They checked in at the nurses' station and the woman behind the desk spoke softly. "May I help you?"

"We're here to see Martha Martin," said Nora.

She reassured them that Martha was awake, and they should go right in. "I have a message for you, if you are Nora or Grace."

"That's us," Grace acknowledged.

"Your sister Diane just called to say that she and your dad will be here in an hour."

They thanked the nurse and continued down the hall to their mother's room, pausing in the doorway. She lay in the bed, propped up on puffy cloud-pillows. When they walked in, Nora's attention went straight to the whites of her mother's eyes, now a murky yellow. Speechless, she wrapped her arms around her mother, substituting hugs for words she couldn't express. Hiding her shock at touching bone, Nora finally uttered, "Mom, you look lovely!"

Grace did much better, her strong voice showing no hesitation. "You'll be out soon, and we'll celebrate your recovery with a juicy jumbo McDonald's cheeseburger and fries."

Their mother gave a faint smile. "All these years I've yearned to be skinny, but not like this. Be careful what you wish for, girls."

They joked about the stacks of cookbooks and clipped recipes that had made their way from kitchen cupboards and drawers, to neat piles on the stairs leading to her mother's basement. Nora wondered how long it had been since her she had eaten real food. A wave of worry came over her, or was it pity?

Noticing the cracked corners of her mother's mouth, Nora fed her ice chips, her hand shaking as she held the spoon to her mother's splintered lips, their web of crevices close to shattering. Her mother's mouth opened like a suckling's. Nora watched her savor the half-spoonfuls, which must have felt like an oasis in the middle of a desert.

Nora imagined she and her mother were silently making amends for all the times they'd stood on different sides of issues; she a dove, her mother a hawk, Nora a liberal, her mother a conservative. Nora fought for racial equality, while her mother clung to Caucasian roots. And now, in the stillness, none of these differences seemed to matter. But there were other issues she had yet to forgive, like the blame for her brother's death.

Now, their mother fluttered in and out of sleep, the sisters sat by her bed, keeping watch. Nora wondered how much longer it would take for Diane and their father to arrive. She hoped they would have an update on Mom's condition. A short time later, Diane and Dad arrived, ushering in renewed vitality with hugs, kisses, and extra-large coffees.

Martha became animated again, laughing at her husband's jokes and smiling at his compliments.

"I dressed up special for this occasion," she said, fingering her lace neckline. The folds of a white cotton gown buoyed her above the covers but did not hide her gauntness. Nora couldn't believe how frail her mother looked. Nora's eyes moved from strand to strand of gray-tinged red hair, then on to rouged cheeks, blue eye shadow and full lashes. She knew the nurse had adorned her for their visit.

Then, without warning, Martha sat up with a jolt and stared at the doorway. "Angelica, is that you?"

"Angelica's not with us, Mom." Nora glimpsed at the empty doorway, a shadow of guilt hovered over her at harboring her daughter's incarceration like a dark secret. Nora knew her mother's deep attachment to Angelica, as if she were the child Martha had lost.

In an awkward silence, her mother stared at the doorway before collapsing back into the pillows. Nora closed her eyes for a moment; an image of the fish dress loomed before her. If only she could slip it on, perhaps she would gain the strength to combat her fear of mortality, and her mother would be full and vivacious instead of weak and waning. Or if Nora were with Kirk, he'd hold her and stroke her hair like her mom might have done, had she not been so overwhelmed by her son's death.

At the end of a long day of tests and small talk, dusk wafted through the windows and settled over the hospital room, twilight's thin veil separating day from night, life from death. The energy the family mustered had now vanished, and they all sat like cemetery markers. Gone was their mother's earlier vibrancy. The rise and fall of the blankets with her breathing lost their rhythm.

A doctor came to the door, and Diane and their father went out in the hallway with him. A short time, they returned.

"We'd better go now," their father said in a soft voice.

Before leaving, Nora touched her lips to her mother's forehead.

Diane whispered, "We'll talk when we get to the house."

They brought a pizza back and sat around the kitchen table. "We met with a doctor yesterday. We wanted you to be part of the meeting, but they needed to schedule emergency surgery right away. The MRI shows a blockage in the bile duct." Diane said.

"Your mom's going to have an operation called a Whipple procedure," said their father. He reached for the yellow-lined pad by the phone, grabbed a sharpened pencil, and began sketching, his reading glasses resting on the lower bridge of his nose. "The bile duct is a thin tube, about four or five inches long.

It goes from the liver to the small intestine and helps digest fats in food. When the duct gets blocked, it causes the symptoms your mother has."

His facial expression, the anatomical drawing, and the undertones of textbook chatter frightened Nora. "Dad, is it cancer?"

His voice cracking, he answered, "Yes. I'm afraid it is."

Nora shuddered.

"Will she need chemotherapy?" asked Grace.

"Most likely," he said.

Without warning, tears streamed down Nora's cheeks. Soon Grace was crying.

"Please don't cry. The prognosis is good, and the surgeon's one of the best in the country."

Perhaps it was the way his voice resonated victory and how his eyes lit up like candles, that touched Nora's spirit and filled her with hope. At that moment, her father became her rock.

"It's been a long day, and tomorrow will be an early one. We need to be at the hospital by seven to see your mother before she goes into surgery." Yawning, he suggested, "Why don't we get some sleep."

As Nora climbed the stairs to her old bedroom, her legs grew heavy. The familiar twin bed with the pineapple posts welcomed her. She sank into clean, crisp sheets and pulled the thick comforter up to her neck. She closed her eyes and heard the familiar night noises of her childhood home—the furnace running, a car passing by, a dog barking—ordinary sounds that would lull her to sleep…

****

I'm … holding Seth in the front seat of the station wagon, my mother racing to the doctor. Rain pounding against the windshield, wipers screaming, tires splashing.

Seth is burning up, his chest rattles and he's breathing hard. "Croup," the doctor says, his shiny stethoscope around his neck. "Give him baby aspirin, run the vaporizer, rub Vicks on his chest. It's very important to give him liquids, check his breathing, and take his temperature every two hours!"

It's morning. I run to my brother's room, expecting the smell of strong medicine and the sound of steam barreling in the vaporizer, but the room is still. He's lying on his stomach. I peer through the crib slats and see his yellow footie pajamas.

"Seth! Seth!" Did he just move?

Reaching through the rails, I poke his foot with my hand. Touch his fingers, cold as stones. I go to the other side of the crib to get a better look. His face, blue as a fresh bruise. His body, still, like the dead bird I once saw in the backyard.

I run to my mother's room and shake her awake. The cuckoo clock in the hallway, sounding angry, and I'm scared. I pull on her arm.

"Seth is blue!" I shout.

My mother lifts her head off the pillow and squints. "Eight o'clock? Oh my God, I slept straight through."

"Seth is blue!" I cry out again.

I follow behind her like a shadow, into his room. Mother scoops him up from the crib, pressing him to her chest, and she's glaring. Screaming, "What did you do to your brother!" but her voice sounds like it's underwater, and she doesn't look like my mother, her face, twisted like the bark of an old tree, her eyes, sunken like craters. She pushes me away.

"Run! Tell Mrs. Clark to call the ambulance!"

Barefoot, in my nightgown, I'm at the neighbor's door, shaking and stuttering.

Back at the house, we find my mother in my brother's room, sitting cross-legged on the floor, wailing and rocking side-to-side. She holds Seth's limp body in her arms; he looks like one of my rag dolls.

A piercing scream. "He's dead. what did you do to him, Nora!"

****

Jarred from sleep, Nora's eyes popped open. She lay in a pool of sweaty sheets, her heart pounding as she recounted the dream several times in her mind. Was it a dream? It felt so real, so familiar as if it actually *had* happened. Yes, it really did happen the way she dreamed it, and nowhere had she hurt her brother; in fact, it was her mother who failed to watch over him.

"I'm innocent!" Nora said aloud, feeling triumphant, yet guilty, as her mother fought for her life in a hospital bed. But how could her mother fail to check on her own son, to cause his death and then cast her own guilt and shame upon Nora? Did her mother not realize how devastating it would be for both of them to dwell in emotional isolation, living the lie in silence?

THOU MUST FORGIVE.

****

They arrived at the hospital early the next morning with a large bouquet of yellow roses and baby's breath, their mother's favorite.

"At least I can still smell," she said, closing her eyes and inhaling the sweet scents. Her smile was weak, but nevertheless it was a smile that Nora hoped connected her mother with past peaceful times in her flower garden.

When the orderly came to take her to surgery, their mother's eyes, brimming with fear, rested on each of the children and their father before she was wheeled away. Nora heard her gasp as if it would be her last breath.

In the waiting room, they retreated into their private worlds, reminding Nora of the silence that permeated the past and the present. Their father worked on a *Times* crossword puzzle he'd tucked in the pocket of his overcoat. Diane buried her nose in a book, while Grace watched a British mystery on television. Nora had brought along schoolwork but was too nervous to concentrate.

By mid-afternoon, attendants allowed the family in the recovery room. They gathered around, taking turns holding her hand. The air felt so much lighter.

When their father asked their mother how she felt, she slurred, "They've got me all drugged up. Otherwise I'd be in a lot of pain."

An orderly wheeled her back to the room and moved her to the bed. When Martha saw the flowers again, her face lit up, and she began to cry.

The family searched for soothing words, babbling reassurances to lift their spirits. *Mom, we love you. You will be fine. Angelica and Eve will visit you soon.* To Nora, the words sounded hollow, even Grace had lost her knack for making conversation, but the more they spoke, the more credible their words sounded.

"The surgery went well," their father said. "I'll be taking you out for lobster at Alfredo's before you know it, Martha." He stood by her bedside, dabbing her face with a cool, damp washcloth.

Diane pulled Grace and Nora aside. "Does Mom know you're leaving tonight?"

"No, I dread telling her," Nora whispered.

Small talk filled the rest of the visit, with their dad spouting jokes that made their mother laugh—weakly. By early evening, she was drifting in and out of sleep.

"It's getting late. We should head back to Maine now," Grace said.

Nora nodded, kissing her mother's forehead, pausing to study her peaceful expression.

Chapter 19

The visit with Angelica opened with a ritual touching of hands across the glass barrier which Nora pretended didn't exist. Seeing her daughter still wearing the pink plastic cross, Nora said a silent prayer. Anything to strengthen Angelica's faith and hope in the unknown.

"Hello, darling. I missed you. How have you been?"

Angelica gave a faint smile. "Staying busy with psych classes and Bible study."

"What about dance?"

She stood up and struck a jazz pose. "It's going fine."

Nora clasped her hands together. "Beautiful!"

"What about you, Mom? Tell me about Grammy, how is she?"

Nora took a deep breath. "Remember me telling you she wasn't feeling well? And then we thought she was getting better. But she ended up in the hospital, which is why we went down again. They did tests."

"What did they find? Anything?"

"A blockage in her bile duct. She had surgery yesterday, and I talked with Diane this morning. She says Grammy's recovery is going well." Nora watched her daughter's face, took a deep breath, and said, "It's cancer."

Angelica sat down on the metal stool and stared at the floor, with her head down. Nora heard sniffling and saw her shoulders shake. Showing a strong front for her daughter's sake, Nora echoed her father's words, "Honey, we've got to stay hopeful. She has the best doctors—experts in their field."

Angelica looked up. "I'll pray for her," she whispered. "When you talk to Grammy, please tell her I love her." She wrapped her fingers around the pink cross.

"I will. Grace and I are going down again after the New Year, but I'm spending Christmas with you. I can't believe it's less than a week away. I can't bring presents, but they gave me a list of what's allowed to send through the mail. You know, they have their restrictions."

Angelica nodded. "That's prison for you. Besides, it's not the material things, Mom. I'd rather have your presence than your presents."

Nora smiled at her daughter's cleverness with words and blew her a kiss. "Before we're out of time, I want to tell you about a dream I had in Connecticut." She recounted the details, explaining how the dream pointed to her innocence in Seth's death. "All this time, I've been imprisoned for something I didn't do," she said, sighing.

Angelica's eyes widened. "You, in prison?"

Nora nodded. "Yes, locked up within myself. A mental prison."

Angelica gave a quizzical look. "Mom, it's not the same, you can't imagine how awful it is in here."

It got quiet, and then Nora let out a deep sigh. "You're right, of course, but to think I've carried this guilt and shame from childhood throughout adulthood … my bars are mental, not metal. And think about it, Grammy's been a prisoner, too, held hostage by a lie."

"Maybe that's the only way she could survive," Angelica added.

"We all have our own demons," uttered Nora. "Private matters that keep us locked in shame."

Angelica pursed her lips and looked away.

"Please forgive me for not having the courage to talk openly about what you were feeling inside or what I was grappling with," Nora said, tearing up.

The warning bell rang.

"I forgive you, Mom. You did the best you could."

"So did you," Nora said. "And so did Grammy."

They reluctantly said their goodbyes. Nora stood alone staring at the empty prisoner cubicle, caught in a fleeting glimpse of her daughter's sad eyes and waving hand. It was an image that stayed with her all the way home.

The phone was ringing when she stepped inside the house.

"Where have you been? I've been trying to reach you."

"Hi, Rosie. I went to Connecticut for a couple days. What's up?"

"I thought you might be ready for your next session."

"Honestly, I don't know, but I want to ask you about a dream I had."

Nora shared the details, ending with, "Rosie, it was so real, it has to be true, right?"

"Maybe, but you won't know for sure until the dream is confirmed in the waking world."

"What do you mean?" Nora asked.

"You'll receive a sign of verification and will recognize it when you see it."

"What if I miss it?"

"I promise you won't."

"I'm innocent of causing my brother's death."

"It's not that simple, Nora. Your past life muddies the water. Even if you are innocent, you must break Marguerita's vow of silence to completely heal."

"Okay, I'll come right over—I know, with the dress."

Nora climbed the attic stairs with timid steps, retrieving the dress and the small framed portrait. She shuddered to think how her first past life journey had ended by almost freezing to death. The last thing she felt like doing was embarking on another dangerous expedition, so close to Christmas. What if she never returned? She knew she must go, but how many regressions would it take to heal, she thought as she headed to Rosie's.

Nora's boots clicked along Rosie's stone walkway. Crows pecking for their morning feed paused and stared, as if they detected something strange was about to happen inside the house. She jarred the stillness with the brass moon door knocker, clutching the picture of Sister Marguerita as the birds flew away.

Rosie stood there, dressed in a dashiki, a swirl of brown and black, with sleeves draped off her shoulders like wings. A jewel-lined V framed her neck, and her hair was wrapped in a turban.

"No muumuu?" Nora asked.

Rosie's beady eyes flickered. "Past life journeys require certain attire, depending on the circumstances."

Such as … ? Nora wanted to ask but said nothing while she removed her shoes, placing them just inside the door. She followed Rosie to the parlor, where scores of lit candles glimmered on tables and shelves. Sunlight dripped through the mostly drawn blinds, casting a shadowy luster over Rosie's face. Last time the psychic had emitted a lush blossom scent, but this time she smelled like a pod of musk. "Have a seat," she said, pointing to the velvet recliner. "You remember the rules, right?"

"I think so. In Marguerita's world, no one can see or hear us. I can move inside her if I wish, or I can choose to stay on the sidelines and observe. You and I can speak with each other anytime, right?"

"Yes, but we can't see each other."

"And you'll bring me back whenever I want?"

"Promise," she answered. "Lie down, get comfortable, and close your eyes. Today I want to take you to your birthplace. We didn't go back far enough last time, remember?"

How could Nora forget being blasted into the arctic? But the memory vanished as the ocean sounds played in the background. Rosie settled into the oversized armchair beside the settee and lulled Nora into a deep hypnotic state.

"We are traveling back in time to the mid-1850s in the Sierra Nevada Mountains of Spain; your name is Marguerita DeRoche, and you are about to join your birth family. Tell me what you see."

****

My blood races through my veins and I shout, "Rosie! A child is coming into focus, a beautiful little girl with a head full of black ringlets bouncing up and down as she runs across the field. She's wearing a long woven wool dress with a white apron over it. Is it Marguerita?"

Rosie breaks out in wild laughter. "We did it! I brought you to your home!"

A man walks behind the child. Tall and angular, he's herding a flock of sheep in from the pasture, tapping at the wooly herd with a long stick.

"Papa!" Marguerita calls out. "Let us find Mother."

"First we must bring the sheep in," he says.

I move closer, running alongside the herd, touching their woolly tufts before I slip inside Marguerita. I feel her pull on her father's rough hand. After the sheep are settled in the barn, we find Mother behind the house, she's hanging laundry across the cord tied between two trees. What a hearty-looking woman, with her ruddy skin and tight, round face. A black braid thick as rope runs down her back, and she wears a shawl knotted around her neck, inside the shawl, pressed against her chest, is Marguerita's baby brother.

Papa points to the sky and tells Mother it may snow during the night. "Look at those grey clouds. The temperature's dropping and it's getting windy. There's a storm brewing."

Mother laughs. "Husband, you worry for nothing. God will protect us."

He shakes his head and starts to walk away. "I'll bring the goats and chickens into the barn and check for firewood in the shed."

Clothes snap on the line, and inside Marguerita, I feel free as the wind. We leave Mother's side and walk toward the cliff and gaze over the edge, pretending the white dots far below are fairy houses. "Marguerita," Mother beckons, and out of nowhere Rosie asks what she is saying.

"She's worried I'm too close to the edge. I ask her if I can visit the village someday. She explains that Mijas is a magical place, but only in my imagination, at five years old. I tell her I believe anything I can imagine is real. She hugs Marguerita and takes her hand, leading us to the house, where I slip outside her."

Inside, there is a large room, with a kitchen area and a big table, and a nook off the room, with a mattress and a wooden box filled with sweaters, pants, and girls' dresses. The space is tiny but has a window which makes it cozy. It must be Marguerita's room.

Marguerita is in the kitchen, stirring a pot that hangs from an iron hook over the hearth. Her mother chops vegetables on the wooden plank counter. I can't stop my mouth and my eyes from watering, these meat and onion smells tickle my nose.

I climb the ladder to the loft and see a large mattress and a drawer with baby blankets lining the inside. When the food is ready, I climb down the ladder and slip back into Marguerita. We all sit at the round wooden table and Papa says grace before we eat lamb stew and biscuits. Afterwards he lights the oil lamp and recites from the large leather Bible until it is time for bed. It is turning dark and windy outside, and I don't want to be alone, so I remain inside Marguerita.

We lie on a straw-filled mattress, covered with a sheepskin blanket. No wonder we have trouble falling asleep, for the wind howls like a pack of wolves, and the window rattles like skeletons dancing. We peek outside and watch the snow fall until we drift off.

Suddenly, a loud crash, and I'm shaken out of sleep. My first thought, *I must leave right now.* But when I try to slip out of Marguerita, I can't budge!

"Rosie, get me out of here!" I scream, but she doesn't answer.

"Papa, where are you!" Marguerita screeches, jumping out of bed and moving toward the kitchen, with me trapped inside her. Knee-deep in piles of snow-covered wood and stone. Oh my God, the storm has caved the roof in, and the ladder and the loft are in pieces. My heart is in my throat, and I can't scream. Where is the rest of the family?

Marguerita wails in pain, for Papa is crushed under the debris, only his feet sticking out. Mother is by the door, with Brother on her chest. We slide through the wreckage to reach them, but they don't move.

Rosie's voice pierces my ears, she tells me I must get help. I have no choice but to face the storm.

Wearing boots and wrapped in Mother's heavy coat and Papa's scarf, Marguerita crawls to the door, with me inside her. Outside, the sheep have broken through the gate, and they are bleating and running in circles. We search for the trail, but it's covered with monstrous drifts of snow. We must find our way down the mountain.

Where are you? Is it Rosie's voice, or am I delirious? I try to speak.

"Lost in the mountains…

"fingers and toes numb…

"ahead, a snowbank... a cave…

"inside … dark … stiff …

"floating…"

****

Nora was back on the recliner, with no sense of how long she'd been lying there. Like the last time, she was covered with layers of blankets.

"That was a close call," Rosie said, wiping her hand across her brow. "I've never experienced not being able to bring someone out of her former self."

"Thank God you did," Nora groaned. "I feel like I've had a near-death experience."

"At least we found out why you were so cold last time. Surviving that blizzard required perseverance, and, oh my, the sorrow of losing your family. But you survived. This is not the time to stop."

"What do you mean?"

"We know what happened. The Roma gypsies rescued you, so you don't have to worry about dying in a snowbank. Please, let's go just a little farther. Perhaps you'll find the dress."

After all, wasn't that, what Nora was seeking? She'd come this far and might as well continue. Who knows when she would return to Rosie's again? Nora agreed, on the condition she would just observe Marguerita, not go inside her.

"Very well," Rosie said.

I see Marguerita wrapped in layers of bright blankets, lying on a stone slab in a large cave lit with torches.

"Mother? Papa? Brother?" Marguerita calls out.

Gypsy women hover over her. They tell her they found her near death, huddled in a cave, hidden from the blizzard, and that they carried her a great distance to their camp in the mountains above Granada.

Between sobs, Marguerita tells them about her home and family in the mountains above Mijas. "Are my parents and my brother alive?"

The gypsies shake their heads. "No, we are sorry. Dreadful, what happened, you are lucky to be alive."

I watch as a beady-eyed woman in a red silk robe chants and waves her arms. She says, "I am Yatobi, High Priestess of the Sacromonte gypsies. It is I who performed healing rituals and saved your life with magic. Our tribe will not cast you out, we will raise you as one of us."

Yatobi appoints a child from the tribe to teach Marguerita the ways of the Sacromontes—about nature, and the worship of sun, moon, and star gods. "That's Heathera, from my last journey," I tell Rosie. "So that's how we became best friends."

"Would you like to stop now?"

"No. I long to know more about my gypsy life, and I must find the dress. Take me forward in her life. I already know what's coming next, we were here in my first regression." No sooner do I make the request than I'm catapulted into Marguerita's life at age ten, landing next to Heathera.

We're sitting by the forge where the men fire and hammer iron to make goods—horseshoes, muskets, and kettles, or gates, hooks, and latches—to sell in the city. Eager to join my friends, I slip inside Marguerita, disregarding my insistence on only observing. "The fire laps like a tongue," I say, licking the air like a cat.

Later, Heathera and I hold hands and trek down the mountain with the tribe, to the city of Granada. A beldame tells us, "While the men sell their iron, you will slip unnoticed, stealthy as cats, into homes and shops to steal whatever you can find." We've done this many times before.

At sunset, we meet the Sacromontes at our special place in the woods, near the edge of the city. The men have done well, stealing horses and mules right under the owners' noses. We bump along in the wagon back to camp. Heathera empties our bag, and her eyes turn starry. "Look at the jewels and gold coins, and food—meat, potatoes, and olives," she says.

Bread, figs, and grapes, too. Tonight, we will fill our stomachs until they pop. We laugh and rub our bellies, sticking them out like balloons.

"I'm not hearing from you. Is something wrong?" Rosie asks.

"I can't talk long. Soldiers in stiff black uniforms are sweeping the caves and storming the camps for men and children, and if they find us, they will take us away."

"Why?"

"Granada's people are frightened. They believe we are cave-dwelling heathens, robbers, witches, and even cannibals. I must hide now."

"Turn over your children, *gitanos*, or we will hang the lot of you!"

I stay inside Marguerita, and I mustn't leave Heathera. We huddle behind a rock, but a soldier spots us. We kick and bite and spit as they drag us away, and I fear I'll never see my gypsy family again. Heathera is luckier; she breaks away and hides in the folds of a beldame's skirt, and the soldiers don't see her. But they stuff me in a cloth bag and tie the top, with only a sliver of light showing and a speck of air to breathe. Now we face the terrible unknown, and I can't stop crying.

After what feels like a lifetime, a soldier unties the bag, setting us free. But where am I?

"What do you see?" asks Rosie, who's following my plight.

"Shadows. But I hear the clicking of shoes and the creak of a gate. In the light of dawn, I see the shape of huge stone building with a tall iron fence. I'm more scared than I've ever been, crouching against the fence and clinging to its railings. Someone is coming but I'm too tired and hungry to hide, and too scared to open my eyes as they carry me off.

The sound of women's voices overtakes my fear, chasing away the cruel soldier visions cemented in my brain. Daring to open my eyes, I'm relieved to find myself seated at a long wooden table with bread and soup before me. *Where are the gypsies?* I ask myself, quickly abandoning my question, too hungry to think about anything other than food.

I'm surrounded by nuns in black-hooded habits with large gold crosses around their bibs. All I can see are their kind-looking faces and wire-rimmed glasses. Today they are a welcome sight, compared to the soldiers, but I miss Heathera and the gypsy family.

As I gulp hot cereal and toast, I hear the nuns talking about me. The most wrinkled of them says, 'The gypsy girl gobbles like she hasn't eaten in a fortnight. What is your name, child?"

"Marguerita."

They tell me I will now live in the village of Mijas at the convent of the Sisters of Charity of the Blessed Virgin Mary. I have a hazy memory of the village. I used to gaze down upon it from the mountains.

I'm thankful to be alive. They tell me I must abide by the Order's rules, but I'm furious with the nuns for removing the silver rings from my ears and stripping me of my flowy skirt and puffy blouse. They dress me in itchy wool undergarments and a heavy gray tunic that ties around my waist with a thick rope. They add another layer of cloth over the tunic, with a hood and an opening for my head.

While I am grateful for the way the nuns receive me, I long for the Sacromontes and the lively music we've danced and sung to. Now I have only the sad chants of monks. Prayers at morning, noon, and night. Daily confession. Memorizing the Bible. Reciting Hail Marys and praying the rosary. Fasting. No talking on Sundays. I feel imprisoned. I wander the halls of the cloister as if I am a ghost. The nuns shake their heads, crossing themselves when they pass me in the dim stairwells. I hear their murmurs. "The child would do well to confess her sins, for we have prayed over her, but she has yet to show contrition."

Time passes but it is hard to keep track of. It has been a great while since Rosie and I have talked, though I miss her less each day. Whether memories of a God-fearing father and mother resurfaced, I will never know, but I feel different now, inside Marguerita, as if we have received a calling from above. I begin to see my time here as a test to be endured. I'm now living a spiritual life. Every morning we walk from the convent to the shrine of *la Virgen de la Peña* to pray and meditate upon her holiness.

"Who?" Rosie asks.

"Rosie, it's good to hear your voice again." I move away from Marguerita. "You've been listening all this time?"

"Yes, I would have stepped in, had you truly needed me. The guides advised me to stand back far enough to let you fend for yourself, and you have done well. I want to hear about this *Virgen de la Peña*."

"She's the Virgin Mary, and overlooks the whitewashed village of Mijas, the very place Marguerita used to dream of visiting. The Sisters of Charity have told us the story of how the statue came to be."

"Tell me."

"A local artist sculpted her of stone in 1586. It marks the spot where *la Virgen* first appeared to shepherds in the foothills. The villagers claimed her as their patron saint of Mijas."

"Really!" exclaims Rosie.

"Oh, but there's more. The sculptor inscribed the stone with *Peña: castigo, dolor, aflicción*. Pain, suffering, punishment, and sorrow. "But the Virgin Mary returned in 1850!"

"That must have excited the villagers."

"Yes. The monks built a chapel around the statue, and my Order honored her with a sacred shroud."

"A shroud?"

"They made it from the finest flax plants in Europe, working many days and nights to separate the strands of stalks, preserving their integrity. They simmered the fibers in an iron pot with a mixture of ground walnut hulls that turned the cloth a deep black—the color of death, mystery, and power. The waxy threads gave a natural luster. The weaving was perfect, without a trace of a knot.

"The Camerlengo of the Holy Roman Church travelled all the way from Madrid for the ceremony and blessed the holy linen, placing it on the granite shoulders of *la Virgen de la Peña*. That is the history of the statue—the patron saint who wears a sacred shroud made by the Sisters of Charity."

"My goodness, that's quite a tale! Let's move forward a few years."

At sixteen, I have finished my formal vows of service to Christ and am prepared to dedicate myself to the life of a nun. I must fulfill the Order's mission to save children, as I was saved. The nuns are at last pleased with me.

But scandalous rumors spread throughout the convent, and beyond, that children are being abused—some of them sexually—by the priests and nuns. The iron hand of the clergy imposes a vow of silence on us to squelch the hearsay. Mother Superior insists it is only by turning inward and listening, that we will receive salvation. She says it is impossible to hear the message of the Gospel in our hearts if our tongues are clanging. God's language is silence, and we must keep this vow throughout our lifetimes, to prove our innocence through martyrdom. Mother Superior imposes the vow upon us.

At first, I wonder how I will rescue foundlings and children from overcrowded orphanages if I'm not allowed to speak. But I soon discover I do not need my voice to show compassion. My manner suffices to communicate the Lord's message.

The government no longer makes formal purges of the *gitanos*, but I am still expected to rescue gypsy children, should I spot them in my travels. My gypsy ties have unraveled, along with any yearning to be with them. It has been six years since I've seen the Sacromontes, and now I am indwelt with a pious spirit.

As I begin my long journey from Mijas to bring orphaned children back from Seville, I pass through the mountains near Granada. A desire to reunite with my Sacromonte family suddenly stirs in my heart, and passion overtakes my thinking. Had the gypsies not rescued me from the blizzard, I would not have survived. The pull on my devotion to religious service is strong, but not powerful enough to keep me from searching cave after cave, seeking a landmark, a special rock or tree where I once played, a link to a gypsy memory.

It is near dusk, and I must get back on the path to Seville. I am filled with guilt at my moment of weakness. I need to forget about the gypsies, lest I bow to sin.

Out of nowhere, someone calls my name, and a figure approaches. I look down at the ground as we pass each other, as the nuns have instructed me to do. Without warning, the stranger pulls me into her arms, and we're twirling and dancing like the sisters we once were.

"Speak to me, Marguerita. Tell me we're still blood sisters."

"Why are you sobbing?" Rosie asks.

"The vow—I mustn't break the vow of silence. I'm feeling conflicted. Please bring me back to the present—*now!*"

****

Nora lay on the velvet recliner. Much time passed before she spoke. "I wanted to tell Heathera how much I missed her and longed to return to my Sacromonte tribe."

Rosie nodded. "That's understandable, for your roots are both Pagan and Christian. There are bound to be conflicts. Do you wish to go back?"

"Yes, only not today. The journey has been difficult, but we unpeeled another layer, I now understand the gravity of my vow of silence. But how was I able to speak?"

"An illusion, isn't it—like all of life. Multiple realities, all happening at once. Perhaps the dress will help you. Is there anything else you'd like to know?"

Nora eyed Rosie with uncertainty. "Are you sure you weren't part of my last life? You remind me of High Priestess Yatobi."

"Oh, really?" Rosie said with a slight twitch. "Let's do another session soon. You made good progress today. Perhaps one more time will do it."

"You mean, I'll break the vow?"

Rosie nodded. "You stood up to your fears today by not allowing them to loom large over you. And you didn't desert Margueria when she was in danger.

Nora felt as if she were gliding over the walkway, one step closer to victory. A feathered friend who'd earlier taken flight now perched on a high branch. She felt his beady eyes on her back and heard his *caw, caw, caw,* which made her think of Carlos Castenada's Don Juan, master of the art of shape shifting into his chosen form—a crow—and set himself free to move beyond human-imposed boundaries, transcending ordinary reality. She thought of Rosie.

It was only when you let your emotions get the best of you that you asked to return to the present."

"One last question, which I'm sure you won't answer."

Rosie winked. "You're right. You must discover the dress for yourself. That's part of the quest."

Chapter 20

On Christmas morning, the phone rang early. Already semi-awake, Nora knew it had to be her daughter making sure that Nora was still coming.

"Hello?" she answered in a dreamy voice. "Merry Christmas!"

But it wasn't Angelica. It was Nora's father, and his voice sounded ragged. "I don't know how else to say it, honey, but we just lost your mother."

Nora felt the blood drain from her head. "No! It didn't happen!" she shrieked.

"Last night she woke up with a fever and sharp pains in her stomach." He choked on his words. "I took her to the Emergency Room and they admitted her for observation. Next thing I know, I get the phone call." As if it were an afterthought, he added, "She was a good woman," and then he sobbed.

Recent chats that had lulled Nora into complacency now pushed against the inside of her chest wall, and anger surfaced. But then she realized it would do no good to cast blame on her father or her sister. *We are a family of denial,* she reminded herself. *None of us can accept mortality.*

He was going to call Grace.

All the regrets she'd ever had regarding her mother snowballed into a piercing cry that broke the stillness of her empty house. Margo climbed into her lap and Nora buried her face in the soft tufts of hair and sobbed into them.

"Why didn't I reach out to her?"

Holding Margo, she walked to the closet and snatched the dress off its hanger. "Speak to me. Say *something* to get me through this nightmare."

It fluttered like the daintiest of birds, or angel wings.

AT LAST, MOTHER AND SON, REUNITED.

A wave of calm settled over Nora, and like a balloon inflating, she filled with strength. She called the prison chaplain and told him what happened, then asked if her daughter could take temporary leave to attend her grandmother's funeral. He explained that her daughter would have to apply for an emergency prison furlough and prove that the relationship was close. Under the circumstances, they would decide by the end of the day. If temporary leave were granted, it could be escorted or unescorted, depending on the risk. They would also look at the inmate's conduct before making a final decision.

Nora pleaded with the chaplain to help her daughter, and he promised to do all he could. She thanked him and asked him to have Angelica call her right away.

"She doesn't know yet."

A collect call came a few minutes later. "Mom, what happened?"

"I'm so sorry, honey. Grammy has died," Nora said, piercing the air with her words.

Nora heard her daughter's high-pitched cry.

"Listen, baby, the chaplain's going to help you get approved for a furlough so you can go to Grammy's funeral. You've got to see him right away."

"Are you still coming today?" asked Angelica.

Nora hesitated. "We'll know by the end of today, and hopefully you'll be with us when we leave tomorrow morning."

"Okay," Angelica murmured.

"I need you to be strong," Nora said. "Do you think you can do that?"

Angelica's "yes" sounded so distant, so weak. If only the sustaining power of the dress could reach her.

Nora called the chaplain and learned that the furlough request was approved, and that Angelica could go unescorted.

"I vouched for your daughter—she's been a great role model," the chaplain added.

"Thank you, sir," Nora said, teary-eyed. Then she called Administration, thanked them, and arranged for picking her daughter up on the way to Connecticut. Angelica would be surprised and elated to find Eve in the car.

The next morning, Nora received a collect call. Angelica was sobbing.

"What's wrong, honey?"

"I got into a fight and now they won't let me go to Grammy's funeral."

"What happened?" Nora asked, trying not to sound alarmed.

Angelica made a guttural sound. "It doesn't matter."

"Yes, it does. Are you okay?"

"Everything's just peachy, Mom. What do you expect me to say? I wake up every morning with a blizzard raging inside me, like all the inmates. Somebody looks at you wrong, and you go off. Do you think I did it on purpose?"

Nora retreated. "Of course not. I'm sorry it happened and that you can't come. Is there someone you can talk to?"

"What do you mean? Like a shrink?" Angelica snapped.

"I was thinking it might help to speak with the chaplain, or a counselor."

"Just let me do my time, okay?"

"Do you want me to see if Kirk can visit you? You could add him to the visitors' list."

Following a long silence, Angelica, sounding lifeless, said, "Whatever."

Nora knew the conversation was over. The chip on her daughter's shoulder would take time to erode. Sometimes her moods were unnerving. *Tough love* came into Nora's head, words she'd heard at support groups. "I'll see you when we get back. I love you."

Angelica hung up without saying goodbye, and Nora wept.

Shame, how cruel it could be. Nora pictured the time she couldn't find Angelica and searched every room in the house, frantically calling out her name. She'd found her tucked in the upstairs linen closet, curled up in a fetal position, her body twitching. She touched her daughter's cold, clammy skin and pulled a needle from her arm.

"Angelica, no, you can't die," Nora had sobbed, shaking uncontrollably. She had crouched in the closet and held Angelica, rocking her as if she were still a baby. Nora had felt lost. Her daughter was a shell of a human at that point. Just flesh she was desperately holding onto, hoping her love would be the life force Angelica needed to stay alive.

Angelica had buried her head in her mother's neck and they cried together. Then Angelica's cry shrank to a whimper, and she whispered, "Mom, I'm sorry. All I've ever wanted to do is make you proud."

****

Nora, Grace, and Eve headed to Connecticut. It felt as if a gray cloud filled the car the whole ride down. A strange sensation overcame Nora when they turned into their parents' driveway and saw their dad's Volvo and their mom's Toyota parked side by side, as if all were status quo.

They trudged through the breezeway and stood at the door, peering into the kitchen through the glass panes. Never again would Nora see her mother standing at the stove, her back to them, steam rising from the pot she was stirring. Nora filled with regret at having missed the chance to mend their relationship with love and forgiveness.

Once inside, they collapsed into Diane's waiting arms.

"Where's Angelica? I thought she was coming," she said.

Shivering, Nora answered, "It didn't work out."

Just then, their father emerged from the next room. He looked hollow, and his face was thinner than Nora remembered two weeks earlier. His usual vibrant blue eyes now had the look of death. He joined his daughters and granddaughter and entered their circle, then wandered from room to room as if he were lost and looking for a place to settle. They took him by the hand and led him to his favorite wingback chair in the den. Diane turned on the TV and found a John Wayne western to distract him from Martha's absence.

Later, the girls headed to the bedroom to begin the arduous process of sorting through their mother's things. Nora felt like an intruder when she emptied the nightstand drawer. A black-and-white photo of Seth at eighteen months, wearing his corduroy overalls. A faded snapshot of the three sisters at Easter, lined up in swishy taffeta dresses, white ankle socks, and black patent leather shoes. At four, five, and seven, they looked so posed with their dimpled smiles and tight-curled home perms. There were other keepsakes: a trimmed newspaper clipping of a poem called "Hollyhocks," which brought to mind the stone cat that sat in their mother's garden.

Nora stared at the miniature 1956 calendar from *Woman's Day*, with a Bible passage for every month, drawings of silhouetted children running through fields, and fresh linens snapping on the line. Emblems of motherhood, a tribute to the simplicity of life, and the exuberance of youth before aging creeps in. A Salada tea tag saying: *The worst form of failure is failing to try.* Nora was surprised her mother had saved such a motto, for most times she acted scared of life.

Then she found a hand-written message copied from Coomaraswamy's *Buddha and the Gospel of Buddhism,* and read it out loud, her voice cracking:

> "Grieve not for me, but mourn for those who stay behind, bound by longings to which the fruit is sorrow… for what confidence have we in life when death is ever at hand? Even were I to return to my kindred by reason of affection, yet we should be divided in the end by death. The meeting and parting of living things is as when clouds having come together drift apart again, or as when the leaves are parted from the trees. There is nothing we may call our own in a union that is but a dream…"

How she longed to touch her mother's hands, whose fingers had scribed the quote in tight strokes on a scrap of paper. "I never knew Grammy knew anything about Eastern philosophies," she said when she finished reading.

Eve slowly nodded her head. "She must have understood more about dying than she let on."

"I can't stand how fleeting life is," Nora said, her eyes moist.

Grace grimaced as she picked up the soiled towels from the bathroom and dropped them in the wastebasket. "The smell of death is all around us."

"It's depressing," Diane said as she pulled the linens off their mother's bed.

Nora wondered when her parents had removed the antique high-poster double bed that had held both of them and replaced it with twin beds.

Diane continued. "Thanks for coming down right away. I've made the funeral arrangements but sorting through her belongings is the hardest part."

"I can't believe she's gone," Grace moaned, then wrapped her arms around Eve. "I wonder what her final moments were like."

"The nurse who was with her said Mom fell apart after Dad left," said Diane.

"Poor Grammy," Eve whispered.

How could their father walk away, as if it were the end of an ordinary day? Nora thought. Sighing, she picked up a paper from her mother's near-empty drawer. Unlike the other mementos, this one looked official with typed words and handwritten signatures. Scanning the heading, she realized it was her brother's Certificate of Death and handed it to her older sister.

Diane cleared her throat. "It says here that Seth died of a bacterial blood infection called sepsis."

So her mother had known the cause of her brother's death. Stunned, Nora didn't know how to feel.

Grace looked at Nora. "This proves you had nothing to do with Seth's death. Mom felt responsible for letting him die when she fell asleep instead of waking up and checking on him that night."

"Or maybe she had to protect herself from Dad. Who knows?" Diane said. "He may have blamed her for being at fault. He always wanted a son."

Grace nodded. "You needed closure. Now you have it."

Nora sat on the edge of her mother's bed, now stripped of its linens, and closed her eyes. Rosie's words echoed inside her: *Your innocence will be confirmed in the waking world.* Nora's absolution felt complete, but bittersweet.

****

The day was dismal—drab and drizzly, fitting for a funeral. Her mother had wished for cremation. The family sat in the front pew. A plain wooden urn adorned the church altar, and alongside the urn was a beautiful color photo. Nora stared at the picture of her mother. Diane had chosen the perfect photo, one that captured their mother in her favorite place, her flower garden, engaged in her favorite pastime, tending her flower children. Whoever had snapped the picture had likely surprised their mother. She was waist-deep in splashes of bright color and wore a floppy sunhat. Bending over, but her face tilted up to the camera, she revealed a full smile.

A wellspring of flowers overtook the altar. Acknowledgements came from people who could count on Martha to touch their lives as a garden club member, library volunteer, bridge club player. That had only come in Martha's later years. Nora knew how inadequate her mother felt, most times not enjoying social obligations, preferring solitude.

The minister recounted, "Martha Martin—a private person, a humble woman, and a giver. There are many rooms in our Father's mansion, and I promise she is living in the best of them."

Nora imagined her mother's favorite pastoral paintings hanging on white walls. The *Tree of Life* china in a corner cupboard. Oak floors padded with indigo and rose oriental rugs. The scent of fresh lilacs in the blue willow vase sitting on a mahogany table. If only she and her mother had discussed the things that mattered.

Nora breathed in her mother's essence, lamenting her loss. She also grieved for Angelica, who should have been there to hear the songbird soloist in the balcony, with an angel's voice floating over the congregation, singing *Ave Maria*, one of Martha's favorites. Angelica would have joined the family after the service, when they plodded toward the car that led the funeral procession to the cemetery.

The ground had not yet frozen, so their mother would be buried next to Seth. Two men in dark suits dug out the small muddy hole with shovels. "That should have been done before now," their father muttered, frowning as the simple wooden box filled with Martha's ashes was lowered, then covered with mud and flowers.

Diane had arranged for a bagpiper to play *Danny Boy*, another of Martha's favorites. The bagpipes crooned across the hill where mourners dressed in raincoats gathered, seeped in sorrow. When it was over, the family trudged toward the car, with Diane on one side of their father and Nora on the other, her hand at her father's elbow. Grace, with one arm around Eve, held the monstrous black umbrella above their heads.

At the reception, Nora felt like a robot as she shook hands, hugged, and cried. "Thank you for coming," she repeated in a listless voice. Children ran around the church hall with cookies and cakes in their pudgy hands, while sick-humored grownups told odd stories. Like the time their mother lost it when company came over for dinner, Diane said she hated meatloaf, and their mother threw a plate at the wall, shattering it to pieces. "I'm not running a hotel here," she screamed, then ran from the kitchen to the bedroom and locked the door.

It was as if the they were expected to share quirky memories for guests to carry home like leftovers. Nora had nothing to say, for her mind had unraveled. Grace must have noticed, because at one point she leaned over and whispered in Nora's ear, "Where's the fish dress when you need it?"

No! Nora must endure this day alone, in all due respect to her mother, who had no one from the family at her deathbed, instead dying in the arms of a stranger. *Martyr Mother* suffers that others may be redeemed, addicted to self-pity, using service and suffering to manipulate. *Shadow Mother:* smothers or abandons her children, instilling guilt. *Mother:* life-giver, nurturer, bestower of unconditional love. *My mother and I have been each of these,* thought Nora. *My mother and I must have loved each other, but fear, guilt, and blame drove a wedge between us.*

Back at their parents' house, their father spoke of their mother, how she was surely at peace with their son, Seth. "You probably remember little about him. You girls were so young."

Nora resisted the urge to tell her father she knew what happened to Seth; perhaps he knew nothing of his wife's sleeping through her watch over their son. It would accomplish nothing to expose her mother now, and for Nora to share how deeply she had suffered through her parents' silence over Seth's death.

But something amazing occurred, her father began to open up, after all these years. "I remember the day it happened. I was in New York, meeting with a client when your mother's frantic phone call came. The rush to LaGuardia. Running through the airport, half delirious, sobbing and calling out, *My son is dead. I've got to get home.*" Their father paused. "I collapsed in the arms of strangers who held me and walked me to the gate, making sure I boarded the right plane."

Were his eyes watering? The girls were silent.

"If I had only been at home, it wouldn't have happened…"

"Dad, no one knew it was going to happen," Diane said, holding his hand.

"Life was never the same after that. We moved to Rochester and I got a job in Met Life's home office, where I wouldn't have to travel anymore. We needed a fresh start."

"Why didn't we stay there?" Grace asked.

"Your mother had a nervous breakdown. At least back in Connecticut we had relatives to help out."

Nora remembered the aunt who had stayed at the house when her mother went off to the hospital, and when her mother came home, a woman named Catherine came to cook and clean and take care of them. Nora could still picture her faded dresses, mended sweaters, shabby shoes, and large spaces where teeth should be. Nora was glad for Catherine's visits, which perked her mother up, especially when the two of them sat at the kitchen table and drank percolated black coffee, its heavy roasted smell drifting through the house. It was unusual for her mother to sit and talk at length with anyone, but Catherine was the exception.

Sometimes when Nora came into the kitchen, the woman-talk shrank to whispers and her mother suddenly stiffened. Catherine would give a weighty sigh, leaving Nora to wonder what secrets they shared. You always knew when Catherine got ready to leave. She'd tie a babushka under her chin and lumber toward the back door, and Nora's mother always slipped a lump of folded bills into Catherine's apron pocket on her way out. Then she'd climb into a rusty station wagon that sounded more like an airplane than a car when she drove off.

Now, sitting in her parents' living room, Nora accepted the way her mind traveled into the past. At last, she could face whatever memories bubbled to the surface, for she knew the truth about her brother's death. What she didn't know, she no longer feared, thanks to Rosie and the dress.

On the ride back to Maine, conversation turned to their dad. "He didn't even notice that Angelica was missing," Nora said.

Grace nodded. "It's probably best, because if you told him the truth about her right now, it would be too much for him."

Nora nodded. "I'm glad Diane's there to keep an eye on Dad, although he seemed lucid today. He's never talked with us that way about Mom *or* Seth."

"He's feeling guilty," Grace said.

"Like the rest of us," Nora added.

"But she kept things inside, which made it hard to know what she was thinking," said Grace.

"Or feeling. But I never reached out or took the time to find out," Nora said.

"What would you want to have known?" Grace asked her sister.

Nora thought for a minute. "What do I wish I'd asked her? Besides about Seth? The details of her life, for starters. Like what toys she played with when she was a little girl. And who was her favorite teacher in school? Was there a dog in her family when she was growing up? How was it when Dad went off to fight in the war? Has she always loved flowers? And why did she blame me when she always knew the truth?"

"If it's any comfort, she told Diane that seventy-two years was long enough to live, and that she'd had a good life," Grace said.

"A good life?" Nora balked. "You've got to be kidding. She was a good martyr. Maybe that was her way of making amends."

Grace sighed. "This year's been a rocky one—breaking up with Thomas, Angelica in prison, and now losing Mom. I'm ready to leave it behind."

"Me, too. I'm going to see Angelica first thing tomorrow, and then I'll spend New Year's Eve with Kirk. You're welcome to come."

"I promised Katrina that Jon and I will celebrate with her, although it might be hard. Actually, I think I'd rather be with Eve before she heads back to China."

"Don't worry, Mom, I'm going to catch up with some old friends before I leave."

Nora gave a paper-thin smile. "At least we can look forward to a new year."

Eve nodded. "Also a new century."

"And the beginning of the next millennium," Nora added, desperate to bury 1999.

Chapter 21

This last morning of the year, it felt good to be home in her own bed, her own bathroom, and in her own kitchen. Today, she would go see Angelica. It frustrated Nora that she couldn't pick up the phone and call her. Calls had to come from the prisoners, collect, and only at certain times. She regretted having missed Christmas Day with her daughter.

As she stood at the sink, she recalled one of her mother's sayings: *Making wishes while doing dishes* (the old-fashioned way, not just rinsing and stacking them in the dishwasher). She wondered what her mother's wishes were, then remembered her teenage years when her mother ran up the stairs, screaming *I wish you were never born*, after she'd found pot in Nora's bedroom. Now, looking out the window by the sink, Nora said aloud, "I forgive you, Mom. Please forgive me."

Her attention wandered to the windowsill. She picked up the amber heart with the Serenity Prayer embossed in pewter, pressing it to her own heart, and thought of Angelica. Almost a week had passed since they'd talked. She worried that Angelica might shut down after her grandmother's death.

****

When Nora stepped into her side of the visiting area, it surprised her to see Angelica standing tall, as if in mountain pose at a yoga class. Relieved to see the pink plastic cross still around her neck, she supposed it might provide comfort. The orange jumpsuit hardly did justice to the young woman who lit up the room.

Was it her imagination, or had Angelica grown since they'd last seen each other? Not physically, but emotionally. Her calm, quiet presence, with humility and grace, amplified her beauty.

"I missed you so much, Mom. They took away phone privileges, so I couldn't call you. I stayed busy with dance and psych classes and tried not to think about Grammy."

Nora recognized the signs of denial she knew all too well. She heard the sadness in her daughter's voice, despite her attempts to conceal it.

"I worried about you, Angelica."

"I'm sorry, Mom. I'm glad you came today. As much as I hated being disciplined for my behavior, it taught me a good lesson. I'm never going to fight again. I'm happy turning my life around."

Their eyes met, and Nora was sure they shared a moment of adoration for each other, which warmed her insides.

Nora shared the details of the funeral service and told Angelica how she found Seth's death certificate. "He died from a blood infection, not from anything I did."

"Then why did Grammy blame you?"

"Remember the dream I had? She couldn't bear the truth that she may have caused Seth to die, even though it was an accident. I became her scapegoat, while she withdrew into her own world. Grampy doesn't know the whole story."

"Wow," Angelica interjected, looking dazed. "You know what Kirk told me when he came to see me Christmas Day? His parents were heroin addicts who died before he was a year old. That's how he ended up in an orphanage, with the nuns."

Nora's brow wrinkled. "Overdosed?"

"Uh-huh. You told Kirk about me, right?"

Nora squirmed in her seat.

"It's okay. I'm not mad. He didn't judge me, and he was easy to talk to."

Nora smiled. "He cares about you very much."

"I told him how the Drug Enforcement Agency burst through the back door when you were at work, and how I showed them my hiding places—inside the couch, in the boom box, under a ceramic cat, taped to the back of a shoe rack. He asked if I was scared."

"Were you?"

"At first, then I felt relieved. I knew if I didn't quit, I would die, and rehab hadn't worked. Now I understand that I had to lose my freedom. As much as I tried to outrun the devil, I couldn't defeat him as a free woman. You know what I've learned here? In the last three decades, almost a million people have died from overdoses. I'm so lucky I'm not one of them."

Nora hid her heartbreak behind a nod.

"And guess what, Mom? I'm not ashamed anymore."

"That makes two of us. I believe all things work together for good."

Angelica gave her mother a look of surprise. "I didn't know you could quote the Bible."

"I know a few verses," Nora said, winking.

Angelica gave a thoughtful look. "Here I am in prison, feeling freer than I've felt in years. Malachi 4, Verse 2: You will go free, leaping with joy like calves let out to pasture." She stood up and did a grand jeté across the concrete floor.

Nora clapped. "I see you're still on your game with ballet."

"Kirk told me I'm building my testimony."

"I'm happy you two connected. When I see him later, I'll tell him how much you enjoyed his visit."

"Thanks, Mom. Are you going out for New Year's Eve?"

"No, we're staying at Kirk's house."

"You know he had another female in his bed while you were gone, right?"

"*What?*"

"Margo insisted on sleeping under the covers."

Nora laughed. "Under the covers?"

"You've taught her bad habits."

"I'll speak with Margo when I see her at Kirk's."

"So, do you love him?"

Nora blushed. "I never thought I'd say it about a man again, but yes, I'm madly in love."

"Hasn't it been kind of quick?"

Chuckling, Nora answered, "Well, yes, but my friend Rosie says it's the energy of the universe. She calls it Divine Time."

"Oh," said Angelica, rolling her eyes."

"Has there ever been someone you've had strong feelings for—like a relationship?" Nora dared to ask.

Angelica gazed into space. "Not really. There's only one thing an addict cares about, and that's the drug. But I don't need to drown myself in heroin anymore." She paused. "God is faithful, he won't let me be tempted beyond what I can bear, and he'll offer me a way out so I can handle it. 1 Corinthians 10:13. I'm beginning to care about my life."

"Amen. So am I," echoed Nora. "It happens when you learn to love yourself."

"What about Eve? Did she leave for China yet?" asked Angelica.

"No, she's going back tomorrow. She wants to visit you again before she leaves but there's no time."

Angelica slowly nodded. "At least we got to see each other while she was here. I'm going to write her a letter."

"She'd like that," Nora said, smiling.

****

Nora sank into an ambrosia bubble bath, candles flickering and gentle harp music playing in the background. She wanted to unwind before launching into New Year's Eve, which had never been one of her favorite holidays with its emphasis on examining one's inadequacies and pledging to do better. She did enough of that on a regular day.

At first, Nora's mind drifted to melancholy thoughts of her mother's passing, but wondrous images of Angelica and Kirk soon pushed them aside. From the bathtub, she could see the fish dress on its satin hanger, hooked over the door and draped with an art deco necklace from her mother's jewelry box. The dress now comforted her; she began to regard it with affection, as if it were a companion and helper.

PLEASED TO SEE A DEEPER LEVEL OF WORTH, NOW
THAT FEAR HATH LOST ITS GRIP AND ALLOWED
THEE TO RECEIVE. WHERE ART THOU TAKING ME?

"As if you don't know," Nora playfully replied. "Please don't embarrass me tonight."

She heard a fluttery laugh.

WELCOME TO THE REALM OF ALL POSSIBILITIES.

Stepping out of the tub, Nora reached for a towel and gently dried her body, admiring its beauty. What a discovery, for so long she'd avoided looking at her below-the-neck anatomy. She reached for the freesia lotion, rubbing it into her skin, prompting a memory of the morning she'd prepared for the massage of her life. A fleeting smile spread across her face as she pictured Romar.

After putting on the fish dress, she gave a final twirl in the mirror and adjusted the necklace, moving it to the left instead of keeping it centered. Katrina had told her that necklaces should always be worn slightly off kilter to attract more attention.

On her way out the door, Nora grabbed the Christmas gift she'd picked up for Kirk at Miss June's shop, along with the picture of Sister Marguerita, and dashed off into the snowy evening.

He was standing in the entryway when Nora arrived, his arms outstretched. Barking and jumping up and down like a yo-yo, Margo scooted by Kirk before hopping into Nora's arms. Nora nuzzled her head in Margo's furry body.

"I missed you, Furball."

"Somebody else missed you, too," Kirk said. "Welcome back, mate." He pulled her into his arms and kissed her, his fiery tongue lapping around hers until she heated up like a furnace. "Oh, baby," he whispered in Nora's ear, rendering her speechless.

Was it the dress, or her own desire to suspend time and savor their shared arousal, as if it were more pleasurable than the act itself?

"Soon," she said, with a coy smile.

Now inside, Margo rejoined Kirk's dogs, Chiller and Mondo as they stretched out on the living room's braided rug in front of the hearth. Nora soaked up the heat of the roaring fire that blazed in the fieldstone fireplace. *As if I need more heat,* she thought. She removed her coat, hat, and boots, setting them near the hearth.

She turned her attention to the Christmas tree, which glittered with star-shaped lights, red glass ornaments, and silver tinsel. "It's gorgeous!" She reached into her overnight bag and pulled out a wrapped package, handing it to Kirk.

"What's this?" he asked, sounding surprised.

"A late Christmas present."

He placed the gift next to the only other one under the tree, which had to be for Nora. She remembered their Early Bird visit to Mystique, when Miss June had whisked him off to the jewelry case.

"A glass of Hennessey?" he asked.

Nora licked her lips. "Sure."

"I'll be right back."

A few minutes later he emerged from the kitchen with two brandy snifters, a tray of cheese and crackers, and a frosted bowl of shrimp cocktail, which he set on the coffee table, then snuggled next to Nora on the loveseat.

"You've been through so much, Nora," he said, putting his arm around her; she rested her head on his shoulder and stared into the fire. " I'm sorry you lost your mom." His voice was soft and comforting.

A picture formed in Nora's mind: the hospital visit when she fed her mother ice chips and they said a voiceless *yes* to letting go of the many differences that had separated them through the years.

"She's at peace now, and I feel as if we made our silent amends." But deep inside, Nora questioned how she really felt. Was it a myth she hid behind to spare herself the grief of a family torn apart, strangers unto themselves? It would have been so much better, if, before her mother passed, they'd spoken about her life and expressed the deepest truths they knew about themselves. But it was not to be.

Now, toasting to the dawn of a new year, Nora was relieved at not having to recount the details of her mother's death, nor finding her brother's death certificate. They'd talked about it on the phone when Nora was in Connecticut and that was enough. Instead, she told Kirk how his visit with Angelica over Christmas meant a great deal to her and her daughter.

"She's amazing."

"Do you think she's through with drugs?" Nora asked.

"She said so, though she admits it will be a daily walk. She's got Jesus now. Hopefully, prison can do what rehab couldn't. She's determined—like her mother."

Nora blushed. "Who, me?"

STAND IN THY POWER!

"I mean, yes, I *am* determined. Angelica told me what happened to your parents. I'm so sorry. I had no idea. Here I've been running my mouth about Angelica's drug problems, which must have stirred up hurtful feelings inside you." She put her arms around him and covered his face with kisses.

"Don't worry, hon, but I'll take the kisses. How do you think she's dealing with her grandmother's death?

"Like her mother, burying herself in work to push away the pain. You know—denial. But I'm working on myself." To Nora, that meant returning to Rosie to continue her past life journey. As much as she wanted to tell Kirk, he would never understand. Or maybe he would, but she wasn't ready.

The next glass of Hennessey went down more smoothly. Nora settled against Kirk's chest. His fingers kneaded her rigid neck and shoulder muscles, turning them to dough. She listened to the sound of the heavy snow against the windows.

It was his idea to take the dogs outside. After bundling up like Nanook of the North, they stepped into a winter wonderland, their boots sinking into layers of white fluff. The air felt sharp, with billowy cotton balls bombarding them from every direction.

Nora pictured herself wearing an ermine mink hooded cloak, her hands tucked into a matching muff, and her feet covered by high-buttoned boots. Was it the dress's doing that filled her with romantic visions of an earlier era? *Imagine Kirk in a long black wool coat, a scarf around his neck, a Russian fur hat, and tall leather boots… he takes her hand and leads her through snowdrifts, ready to catch her, should she lose her balance. Her mind travels to a Doctor Zhivago scene, and the words spill out: Somewhere we'll meet again, my love.*

"I love you to the ends of the earth," Nora called out.

"I'm hard of hearing. *Eh,* what did you say?"

"I SAID I LOVE YOU, KIRK KLOPPENHEIMER!" She shouted with such force she imagined she could knock the shutters off every house in the neighborhood.

"That's better," he said, enveloping her in his arms. The dogs, in a high-pitched barking tizzy, ran circles around them. Then he said, "Will you marry me, Nora?"

"Yes!" she declared, secretly marveling at the fish dress's influence.

AT LAST, A HIGHER LEVEL OF SELF-WORTH.

They raced to the door, brushed themselves and the dogs off as best they could, opened it and dropped their winter gear by the fireplace before snuggling on the hearth like lovers on a park bench. Snowflakes melted on the bridge of Kirk's nose and trickled onto Nora's hair.

"You look gorgeous tonight," he whispered, leaning his chest against hers and running his hands down the small of her back. He kissed her neck and into the scoop of the dress. Nora felt the dress vibrate and swore it was glowing.

"It's settled. We're getting married in 2000," he announced. "Let's open the presents. You first."

Nora carefully unwrapped the silver foil, expecting a ring. When she lifted the cover, it surprised her to see a magical-looking seashell jewelry case with a silk pillow that held the most brilliant moonstone necklace Nora had ever seen. Breathless, she resonated with its lunar energy and feminine spirit, admiring its rainbow iridescence.

"Kirk," she whispered, "it's out of this world."

He smiled and put his arms around her. "*You're* out of this world."

She pushed him away with a light touch. "I hope that's a compliment."

"It is. Miss June says it's a stone of protection and abundance; I thought it was perfect. Aren't you a moon child?"

"Yes, a July baby. It *is* perfect. I used to have a moonstone, but I lost it."

Nora recalled that the crystal attunes to cycles of time and enhances intuition. *I'll definitely wear it on my next past life journey,* she thought, then suddenly remembered she hadn't called Rosie, who by now was probably wondering why Nora hadn't returned for another session. The call could wait until morning.

"Thank you, Kirk. Now open your gift."

Kirk shook the empty-sounding box. "Thank God it's not a book of spells."

Nora made a face, and Kirk said, "After all, we *were* at a magic shop."

Nora laughed. "I'm into angels and crystals, not witchcraft."

"Just checking. Rosie's a strange bird."

Nora's heart raced. *What if he thinks it's too weird?*

Kirk slowly unwrapped the package, revealing the wooden box. He stared at the cover, running his fingers across the wood grain and rubbing the crystals.

"Stunning! What are they?"

"Carnelian. For truth, love, and faith."

"Till death do us part," he said, carefully placing the box on the coffee table. "Thank you, darling. My first treasure box."

Following a long kiss, he popped the cork off a champagne bottle. Nora screamed when it ricocheted off the ceiling and bounced into the fire. They laughed like innocent children, while Kirk filled their glasses.

"To Nora, my future wife."

"To Kirk, my future husband."

"Time to make New Year's resolutions," Kirk announced. "Did you make one?"

Nora giggled. "Yes, more lovemaking."

Without a word, he scooped her up and gently laid her on the rug in front of the hearth.

YESSSSSSSSSSSSS!

Chapter 22

"Good morning, Nora. I'm glad you called. I was worried."

Nora cleared her throat. "I apologize for not calling sooner. My mother passed away Christmas morning, and we had to rush to Connecticut."

"I'm sorry. Are you okay?"

"It's hard, but we're managing."

"How's your daughter?"

"She's holding up fairly well. I'd like to see you."

"For past life regression?"

Nora hesitated. "Yes, I think it's time." Lately she'd been feeling the pull of the dress to draw her back into Marguerita's world so she could finally break the vow of silence.

"Tomorrow?" asked Rosie.

"Can't do it. I've got a busy week—back to school, doctor's appointment, but Saturday will work."

"That's fine. Come at ten."

****

Nora paced back and forth in the gynecologist's waiting room, experiencing the usual jitters she felt at every annual visit. She settled in a seat by the magazine rack and picked up a random magazine, thumbing through its pages as her eyes passed over the print. Several minutes later she followed the assistant to the examining room, exchanged her clothes for a draping sheet, then lay on the table. While she waited, her anxiety filled every corner of the room.

After the exam was over, the doctor called her into her office.

"We'll send out your pap smear and have the results back in a week. I want to go over your recent mammogram." Her fingertips tapped on the official-looking documents lying on the desk between them. She pulled out the film, displayed it on a lit screen, and pointed to a dark mass.

"A suspicious area has shown up on the same breast you had cancer in seven years ago. When I saw it, I asked Radiology to send me your previous films." She lined up several more slides across the screen. "If you look at the one from five years ago, it's normal. Moving forward, I notice a small dot in '97, and a larger one now. I see Dr. Weiss did your surgery. I'll have my receptionist make an appointment for you. Check with her on your way out."

Nora's heart pounded like a base drum. "What are the chances it's cancer?"

The doctor reached across the desk and squeezed Nora's hand. "Let's wait and see what the biopsy shows. In the meantime, try to stop worrying."

But she couldn't. When she left the doctor's office, her mind swirled with memories of a double lumpectomy and the weeks of radiation she'd gone through. She couldn't stop herself from being hijacked by her own emotions. *I can't bear the thought of dying, of leaving Angelica. And Kirk. And Margo.*

She ran to the parking lot as if she could escape the bad news, then huddled in her car, too stunned to drive. Nora the victim, the walking wounded, held hostage by killer cancer. *Should I have been peering around every corner for the signs?*

Nora put the key in the ignition and slammed into reverse without looking behind her. On the main road, she drove like a wild woman, screaming, "Out of my way." She darted to the left of two cars stopped in front of her and heard a driver yell, "You asshole!" and saw him raise his middle finger. Just then, she came within inches of hitting the pedestrian who was crossing the street. *What am I doing? I need to get hold of myself before I hurt someone.* Trembling, she slowed the car to a crawl the rest of the way home.

The second Nora walked in the door, she called her sister, sobbing and spewing out the bad news.

"Calm down," Grace said. "Wait for the results. When is the biopsy?"

"The day after tomorrow." Nora took a deep breath. "Shouldn't I tell Angelica? How about Kirk?"

"Don't say anything until you know for sure. People don't need to be scared when it's probably nothing."

It was a relief to hear Grace's response. Nora wanted to hold off telling her daughter anything until she absolutely had to. Angelica knew nothing of the first bout with breast cancer, and Nora hoped to keep it that way. She wasn't as concerned about telling Kirk, she was certain he would be a rock to lean on.

"I'm going with you for the biopsy," Grace said. "Do you need me now?"

All at once, Nora felt utterly exhausted. "I'll be okay. Thanks for offering, Grace."

"Have a glass of wine and don't think about it tonight."

She took her sister's advice about the wine and ended up calling Rosie. How could she possibly take a past life journey, with cancer on her mind?

"Hi, this is Rosie Deerborn. I'm sorry I'm not available to take your call right now. Please leave a message, and I'll get back to you as quickly as I can. Have a sparkling day!"

"Sparkling, my ass," said Nora, fuming. She hung up without leaving a message.

Though the house turned dark with dusk falling, Nora left the lights off and lit a candle. After pouring another glass of wine, she collapsed on the living room couch and sobbed. The slightest touch of a hand stroked her hair, and she heard a gentle whisper in her ear:

THOU HATH THE STRENGTH AND UNCONDITIONAL LOVE OF A HIGHER POWER AS THE RUDDER OF THY SHIP.

That's the last she remembered until awakening at daybreak in the same spot and still wearing her street clothes. The candle was no longer burning. Margo was curled up in her arms.

Nora tried to banish thoughts of cancer by busying herself with tasks on her to-do list: *Go to work, walk Margo, clean house, write letter to Angelica.* Kirk was away at a Miracle Ear conference for the week, and by then she would know for sure whether she had cancer.

When Angelica called, Nora steered the conversation away from herself and toward her daughter. The news was not the kind you share over the phone, so they talked about Angelica's studies, Nora's students, and Kirk's travels. She mentioned that Grace might come with her on the next visit. Before they said goodbye, Nora told her daughter that when she got out, they would plant a weeping willow tree in the back yard in honor or Grammy, and Angelica said she would like that.

****

Nora met with the surgeon. He welcomed the sisters into his office with a smile and an iron clad handshake. "We will do the same thing we did before, a stereotactic breast biopsy. Relatively painless. We'll numb the breast and collect multiple samples of tissue, using a hollow needle. You might feel some pressure."

Nora's nerves flared, even though she'd been through this before. "How soon will we get the results?"

"We should have them in two or three days."

Nora's body stiffened on the examining table. Bright lights bore down, and the room reeked of hospital antiseptic. First the pin prick, then the numbing, but not enough to quell the pain. It felt like the flesh of her breast was being sliced up into pieces, like a pizza. When it was over, it comforted her to find Grace in the waiting room, reading a British mystery paperback she'd brought along.

****

Nora and Grace met with the doctor for the follow-up visit. The biopsy showed invasive cancer in the left breast, extending beyond the ducts and into the tissue.

Nora cringed. "What does that mean? Am I going to die?"

"I can't answer that question, Nora. The tests will determine the stage, and the stage will dictate the treatment options, which are yours to make."

Disturbing images floated through Nora's mind—her body minus its breasts, fleshy tissue scooped out like the carving of a pumpkin with only its pithy pulp remaining. Breasts discarded, leaving two gaping holes where once her daughter had nursed. She crossed her arms over her chest as if to guard against further intrusion. Tears welled up in her eyes, and she began to cry. "I'm overwhelmed. Will I need chemo this time?" she asked, clutching the strands of her hair.

His voice softened. "One step at a time."

Grace's hand rested on Nora's shoulder.

"I recommend the Cancer Forum in Portland. The better informed you are, the more grounded you'll be in figuring out what's best. I'm glad you have your sister for support, but it's also helpful to meet people in the same situation as yourself." He gave her a brochure. "My receptionist will call you to let you know the surgery date." He gave her hand a gentle squeeze.

On the way home, the sisters talked about the best way for Nora to tell Angelica. "Will you come with me, Grace?"

"Of course."

"I can't imagine what I'd do without you. Angelica is my big worry, not knowing how she'll take the news. I'm sure Kirk will stand by me. I'll tell him when he stops by on his way back from his conference tonight."

"Thank God you can count on him as your pillar."

"I'll need him for strength, that's for sure. I feel fragile, like if one more bad thing happens, I'll shatter."

Grace said, "We've spent most of our lives running around behind others, trying to fix them, depleting ourselves, haven't we?"

"I suppose." Nora's fear of dying crept in again, just the way she imagined it had for her mother before she breathed her last breath.

*ALL THOU NEEDEST DO IS SEE THE NEXT FIFTY
FEET OF THE JOURNEY.*

Chapter 23

Nora heard Kirk's special tap on the back door and ran to open it. He greeted her with hungry eyes, then twirled her around and drew her to him. Their kiss lingered like an echo.

"I missed you," he whispered in her ear.

"I missed you, too," she whispered back, and then her voice turned serious. "Kirk, come sit down, I've got something to tell you." Taking him by the hand, she led him to the living room couch.

"You're pregnant!"

"Not exactly." She bit her lip. "The cancer ... came back."

He got up and poured himself a shot glass of whiskey, his hands trembling.

"Why didn't you tell me?" His voice had a sharp edge to it.

"I just got the results today." It was going so wrong, not at all the way Nora pictured it would happen.

His eyes narrowed. His words penetrated her like thorns of a rose. "This changes everything, Nora."

She choked up, struggling to find her voice. "What do you mean?"

"I do love you, but I feel like I'm reliving the nightmare of losing Janine, and that almost killed me. I went through it once, and I'm *not* going through it again." He clenched his jaw and locked his arms together.

Nora had never seen him so resolute about anything. Abandonment and betrayal bubbled inside her, and she felt as if she might shatter into ten million pieces.

"What happened to the man whose love was enduring, and who would go to the ends of the earth to defend his woman? You're supposed to hold me in your arms and tell me everything will be all right, that we'll get over this hurdle together. I'm sorry you lost your wife, but didn't you tell me you wanted to get on with your life, and that's the way she would have wanted it?"

His voice cracked. "Yes, and I meant it, but never in a million years did I imagine it would happen again. What are the odds of that? Reliving cancer with the woman I love isn't my idea of getting on with my life. I can't go through it again. I wish I could promise to be here for you, Nora, but I'd be lying." He covered his face with his hands.

"Oh, *stop*! Do you think anyone is spared trouble? Please leave *now* and take your baggage with you." She started to get up from the couch, her anger blazing,

He grabbed her hand, as if trying to catch something that was slipping away. "Try to understand that I never imagined death would be banging at my door so soon again," he pleaded.

"Must you equate cancer with death?" Nora asked.

Kirk stood up and wrung his hands and hung his head, looking like a scolded child instead of the man she'd envisioned would envelop her, a big bear of a man holding her in his arms, providing protection and reassurance.

"Nora, I'm not the tough guy you thought I was, or even *I* thought I was."

"Why can't you be here for me?" she begged, watching him blur before her eyes. She wanted to shake him like the fish dress until he spilled out the words she longed to hear. She looked into his eyes, expecting to see their blueness, instead she saw gray.

"I'm sorry, Nora," he said, his voice fading into silence.

"Me too! I'm sorry we ever met!" she screamed, filling with rage and hurt. "Here, take your damn moonstone necklace, you coward. So much for protection and abundance." She ripped it from her neck, and the necklace that he'd given her on New Year's flew across the room, the crystal shattering and scattering into pieces.

As if in slow motion, he picked up the pieces and walked out the door. She watched him step inside his car and creep away, not even turning his head to look back. Gone, just like that, as her mother's Buddhist quote had described: *The meeting and parting of living things is as when clouds, having come together, drift apart again, or as when the leaves are parted from the trees.*

Later, Nora found herself sitting cross-legged on the floor, rocking back and forth, her arms folded across her chest, her hands clutching her elbows, her eyes staring into space. Margo was licking her toes. She wondered how long she'd been that way. The phone was ringing but she couldn't move across the room to answer it. *What if it's Angelica?* she gasped. With every ounce of strength, she pulled herself to a standing position and picked up the receiver. "Angelica?"

"What's wrong, Nora?"

"Grace, it's you."

"Sorry to disappoint you. Are you okay? You sound awful."

Through her sobs, Nora muttered, "Kirk bailed on me."

"You're kidding. What happened? I'm coming right over."

Minutes later, Grace arrived with a jumbo-sized bottle of wine and poured two glasses.

"I can't believe he's walking away. He's not the one if he deserts the ship when it's sinking." She paused. "Not to say it *is* sinking. Either way, Kirk is an asshole."

"True, but I can't make him stay." Nora reached for her sister's hand. "Grace, I'm terrified of dying. What will happen to Angelica?"

"Stop it! Don't be doom and gloom. You beat cancer once, and there's nothing to say you can't do it again." She paused. "Where the hell is the fish dress when you need it, if it's so powerful?"

"In the closet, right where it will stay. If it were as mighty as Rosie says, my daughter would be with me, I wouldn't have cancer, and Kirk wouldn't have left. Katrina was right when she said to burn it."

Nora grabbed the scissors and walked to the refrigerator, snatching Kirk's picture from behind the *Live for Today* magnet.

"I won't be needing this anymore." After snipping him into tiny pieces that tumbled helplessly into the trash, she pulled out the *Golden Pagoda* fortunes they'd gotten on their first date—scraps of paper, meshed together in the tucks of her purse. Her voice wavering, she began to read aloud, "Thorns protect a rose but withhold them from your love. Be gentle, fiercely defending ... I can't go on." She broke down, whimpering.

"That sure didn't happen," Grace chimed in.

"He had the nerve to say he's been through fire. Watch this." Nora held a match to his fortune. "Burn, baby, burn."

"You go, girl. The same way you'll burn that cancer right out of your body forever."

Nora grabbed an oyster shell from under the kitchen sink. "Time to get rid of negativity. You don't mind if I smudge, do you?"

Grace winced. "Good God, do you have to do it right now? Too New Age for me. Can't you wait until after I leave?"

"Please don't go yet. Let's walk. I could use some fresh air."

Nora welcomed the chilly arctic blast, inhaling it up her nostrils as if she were breathing in the heavens, and immediately her head cleared up. She heard the mournful sounds of the foghorn in the distance, making them her own. The clock bells tolled in the East Side's chapel.

"Grace, I don't know if this has anything to do with Kirk and me breaking up, but I can't stop thinking about Angelica's father. Right now, I'm missing the hell out of him. We loved each other so much and had dreams for an amazing future together as a family."

"I know what you mean," Grace replied. "I often think about how I came to Rocky Harbor twenty-five years ago in search of a new life. I was working at the local diner when I fell for Josh. A bricklayer, a local boy. It wasn't long before we got married and had our sweet baby Eve. Like you, we expected to spend the rest of our lives together. It's funny, how things happen. We just have to keep going and hope for the best."

The sisters stayed wrapped in silence for the rest of the walk, as their boots crunched along the crusty sidewalk. When they got home, Grace asked Nora if she wanted her to spend the night. Nora reassured her she would be okay.

"I'll do my smudging. We'll talk in the morning. Thanks, Grace."

Nora stood outside and watched the Green Hornet ease out of the driveway and onto the main road. As soon as she returned inside, she reached under the sink and grabbed the bag of herbs and broke the leaves into the ceramic clawfoot shell, lighting them. When the flames turned to smoke, she picked up the crow feather wand and waved the smoky negative energy out through the cracked-open windows. She smudged her whole house and then her body, dotting the feather into the middle of her chest. Oh, how she savored the cleansing earthy aroma of white sage.

She stumbled to bed, purposely not glancing in the fish dress's direction, nor toward Marguerita. Just before drifting off to sleep, Nora swore she heard a low *HMMM* coming from the closet, followed by *ADVERSTY BUILDETH STRENGTH.*

In the morning, harboring a slight headache, Nora called the spa. "I'd like to book an appointment for today with Romar, please."

She lathered her skin with freesia lotion and stepped into the same lace bikinis she'd worn the first time. No bra, just a T-shirt and sweats, and she was out the door. She vowed not to think about cancer today, and Kirk could go screw himself.

When she arrived at the massage parlor, she smiled at the receptionist. In the dressing room, she removed every piece of clothing. This time there would be no cowering or pacing while she waited.

Romar tapped softly and welcomed her with a light *Good morning.* She followed him at a brisk clip to the same room with the three little windows overlooking a Zen garden, and hopped onto the massage table, surrounded by floating candles and chant music. She hoped he would do her feet again.

As she lay on her stomach, his fingers massaged her back side into oblivion, then he turned her over, carefully draping the sheet. As if in slow motion, he worked his way down the front of her body, and she succumbed to his tantalizing touch through the silk sheet.

He traced each toe with his fingers. Her lower body started to quiver, and she arched her back, kicking the sheet aside. He hesitated for only a moment.

When she was alone again, she felt abandoned, overcome by a peculiar sensation of feeling full of emptiness. *What am I doing to myself?*

When she reached home, she ran to the closet and snatched the fish dress off its hanger, twisting and shaking its bones and swirls.

"My boyfriend left me when I spoke the truth, and now I might die of cancer. The only bright spot in my life is Angelica, and I'm sure you had nothing to do with that. Since you've been around, I've been bombarded, beat up, chewed up, and spit out."

The dress pulled away.

THOU ART HURTING ME, PLEASE STOP!
THOU SHALT HARDLY BE PLEASED WITH SELF,
RETURNING TO THINE OLD DESTRUCTIVE WAYS,
AS IF SLEEPING WITH A STRANGER WILL MAKE
THEE FEEL WHOLE. THINK MORE HIGHLY
OF THYSELF. GREATER FAITH AND PERSEVERANCE
ARE REQUIRED OF THEE.
AND BETTER DECISIONS. YEESSSSSSSS.

Nora melted, blubbering into the dress, and it wrapped itself around her as she lapsed into memories of death, blame, shame, and toxic relationships. And now, Romar.

THOU NEVER RECOVERED, FALLING DEEPER AND
DEEPER INTO AN EMOTIONAL ABYSS.

Nora felt her hair being stroked.

THERE'S AN ORDER TO CHAOS WHEN A HIGHER
POWER IS IN IT. THOU ART BEING REPOSITIONED
TO GROW.

The dress folded her into its skeletons, crisscrosses, and tribal symbols, filling her emptiness with a new emotion that flowed like the gentle rippling of a pebble tossed into a pool of water.

I AM AN ECLECTIC MIX OF ASCENDED MASTERS—
CHRISTIAN AND PAGAN—OFFERING FORGIVENESS
AND HOPE.

Wrapped in the dress, Nora crawled onto her bed, tucking her body into a fetal position. She drifted off to sleep, floating timeless, suspended between physical and mystical worlds of past, present, and future.

The next morning, a call from Thomas awakened her. He'd heard about her breast cancer.

"It's amazing how news spreads like the flu in a small town," Nora said.

Thomas chuckled. "We're here to help you through this, Nora."

Like the full sun at high noon, she felt his warmth. "Thanks, Thomas. How're you doing?"

"Same old, one drama after another. Mrs. Carver is convinced she has terminal brain cancer but she's such a diva. I'm sure her dizziness is age appropriate. I've got to take her for tests. She doesn't want her husband to know, so please keep it to yourself."

"Who am I going to tell?"

"You women can't keep a secret. Like your sister."

Nora knew he'd manage to slip Grace into the conversation. "What a tremendous help she is."

"That's Grace. She'd give anyone the shirt off her back." He let out a huge sigh. "I love that woman, but she just doesn't get that my job comes first."

"You men always have some kind of excuse for not committing," Nora quipped.

"Ouch, that hurts!"

Nora could picture him grimacing. "Sorry, Thomas, I don't mean to take it out on you. I'm not in the best of moods. On top of everything else, Kirk broke up with me."

"*What?*"

"Cancer hit too close to home. He lost his wife to cancer a few years ago."

"What's that have to do with it?"

"He's afraid to go through the same nightmare with me."

"That's too bad. Do you want me to talk to him?"

"You're a sweetheart, but it would do no good. Let me know how Mrs. Carver makes out."

"I will. Gotta run—it's time for Pippette's grooming appointment."

Chapter 24

"Are you sure she won't mind?" Grace asked.

"Absolutely. You're like her second mother."

"Yes, but do you really want to tell her about your cancer or your break-up with Kirk, with me there?"

"I need your moral support."

"How are you doing, anyway?" Grace ask in a soft, caring way.

"I'm nervous about telling Angelica."

"Kids are supposed to have more resilience than we give them credit for."

"Outwardly, anyway. I worry about what she feels inside. She's barely had time to recover from Grammy's death."

"Maybe you should've worn the dress," Grace said, light-heartedly.

"No, not today." She was not about to mention her act of desperation at the massage parlor, nor the confrontation with the dress. "I'm saving it for my next past life episode."

"The other night, you were ready to burn the damn thing."

Nora smiled thinly. "The dress and I have reached an agreement."

Grace raised an eyebrow.

Angelica's face lit up like a bonfire. "Mommy! Auntie Grace! What a nice surprise."

She looked robust, and Nora beamed at seeing tears of joy instead of sorrow. *She really has changed,* Nora thought. At that moment she wanted nothing more than to spare Angelica from bad news, but she knew she needed to be truthful about her cancer setback.

"How've you been, honey?" Nora asked.

"Great, other than I can't hug you and Auntie Grace. Did Eve get off okay?"

Grace sighed. "Yes, and I'm missing her already."

"Me, too. I can't wait to see her again. I loved it when you all came and visited, and we talked about our good times together. By the way, Mom, Psych classes are going well, and so is dance. You'd be proud of me."

"We already are," Nora said.

Grace smiled. "That's for sure. It's so good to see you, Angelica. I miss you and think about you all the time."

Angelica blew Grace a kiss, and Grace caught it and sent it back.

Nora saw a flash of pink at Angelica's neck. "I see you're still wearing the cross."

"Yes, but I'm not so over the top."

"What do you mean?" Nora asked.

"I was flaunting the cross and spouting Bible verses. It was all new to me, but it didn't go over so great with some of the girls here. Now I see the bigger picture. There's a higher power that's greater than us, and maybe there's more than one way to know God."

"Oh," exclaimed Nora, calling to mind the dress's mix of Paganism and Christianity for strength. She hated to ruin Angelica's upbeat mood and wanted to break the news gently. "Do you remember me telling you to be strong when we found out that Grammy passed?"

Angelica nodded, her lip quivering as if she anticipated more bad news was coming.

Nora wished there were bars she could reach through to hold her daughter's hands. "I'm asking you to be just as strong today."

"What is it, Mom? Just tell me."

Nora cleared the frog in her throat. "I have breast cancer, and it's invasive." As much as Nora wanted to be open with her daughter, it would be cruel to tell her about the first time.

Their eyes met, and Nora saw her daughter's lost look and heard her sobs. "I'm sorry, I'm sure it wasn't what you expected." If only Nora could cradle Angelica in her arms.

"We *will* get through this. Our family is as strong as iron." Grace leaned forward toward Angelica, placing her hands on the ledge between them. "Your mother's not just a survivor, she's a *thriver*."

Angelica folded her hands as if she were praying. "Mom, we'll help you get better. Does Kirk know?"

"Yes, but we're not together anymore."

"Oh, Mom," Angelica gasped. "I *knew* it! I hate men!" She yanked the cross from her neck and tiny pink beads scattered in the air like shrapnel.

"He couldn't handle it when I told him I have cancer. It hit too close to home. He lost his wife to cancer a few years back. I was furious, but I understand."

"I never could figure out why they call women the weaker sex. Seems to me, it's the other way around," Grace said. "We three are living proof."

Nora nodded. "You've got that right."

Angelica added a weak *Amen.*

When visiting time ended, Nora and Grace touched their fingers with Angelica's across the glass, and they all echoed their love for each other.

****

Nora wore the dress to the Cancer Forum, hoping it would offset the anxiety she felt over having to walk around with cancer seeking to destroy her insides. Surgery couldn't come soon enough. She found the Convention Center parking lot and grabbed her work bag from the back seat, in case she found a spare minute.

A scolding tap touched her hand.

*REMOVE THYSELF FROM CHAINS THAT BIND WITH
PERFECTION AND APPROVAL SEEKING.*

She chuckled to think that the maintenance man at school had told her the same thing, though he used different words. *Nora, if you died today, they'd have someone else doing your job tomorrow.*

This need to never miss a day of work. She took life way too seriously. It was time to learn how to just wander through a day, like Rosie had told her. Maybe that was one reason cancer was clubbing her over the head.

Inside the auditorium, bursts of pink and white balloons hanging from the ceiling welcomed Nora. Bubbles blasted from the stage, and she could smell buttery popcorn nearby.

Quietly slipping into the back row of seats, she gazed at the stunning middle-aged woman who stood at the podium. Her straight ash blonde hair rested perfectly on her shoulders. Nora wondered if she was wearing a wig. The woman's face was thin but not gaunt, her makeup subtle, not overdone and clownish like someone desperate to cover up disease.

The woman bellowed out to the audience, "I've learned to accept nothing less than success. You're looking at someone who's had cancer four times." She held up a hand and counted on her fingers. "Twice in my breasts, once in my lungs, and recently in my brain. I've had more chemo cocktails than most people have had glasses of milk in their lives, and guess what, friends? I emerge stronger from each ordeal. You create what you think about, so stop seeing yourselves as victims. Am I letting cancer stop me from living?"

"No!" the audience shouted boisterously.

"Absolutely not! Tomorrow I leave for a two-month tour of Europe."

The crowd clapped and cheered even louder. The speaker gave a broad smile, waving a shiny pink cover in the air. "Thank you for attending the premiere of my book signing. You've been a fabulous audience."

People were on their feet, applauding before joining the long line waiting to purchase books. Nora watched the speaker move around the room and hand copies to those too weak to stand. Nora shuddered to think this might be the last book for some.

She stopped at the ladies' room before heading to the foyer where free massages and Reiki sessions were being held. Convention center bathrooms were wonderful, with their lounges with puffy sofas, soft lighted mirrors, and sinks with brass fixtures. Nora sank into a sofa to scan the program. It felt good to be away from work, to be a nameless face in the crowd and not have to answer to anybody.

She looked up and saw a stranger standing over her. Struck by the woman's face, whose gray-green eyes reminded Nora of sea foam, she could almost hear strong surf as she imagined thick lashes rolling off the eyes, accented with silver and lined with charcoal. The woman's glamour defied age.

"Excuse me," the stranger said. "Sorry to intrude, but I must ask you a question."

"I hope I can be of help. Please, sit down," Nora said.

The woman smiled as her bones creaked onto the cushions. "Thank you. Oh, that feels good. I've been so tired." Her chin-length hair had just the right amount of poof and color, a proper shade of blonde, bleached but not brassy. She wore a classic cotton dress from Talbot's.

"May I ask where you got that dress?" the woman asked, looking straight at Nora.

Not again, Nora thought. *Let me guess. She loves the way it looks and wants one for herself.*

"I said, *where* did you get your dress?"

Urgency in the elderly lady's voice snapped Nora to attention. She'd promised Thomas she'd never tell anyone, yet when asked by this stranger, she found it difficult to lie.

"It was a gift from a friend."

The woman's face lost its beauty, seeming to explode with wrinkles. "Was it Thomas?" she asked in a sharp voice.

Oh my God, Nora thought. *"Am I sitting with Thomas's boss?"*

Before she could answer, the woman said, "I can't believe he'd do this to me. Who does he think he is to defy my orders? I should fire him on principle!" She stood up, huffing and puffing.

Nora feared the old woman would collapse. "Please calm down, Mrs. Carver. I can explain everything. My name is Nora Jenkins, and I'm honored to meet you." She reached out to shake her hand.

"I'm not happy to meet *you*," Mrs. Carver snapped, holding her hand at bay.

"Please, it's all my fault," Nora pleaded.

Mrs. Carver put a shaky hand to her forehead and closed her eyes, her face paling. "I must sit down again," she said, grasping for Nora's hand.

"Are you okay?" Nora asked, carefully guiding Mrs. Carver back to the couch and crouching beside her. She, fanned the woman's face with the program.

With her eyes closed, Mrs. Carver whispered, "It'll pass in a few minutes. It's just another head explosion."

"May I get you something to drink?" Without waiting for a response, Nora pulled a Poland Spring from her purse and twisted the top off.

"Thank you, dear," Mrs. Carver answered, her tone softening. Eyes half-opened, she took tiny sips of water, her head bobbling like a kewpie doll. They sat in silence for several minutes, until the elderly woman regained composure.

Nora shared how she came to acquire the dress, insisting it was all her fault, not Thomas's. By the time Nora finished, Mrs. Carver's wrath had dissolved, and she agreed Thomas should bear no blame.

"Instead, I should be upset with *you*, but I believe the dress was meant to be in your hands, just as it ended up in mine three years ago."

It took little prompting for Mrs. Carver to tell her story. "While my husband and I were vacationing in Spain, we thought it would be exciting to take the ferry from Gibraltar to Morocco, so we could say we'd been to Africa. We've visited every other continent, even Antarctica."

"Are you sure you're up to talking?" Nora asked. Right before her eyes, Mrs. Carver transformed back into the age-defying beauty Nora had observed when she first saw her.

"I feel renewed," she answered in a full voice. "When we reached Marrakech, I wanted to tour a casbah. It was like crossing into another world—narrow alleys lined with beggars and vendors, mostly men and boys dressed in rags, reaching their twig-thin arms out for American money and chasing after us if we refused to buy their goods. The only women on the streets wore scarves revealing just their eyes, and shawls to hide their hunched backs. It was very interesting but quite frightening. They had warned us to stay with the guide."

"I heard they don't treat women very well."

"You mostly see boys, men, and ancient women in the streets. People of the casbah treat girls and young women like second class citizens, disrespecting and hiding them behind dark windows and closed doors. But I saw the curtains move aside, ever so slightly, as they peered down at us." She paused, frowning.

"Somehow, I got separated from my husband and found myself in the middle of a crowded marketplace seething with beggars, some of them blind, others without an arm or a leg. The poverty unnerved me, but when I tried to find my way out, one of the wretches held a dress in front of me. I was drawn to it immediately. I had to have that dress at any cost, so I emptied my purse into the old man's palm. As soon as he handed me the dress, I made my way back to the group as if by magic. I felt compelled to say nothing about what occurred, not even to my husband, and I tucked the dress into my satchel."

Despite Mrs. Carver's glowing appearance and strong voice, Nora worried that she might collapse. "Please, as much as I want to hear more, I think you should rest."

"On the contrary, I haven't felt this good in months. I insist on telling you *now*, so let me continue. On the ferry ride back to Spain, I had a second encounter, this time with two gypsies who followed me into the ladies' room. They said they saw me in the casbah and described in detail how I bought the dress from a beggar. The gypsies warned me it was full of danger, explaining that I didn't understand the karma attached to it. They demanded I give them the dress. Of course, I refused. The scoundrels got angry and demanded money. I told them I had no money, that I'd given it all to the beggar. They insisted I give them my rings.

Mrs. Carver began to weave back and forth in her seat. "I felt like I was in a trance and would do anything to keep the dress, so I took the rings—my precious diamond and sapphire—and handed them over. But that wasn't the end of it. They pulled out a leather journal and told me it held secrets of the dress, insisting I give them the jewelry in my satchel in exchange for the book. When they saw me hesitate, they convinced me that the price of knowledge is high, but necessary." Mrs. Carver's eyes grew wide as full moons. "Nora, there's so much to tell you about this dress, I don't know where to begin." She touched Nora's arm, her hand trembling.

"What kind of power does it have?" she asked.

"It gives its owner the desire for self-reflection and self-improvement. But the wearer must show great strength through faith and persevere through unimaginable challenges."

"Desire alone isn't enough to gain power?" asked Nora.

The old woman gave a deep sigh. "I wish it were that easy. You must also face your transgressions, but I couldn't do it."

"Why, what happened?"

"When I got back to the States, I started having nightmares about my first husband's death." Clutching at the sleeves of the dress, she lowered her voice. "They became more excruciating than my waking world and took over my life, nearly consuming me. Listen closely to what I am about to tell you, only because my time is short. I must confess to someone who won't condemn me in my last days."

"I promise," Nora said, nodding, though she didn't comprehend the depth of the woman's words. "Mrs. Carver, please don't think your life is over."

"Everyone believes it was natural causes—my husband's death—but that's not the truth. *I killed him!*"

Keeping a steady gaze, Nora hid the fact that Thomas had said as much.

"He was a cruel man who showed a different side to the rest of the world. Everyone loved him, but behind closed doors he was a tyrant. I prayed that things would get better, but they didn't. Then I started praying he would die. Finally, I couldn't take his abuse any longer, so I poisoned him, torturing him slowly like he had done to me over the years. I slipped antifreeze into his drinks, at first just a little, but over time I increased the dose. When he died, it looked like a heart attack."

Nora rubbed the woman's shoulders until she regained her composure.

"Do you know they've added a bitter taste to antifreeze these days, so we can't do that anymore. Anyway, I justified to myself what I'd done—until I got the dress. That's when I started reliving the memories. They were more terrifying than the actual act of killing him. Shame and guilt were too much to bear, but I blamed the dress. It was a curse because I wasn't ready to confront the truth. I had to get rid of it, and the only way I could think of was to send it back, but not to Morocco. I decided to send it to a church in Spain."

"But why did you want to return it to a chapel in Spain, when you bought it in a Moroccan casbah?"

"I'm too tired for another long story, my dear. You must read the diary that came from the gypsies. It will tell you how Marguerita DeRoche became entwined with the dress."

Marguerita DeRoche, the very person I was in my last life! It's all strange yet wonderful, but I'm learning to expect such coincidences, Nora thought, her heart racing.

"I'll see that Thomas gets the journal to you. It's written in Romani Spanish, but I had it translated. You should keep the dress. I've said enough, and all at once I am beyond tired." Her eyelashes fluttered, no longer resembling strong surf. She looked as if she were wilting.

Nora gave her another sip of water. "Mrs. Carver, you just came to terms with your past mistakes when you confessed to me. The dress will help you now. You could use protection and healing. Please take it back."

"No, my dear, this dress has a mind of its own, and it has chosen you. I'm at the end of my journey, while you're in the midst of yours. It's too late for me. I'm at this conference simply to figure out how to accept my mortality. Perhaps you can do what I couldn't. I know you're going through a lot, so keep the dress, for with it there is hope. Eighty-five years is long enough on this earth. I'm ready to move on."

Nora felt a nudge.

IT IS THY DESTINY.

On the drive home, she thought about how trapped Mrs. Carver must have felt to resort to taking another person's life. But Nora didn't judge her. Lord knows how many times *she'd* yearned to harm James. More important, Mrs. Carver had confirmed Nora's hunches about the dress—that while it made her feel temporarily on top of the world, its greater power was in helping its recipient to confront her flaws, seek the truth, and learn the lessons that would lead to growth. With cancer bearing down upon her, Nora needed every available piece of artillery. The magic of the dress rose up inside, as she felt its power to move her toward healing. She was ready to return to her past life as Marguerita.

Chapter 25

Nora lay on the couch in Rosie's candle-lit parlor, relaxing into puffy velvet pillows. Her eyelids grew heavy, and she began to free-float in the black sea of the fish dress covering her body.

"This may be your final journey," she heard Rosie say.

She sat up with a jolt. "I'm not coming back?"

Rosie chuckled. "Sorry, I didn't mean to alarm you. I predict you'll break the vow of silence this time."

"What about the dress? I haven't seen it once this whole trip, and it's supposed to be helping me."

Rosie glanced off into the distance. "You will, soon."

Soon, always soon, Nora said to herself. Before long, she was swept into the depths of her own imagination where she encountered rogue waves through which she must pass, obstacles to conquer, and victories to secure.

****

A voice calls out. "Tell me where you are." I recognized it as Rosie's but can't see anything through the thick haze that separates us.

At last my eyes adjust. "I'm deep in the Sierra Nevada Mountains of Spain. The same spot where Heathera and I found each other on the path to Seville, but you brought me back to the present.

"At your insistence," Rosie reminds me.

It all comes back to me—I was torn—wanting to speak but scared to break the vow of silence. I am no longer afraid. Now I am back in the arms of my beloved Heathera, whose blazing red hair and brown sugar skin have only magnified in beauty. She tells me that although I hide my black curls, she would recognize my walnut eyes and the slope of my nose anywhere. She's walked these hills for six years searching for me.

Entwining our pinky fingers, we renew our promise as blood sisters. Not needing speech to bind us, my vow of silence holds. Heathera talks, and I nod my head in agreement, shake it to show disapproval, and shrug my shoulders if I'm not sure. My hands move in different ways to signal what becomes our private language.

A cool breeze passes over me, it's Rosie asking how I am. I tell her that Heathera seems puzzled by my new life. When she touches the gold crucifix around my neck, she says, "That isn't our God. Have you forgotten that we have many? Our gods are the elements of Nature, we worship Sky, Water, Earth, Air, Fire, Sun, and Moon. And we celebrate life, not punish ourselves in silence, guilt, and sacrifice."

She leads me toward a group of gypsies juggling colorful glass bottles, casting prisms in the sun. I hang back and kneel behind a rock, bowing my head. My lips and fingers move silently across my rosary. When I rejoin them, I detect a sad look beneath Heathera's thin smile, as if my gypsy sister remembers our childhood laughter, secret-telling, foxglove-picking, and pretending to be gypsy queens whirling and twirling with silk scarves. How different I must seem to her now.

Rosie clears her throat, signaling her desire to know more.

I whisper from inside Marguerita. "Heathera still acts like a child, with her love of fun and play. Sometimes I wonder if I would be more like her, had I hidden under a beldame's skirt that day the soldiers came. If she were to ask me if I miss our old life, and if I were to speak honestly, I would tell her how conflicted I feel, secretly going back and forth between the Sacromontes and the Sisters of Charity."

"It's difficult to serve two masters," Rosie whispers. "Let's move on."

Under an August full moon, the tribe prepares for a fertility celebration to honor Nature's harvest. I admire my dear Heathera, wrapped in a sea of red silk from the bolt of Granada's fine fabrics, its folds cascading over her bountiful breasts, around wide hips and down sinewy legs. Doused with myrrh, her body's potent scent puts her in feline heat. Hair blazing like a lion's mane, she reflects the glow of fire. Crystal necklaces shimmer against her chest. Gold hoop earrings tug at her lobes, and her eyes shine bright as emeralds.

Drab layers of clothing hang like weights as if cementing me to the ground, and my undergarments press flat against my breasts like a shield, suppressing any inkling of sexuality from pulsing through my twig-thin body. Inside these rugged buckled boots, my feet suffocate while Heathera goes barefoot, her toes adorned with fine rings and her toenails tinted with henna. I feel insufficient next to my best friend, whose body has become that of a grown woman, while mine has shrunk to that of a child. Look at her, flirting with strangers who pass through the camp.

It is near dark. The celebration comes to life with fire, food, wine, and music. Heathera weaves through the crowd of men, her hips making wide pendulum sweeps. As night wears on, she continues to dance and drink, pulling men from around the fire to join in her frenzy, as if possessed. She pushes her breasts in their faces, grinding her pelvis against their groins. The beldames and some of the younger women gossip, shaking their heads back and forth. "Look at her. She should know better than to act like a whore."

I try to pull her away, but she shoos me off, cursing loudly. the men laugh. The beldames say, "Let her be drunk and lie in her own vomit," and they retreat.

The hurt inflicted by Heathera gouges my heart. I follow the beldames into the shadows and huddle in a corner of the cave, praying in silence for forgiveness for having cast judgment upon my best friend. *Father, help me do unto others as you would have them do unto me.*

The next morning, I find her crumpled up in the underbrush, asleep, still dressed in silks, though now they are soiled and torn. I shake her awake and help her to camp, her body damp and heavy against mine. I place her in a cave and kiss her forehead, watching her stir and offer a weak smile before I depart.

I hear Rosie's voice in my ear. "Come, let's move forward in time. You have children to save."

Months later I return to the gypsy camp to find Heathera, who is glad to see me. She leads me along the path to the secret spot we shared as children, and we sit on our flat rock. She takes my hands and places them on her belly, rounder than I ever remember. I feel sudden movement and pull my hands away. Together we weep, and the wind sends our sobs skyward.

Rosie's voice comes to me. "Why are you crying, dear?"

"Heathera gave herself to a stranger, and now a baby is on the way. I fear there will be retribution to pay in the Sacromonte camp."

Word spreads like wildfire through the tribe: Heathera is with child. Yatobi calls a meeting and tells us that trouble brews. She must summon Fire, Moon, and Earth, along with the ghosts of Indian ancestors, to perform a cleansing and healing ceremony after the birth, so that the child will live, and the gypsies will be spared from any curses. The tribe pledges to support Heathera for the sake of saving the infant, for gypsies bind together like a tight weave of fabric, and karma passes not only from generation to generation but within tribes.

I worry that tribal powers alone will be insufficient. When I leave the gypsy camp, I take matters into my own hands. I return to the Sisters of Charity convent and steal the holy cloak of la Virgen de la Peña from the chapel at Mijas. The nuns are in an uproar when they discover that the shroud is missing, but I remain calm, carrying out my vows with perfection.

As the time of birth approaches, I conceal the shroud in the folds of my tunic and leave the convent. I trek through the mountains of Andulasia to the gypsy camp, and there I hide in a cave and cut and stitch the shroud into a ceremonial dress.

In the distance, I hear a gasp.

"What is it, Rosie?" I ask.

"What have you done?"

"I'm using Christian power to strengthen the child's chances of survival."

Rosie sighs.

"I will give the dress to High Priestess Yatobi, who knows not where it came from. She will imbue the cloth with Sacromonte symbols. How pleased I will be with this blended masterpiece. We must place faith in both Christian and Pagan anointing to raise the dress's power to cleanse Heathera and her soon-to-be-born child."

"Through joining Catholic and Pagan energies?" asks Rosie.

"Yes, they will receive the grace of God—the Creator Himself—under the guise of Mother Earth and Father Sky."

Rosie's sigh deepens. "We shall see. Let's move forward."

****

Heathera's daughter is born ill and near death. The ceremony takes place at midnight in the chambers of the largest Sacromonte cave, with its painted walls of gypsy legends and nature idols. Flames rise from stakes dug into the earth's floor. Yatobi lays the newborn on a flat rock and chants mystical sounds, echoing mantras inherited from her great-grandmother. Drums declare war against bad spirits as we encircle the ceremonial fire.

Heathera cowers in a shadowy corner of the cave. I wish I could tell her that the dress will protect her, and her daughter will live. Wait—she is not alone. I see the luster of light hover over her, and in a flash, it disappears.

"Come to me, child," the High Priestess commands, and the circle opens. Heathera emerges from the shadows and moves toward Yatobi, who stands near the fire. Illuminated by its brilliance, Heathera is stunning, despite her head shaven of its flagrant mane. Surely, she is the most beautiful woman on earth.

Face to face with the High Priestess, Heathera stands statuesque in the ceremonial dress that entrances me, with its tribal symbols—spirals, criss-crosses, heart shapes, crescent moons, and mermaid combs. Oh, no! Sea creatures with dorsal and tail fins, fish skeletons with gills and eye sockets, swirling through the netting, frenetic, chasing—Christian Symbols that I thought were hidden in the fabric's weave. A sickening thought overcomes me: Virgen de la Peña has appeared and made her Diego known. *What if Yatobi discovers that I have deceived the Sacromontes?*

The High Priestess raises her arms to receive Heathera, but at the last moment she retreats. "Remove the dress," Yatobi orders in a voice no one dares defy. "These are not the symbols of the Sacromontes," she screeches, pointing to the now glowing fish. She glares at me and screams, "What evil have you released, Marguerita?"

I long to speak but the vow of silence chokes me.

Yatobi's piercing pitch reverberates throughout the cave. "You must tell us what you have done, or Heathera and the infant will die. There will be cursing and gnashing of teeth, great sorrow in our tribe, for you have angered the gods. Break your silence *now*!"

I kneel before Yatobi on the cave floor, which trembles at her looming presence. Through the flames, I see Rosie's face and her voice, strong and urgent. "Now is the time to break the vow of silence and speak your truth!"

Like the full moon, I rise, shouting, "Spare Heathera and the infant. *I* stole the Virgin Mary's shroud and created a dress made of Christian and Pagan energies. I am a traitor to both, my fate is in your hands, High Priestess Yatobi."

I collapse on the hard, cold floor, and the cave is shaking me, shaking me, shaking me.

****

Nora rubbed her eyes. She was lying on the parlor sofa, and Rosie was shaking her. "Welcome back, Nora." Had she dreamed of floating across time and through space, or had she truly traveled into another dimension?

Rosie was smiling. "You did it!"

"Did what?" Nora said, feeling dizzy.

"Don't you remember? You broke the vow of silence and freed yourself from the past. I pulled you back because your energies belong in the here and now again."

When Nora's senses returned, it surprised her how much lighter she felt, as if she'd left behind baggage—the mental and emotional kind she'd been carrying throughout her life. "I feel like a new person," she said, stretching her arms above her head.

"You should. You found your true voice."

"Don't I need to finish my life as Marguerita?"

"Why? Your work is done. In fact, go *have* a margarita."

Nora gave a giddy laugh. "Not a bad idea, Rosie. But what should I do with the dress?"

"We'll talk about that later. You've got other things to think about now, like conquering cancer."

Chapter 26

The day of Nora's surgery, Grace brought her to the hospital. The sisters sat in a private lounge, cracking sick humor jokes to ease Nora's anxiety until they came and wheeled her off to surgery.

After sedation, she lapsed into a stupor, remembering nothing until she awoke several hours later, feeling as if she'd been run over by a steamroller. Her first lucid thought was how thankful she felt to be alive. Grace, whom she called her Florence Nightingale, was there. Nora surveyed the roll of gauze wrapped around her upper body, covering the missing breast and the remaining one that would be nipped and tucked during reconstruction.

She felt the pain of drainage tubes and swollen tissue. But the greatest pain was in her heart, for she thought most about missing her daughter. Much more than missing Kirk, whom she'd written out of her life, despite still loving him, though she would never admit it. "I'm happy you're here with me," she told her sister, "but I wish Angelica could be here, too."

"She's here!" Grace held up the photo of Angelica that Nora had brought to the hospital.

During recovery at home, a steady stream of friends and coworkers knocked on Nora's door, delivering tuna casseroles, meatloaf, and shepherd's pie, along with fresh vegetables and home-baked bread. People she barely knew gifted her with everything from Irish linen bookmarks trimmed in lace and decorated with crocheted flowers, to carved wooden angels and inspirational books penned by cancer survivors. She realized that until now, she'd rarely accepted help from others, or even asked.

Angelica called every day. "How are you feeling, Mom?"

"Fantastic, now that I hear your voice," she would answer, hiding her tiredness and pain.

Letters arrived daily. *Hi Mom. This morning I had pancakes for breakfast. Not as good as yours but they'll do. It was my turn to wash dishes, which is better than scrubbing toilets. The best part of my day is psychology class. We talk about the part of your brain that has to do with emotional intelligence, and how we need to get the bad memories out of our minds, to heal. Can't wait to be home in 197 days. Love you, Angelica.*

Despite often feeling weak, Nora always wrote back right away. She wanted to keep the letters flowing. They recorded the days until her release. Nora drew large Xs on the guardian angel calendar that hung by her bed, and Angelica etched notches with a pen on the leg of a wooden bench in her cell, much like a counting stick.

At Nora's post-surgery visit, the doctor shared good news about the cancer: it went beyond the ducts and into the breast tissue, but margins were clear, and the lymph nodes were clean. There would be chemotherapy because the cancer was invasive. The doctor said, "Radiation's not an option. We used it in your previous bout with cancer."

Nora shuddered at the word *chemotherapy*; she pictured her hair falling out in gigantic clumps and having to hide her bald head under a babushka. A telltale sign of being victimized by cancer. Her long hair was the footprint she wanted to leave behind. "I was hoping I wouldn't have to lose my hair," she said, touching its strands.

Six weeks later, on the day of Nora's first appointment for chemo, Grace pulled in the driveway.

"Good morning," Nora said in a cheery voice, masking trepidation as she slid into the front seat.

"Morning, Mommy."

Nora whipped her head around and saw Angelica crouched in the back seat.

"Oh my God, I can't believe it!" She bolted from the car and pulled open the back door. Mother and daughter gushed with tears, and a moment later they danced circles in the driveway.

"How did you get out?" Nora asked, still in shock.

"I sprung her," Grace said, grinning as she stood beside them.

"Are you really out?" Nora asked, breathing in fresh life from their hugs and kisses. "Or just on a pass?"

Angelica's smile stretched across her face. "I'm released six months early for good behavior."

The new young doctor began their meeting by sharing that he'd recently joined the practice after leaving California, where he'd been involved in cancer research. When Nora asked him about chemotherapy, she was amazed to hear him say, "We'll save the heavy artillery for now."

"I don't have to go bald?"

He smiled. "Not at all. You'll be taking a new wonder drug without the awful side effects of chemotherapy.

"*Hallelujah!*" the girls erupted with cheers, affirming that the West Coast transplant had brought the latest breast cancer research in the form of a pill that would be the antidote to Nora's fears and a link to her recovery.

Later, at home, Angelica made promises. "I'll take you to your reconstruction appointments and do the grocery shopping and laundry. I'll walk Margo and bring you breakfast in bed, and whatever else will make your life easier."

"Thank you, darling. I'm happy you're back home." Gazing into Angelica's eyes, Nora knew that while she needed her daughter's help with recovery, she also needed to help her daughter through *her* recovery. Angelica had been clean for over eighteen months, but that wasn't enough to be out of the woods. There would always be the risk of relapse. Nora retrieved the royal blue angel from the curio cabinet and held it up to Angelica. "Meet Archangel Uriel."

Angelica gave it a curious look. "What's that for?"

"According to Miss June, the Mystique lady, he wards off negativity. Also releases karma and teaches forgiveness."

"He? I thought angels are female."

Nora smiled. "No, most are male." She handed the carved stone to her daughter, along with a royal blue velvet pouch.

Angelica let the angel rest in her palm before sliding it into the pouch. "Thanks, Mom. What am I supposed to do with him?"

"Just keep him close. Lapis lazuli's a powerful healing stone."

Nora guessed that her daughter would throw the talisman in a dresser drawer and forget about it. That was okay, for Nora knew better than to rely solely on the power of angels, just as Marguerita hadn't trusted just one entity when she combined Christianity with Paganism to enhance the healing power of the dress.

Alone in her bedroom, Nora slipped on the dress, turned in the mirror, and pleaded for one more favor. "Please help me heal my daughter, as you have healed me." Hearing only the sound of silence, she again petitioned and heard a small voice inside.

TEACH HER ABOUT THE POWER OF UNCONDITIONAL LOVE, FORGIVENESS, AND GRATITUDE.

Simple but not easy, especially when applying it to oneself.

During recovery, Nora felt a strong urge to connect with nature, as if its forces were beckoning her. She and Angelica walked the beaches in search of unique shells, sand dollars and beach glass to add to the vases sitting on the porch. When thoughts of Kirk and *Simple Pleasures* drifted into her mind, she sent them away.

Nora and her daughter also took walks in a nearby nature preserve. Deep in the woods, Nora sensed gypsy energy and heard the crackling of twigs along the path, although she saw no one. It was as if Heathera were walking alongside them.

On one of their walks, Nora told Angelica that this day they would experience *the simple beauty of life*. When they reached a grove of dogwood, Nora curtsied before a tree.

Despite her daughter's doubting look, Nora said, "This beautiful tree has its own personality. Look how its branches reach out and touch my arm. *Hello*, tree, I see the essence of God within you. You are alive and have a consciousness and a presence, and I honor you today."

"Mom, when did you start talking to trees?"

Nora knelt before the tree. "I get a sense of peace and healing when I'm in the woods."

Angelica ran to the tree and poked her head in the spot where branches grow up from its core.

"*Hello* Tree," she greeted, then peeked through the branches. "*Hello* Mother."

They switched places and Nora, tucked in the dogwood, glanced at Angelica and chanted, "Oh, beloved human, we honor you and hope that our leaves have gracefully brushed your skin and delighted you today. We desire that you see how the wind shimmers our leaves in sunlight. Take the song and let it dance upon your heart. We wish you well, go merrily upon your way, dear one."

"Mom, I can't believe we're doing this," Angelica said with a light laugh. Then she did something that surprised her mother: she grabbed Nora's hands and together they twirled like whirligigs.

Perhaps only Nora heard the rustling in the grove.

SUCH FANCIFUL PLAY DEEPENS THE BOND AND RECAPTURES A SLIVER OF ORIGINAL INNOCENCE. NEVER FORGET THAT THE DAUGHTER WAS ONCE A CHILD.

Over the next few months, Angelica continued her advocate training and sometimes filled in at the bed-and-breakfast when they needed her. Nora taught her how to meditate, sitting cross-legged on yoga mats, immersed in the scent of lavender candles and mesmerized by mystic music. Breathing up and down their bodies, into the earth and up to the sky, they found their third eyes and recited affirmations. *Every day I'm learning to love and appreciate myself more and more, and the more I have to give to others. I have loving, satisfying relationships in my life. I am now attuned to my higher purpose.*

During recovery and her hiatus from work, Nora threw herself into story writing for the first time in years. She started writing a novel, interweaving shame and isolation with magical elements of a fish dress. In her writing, she spoke to the inadequacy as a mother, the failure as a daughter, the shattering of relationships, and the silenced voice, the untapped creative gifts… memories of brokenness. But her book would offer hope through the transformative power of forgiveness and love, especially of self, to heal. *I will create a new life story,* she thought.

****

One afternoon while she was working on her book, Thomas stopped by. Nora looked closely at his face, red and splotchy, and knew he'd been crying.

"Are you okay?"

"Mrs. Carver died last night. It turns out she had terminal brain cancer but kept it a secret."

Nora wrapped her arms tight around him. "I'm sorry, I should've told you I met her at the Cancer Forum, but I promised I wouldn't say anything. She didn't want anyone to know."

He let out a heavy sigh. "She had her moments, but I'll miss her."

"I'm glad I got to meet her. How's Mr. Carver?"

"A wreck. Nobody in the family can function so I have to make all the arrangements."

"What can I do to help, Thomas?"

"Let Grace know. I've got to run."

A minute later, he was back. Scratching his head, he said, "I almost forgot. This was on her night table, with your name on it." He handed her a package and rushed off.

She knew what it was. Alone in the house, Nora ripped off the wrapping, her heart pumping with excitement. She settled on the couch and ran her hands over the leather binding cracked with the passage of time. Her fingers tingled when she turned to the first page and began to read…

Marguerita de Roche: My Legacy

Andulasia, Spain

1870

At last I tell my story by filling the pages of this journal. I gleaned some details from others who told me about my early years. Let this be my final act of contrition, and may the finder of this book, after reading my words, reflect on the mysteries of life, its twists and turns, how honorable intentions can become tainted by human folly.

I was born in the mountains of Granada, Spain in 1850 but memories of my family are scant…

Nora instantly connected with Marguerita, as the words rang true to what she had experienced in her past life regressions. She read about the blizzard and the death of Marguerita's family when she was five, and the cave-dwelling Sacromontes who rescued and raised her as a gypsy, about her best friend Heathera, the government's purge, and being kidnapped by soldiers and taken to the Sisters of Charity when she was ten. How she became a nun and took a vow of silence, later rediscovering her old gypsy tribe.

Reading on, Nora pictured Heathera, her wanton behavior, and the birth of the illegitimate child, born gravely ill. She recalled Yatobi calling for a ceremony to save the infant and forgive the mother, along with protecting the Sacromontes,. and how Marguerita stole the Virgin Mary's shroud and fashioned it into a dress that Yatobi imbued with Pagan energies, unaware of the dress's Christian origin.

It was while reading through the ceremony scene that the journal took a different turn than Nora remembered. Surprised, she kept reading, wondering when Marguerita would break her silence, as Nora had done when she relived those frightful moments.

We formed a circle around the High Priestess, who laid the infant on a smooth flat rock out of reach of the flames. Yatobi summoned Heathera from the shadows at the far corner of the cave, and the circle opened to allow her in.

"Come to me," Yatobi commanded, raising her arms to receive Heathera in the dress, its fish skeletons veiled by the tribal symbols which swirled through the netting. Heathera stood statuesque, stunning, despite her head being shaven of its fiery red mane. "Remove the dress," Yatobi ordered.

I saw my friend's terror-filled eyes fix upon a ring of flame encircling her daughter. The dress dropped to the ground, and Heathera shrank with shame into her nakedness.

Yatobi glared at me and called out in a low, threatening voice. "These are not the symbols of the Sacromontes. What evil have you released, Marguerita?"

I longed to speak but the vow of silence choked me.

Yatobi drew in several breaths and appealed to me in a kinder voice. "We found you near death and restored you, raising you as a Sacromonte until the enemy took you and poisoned you with its thinking. When you returned, we treated you as if you had never left. You must break your silence now, so whatever curse you caused can be undone."

I clung to my silence, unable to speak. I wanted Heathera to know that she could receive protection from the Virgin Mary, though I wrestled with my allegiance to the Sacromontes.

Yatobi's voice pierced me. "Speak now and tell us what you have done, before it is too late. You have angered the gods."

Suddenly the fire lashed out, its tongue nipping at Heathera's paled skin, casting it in reds and blues. The heat swelled, and I felt faint. Yatobi's face writhed as if she were sucking the child's sickness and the mother's shame into her own body.

Without warning, Heathera leaped into the fire, and the infant gave a sharp cry. I stood in horror as her mother took a sudden last breath, deafening as death, skin melting off bones. The smell of burnt flesh sickened me.

Shocked, Nora looked up from the journal. "Oh my God! Why didn't Rosie tell me?"

Yatobi lurched forward, convulsing, speaking in tongues. We had seen her magic before and knew this time was different, that tragedy was upon us. Cat wails of the gypsies echoed throughout the cave, seeping into the night air. The High Sorceress, her voice faint, said, "A demonic spirit persists." She picked up the dress with the infant inside and held it to her chest. Then she glared at me through a lingering silence then screeched, "It is the dress. Leave now, Marguerita. Take the dress and the child with you, for they, too, are tainted. It is our daughter's blood upon your hands."

The High Priestess stood like a stone pillar, while the others huddled around the fire as if waiting for Heathera to rise from the ashes.

Clutching the infant, I fled from the Sacromonte camp, my insides retching. We moved through the black night, reaching the iron gates of the convent by morning. Weary, I placed the child into the welcoming arms of wide-eyed Mother Superior, who signaled to the nuns. Several minutes later, one returned with a cloth dripping with goat's milk, and the infant suckled.

The nuns did not recognize the dress as the stolen shroud when they removed it from the baby and hung it by the church robes, then sponged her with cool water from the well. They made a diaper from a collar and wrapped her in an altar cloth. They rocked her to sleep in a wooden cradle, allowing me to curl up and rest on a nearby bench. Perhaps they sensed my heaviness. I closed my eyes and tried to sleep but visions of Heathera visited me.

When the sisters retired to their sleeping quarters, I fed the child, holding her in my arms. Memories of songs the gypsies sang when we were children filled my head. I wanted to sing to the child, but the vow of silence contained me. It was after midnight when I settled her in the cradle, stroked her tender cheeks, and brushed her forehead with my lips. I longed to feel the touch of my best friend and smell the same scent of myrrh on her daughter.

Nora paused. "Marguerita, if only you had broken your silence, none of this would have happened, and I wouldn't have inherited the vow."

I can only describe myself as being in a deep trance when I stepped away from the cradle and removed the dress from its hook, concealing it under my cloak. I slipped out of the convent, leaving the infant behind. As I ran to the sanctuary, I remember clutching my chest and thinking "I can't breathe."

When at last I reached la Virgen de la Peña, I knelt before her. Slowly my breath returned. I wept, then recited in my mind the mysteries of the rosary, having learned them from the nuns before we took our vows of silence "Father, give me a deeper understanding of the cross I carry. That we must endure despicable trials to strengthen us is a mystery. Help me learn from your long suffering, your fortitude, your perseverance. And when I fear the future, when I'm too afraid or too tired to take another step, send me a helper. I pray for the virtue of forgiveness and justice." Beads of the rosary passed through my cold fingers, and the words rang hollow.

A voice echoed inside my head. "Marguerita, your faith is insufficient. You should know the Lord already paid the ransom. He alone could pardon the Sacromonte woman, heal the innocent child, and forgive you. God is the giver of mercy and grace, but you cut off the power of Christ when you failed to believe in the fullness of His love, turning instead to heathen magic. No one can serve two masters, for affections and obedience will be divided, and you will fall."

Sobbing, I folded the dress and placed it by the shrine, shielding my face from hers in shame. I retreated to a pew in the back of the chapel where I have been writing this account of my life. Soon it will be time to face la Virgen de la Peña and place the journal at her feet, by the dress.

Then I will travel by night through the Sierra Nevadas, so the Sacromontes won't spot me on my way to pay a final visit to the cliffs of my birthplace. Having desecrated loved ones, I am beyond redemption. As I jump to my grave, I will think of Heathera, whose death I caused. Fire consumed her, as earth will swallow me. I wonder, was there a god to meet my best friend? Will there be a god to meet me?

Marguerita de Roche

Nora closed her eyes and rested her head against the back of the couch, reflecting on the tragic journey Marguerita had taken.

"I can't believe I committed suicide in my last lifetime. No wonder I'm such a mess."

She picked up the phone and called Rosie. "I need to see you right away."

Chapter 27

Rosie greeted Nora in a blue lotus print muumuu.

"No fish dress today? How are you feeling?"

"A little weak, but better." Nora held out the journal, her hands shaking.

"What have we here?" Rosie asked.

"Marguerita's journal."

Rosie's eyes grew to the size of sand dollars. "You're kidding!" she said, taking the book from Nora's outstretched hands. "Where did you get this?"

"Not important," Nora bristled. "I need you to explain why you didn't tell me."

Rosie's eyes shifted. "Tell you what?"

"About Heathera's horrible death, and Marguerita's terrible end. I can only guess what disaster the infant faced. Is that why you pulled me from her world?"

Rosie's eyes darted across the pages of the journal. Stretching out a sigh, she said, "I'm sorry, Nora. I didn't mean to deceive you. I confess—in your last life regression, I saw your fate, and Heathera's. You *had* to break the vow of silence to free yourself from the shame surrounding your brother's death. When I brought you back into the present, I was trying to protect you from unnecessary pain and sorrow of your last lifetime, had you not broken the vow."

"It's too late. I already know that I took my own life."

They sat in silence until Rosie asked, "How can you be sure Marguerita committed suicide?"

"It says so right here," Nora answered, pointing to the final passage.

Rosie shook her head. "She *intended* to jump off the cliff, but is there proof she did? Things aren't necessarily what they appear to be. How do you know she didn't find hope at the last minute, as she stared out over the cliffs? Perhaps she had a memory—a happy memory of a young child gazing over the edge, the wind brushing her skin with the touch of her mother's lips upon her cheek. As I've told you before, there's a thin line between illusion and truth, especially in matters pertaining to life and death."

Nora's mind filled with the horror she imagined Marguerita experienced at causing the death of her best friend Heathera, and perhaps the child. Nora had reached the same depths of depression and isolation when she believed she had failed to save her brother. Both Nora and Marguerita had experienced the devastating effects of being caught in vows of silence.

Rosie's voice softened. "With life and death, sometimes we can't explain why things happen the way they do. It's best not to add anything to it, otherwise, you'll drive yourself crazy with *what if...? I should've...or why didn't I...?*"

Sighing, Nora said, "That's true. Like with Seth. And my mother."

"The past casts a long shadow. It's best to leave the sadness behind and hold on to the positive memories, using them to fuel the present and your dreams for the future. "

"And help my daughter live hers."

"Yes, but ultimately she's on her own path, and don't overlook free will."

Nora nodded. "I'm thankful that Angelica and I have reconciled. I understand she must travel her own path, but it's hard to let go."

"You can do it. You've done the work and learned the life lessons about relationship and self-love. Soon it will be time to return the dress to its rightful place—Mijas, Spain."

"It all makes sense now. Except I thought I'd found my soulmate but apparently not, so how have I learned the relationship lesson?" asked Nora.

"You never know what life brings, but you can count on one thing: it's about change, and you must be open to it."

They stood up, and Rosie handed the journal to Nora. "I'll be leaving for Mexico in a few days—off to follow in Carlos Castaneda's footsteps."

"To study shamanism with Don Juan?" Nora asked, winking.

Rosie's eyes sparkled. "Ah, you're familiar with his quest for knowledge. I'll be staying with the Yaqui tribe."

Nora frowned. "Will I ever see you again?"

A robust belly laugh filled every corner of the room. "I'll be back in a few months. How about a hug?"

Nora leaned into Rosie and felt an energetic zap surge through her body. She stepped away, unsure of what had just happened.

"I wore this dress for you," Rosie explained, smiling. "Not the usual white lotus blossoms, but ocean blue, the color of strength."

"I feel it," said Nora. "Thanks, Rosie. I'll miss you." They strolled arm-in-arm to the red door. On her way out, she lifted the moon-shaped knocker and waited for the *thud* before stepping onto the stone pathway, envisioning the trip Rosie had promised she'd take someday.

Nora wrote to the Sisters of Charity to arrange for the return of the dress to la Virgen de la Peña Sanctuary. It was time to tell Angelica. That evening, when her daughter returned from class, they sat in the living room with two cups of tea and a plate of sugar cookies. "I want to tell you about the fish dress," Nora began.

Angelica smiled. "You mean that weird dress you wore when you visited me in prison?"

"That's the one. Trust me, the universe always provides what we need, even if it looks like a wolf in sheep's clothing, or maybe a sheep in wolf's clothing."

She could tell by the puzzled look on Angelica's face that her daughter didn't understand the point of the analogy, nonetheless, she snuggled up and listened as Nora read the diary, stopping along the way to answer her daughter's questions, beginning with, "Who's Marguerita?" Nora pulled out the framed picture of the nun and continued reading.

It was when Marguerita stole the Virgin Mary's shroud that Angelica said, "Her motives were pure and worthy. She wasn't perfect, but don't we all have certain things in our lives that make us imperfect?"

And Nora said, "Yes, we're only human."

"Why did Heathera leap into the fire?" asked Angelica.

"She thought she had to sacrifice her own life in order for her daughter to live," Nora answered.

Angelica was silent during the rest of the reading. When it was over, she asked, "Why didn't Marguerita speak up?"

"She was caught between allegiance to both the gypsies and the nuns."

"What a tragedy. I wonder what happened to the baby."

"I'm sure the Sisters of Charity raised her to become one of them. We can only hope she lived a good life."

"What does this have to do with you, Mom?"

Nora hesitated. "It's complicated." She talked about Rosie, the dress, and past life regression. "Supposedly I was Sister Marguerita in my last life," Nora said, holding up the nun's picture again.

Angelica squinted at her mother. "I can't believe you went through all that. Are you sure it really happened?"

Nora looked her daughter in the eye. "Sometimes it's hard to know the difference between truth and illusion. This dress speaks to me."

"You expect me to believe that?"

"No, not necessarily. It's your choice."

"May I try it on?" Angelica asked in a shy voice.

"I suppose it won't hurt. Just remember, it chooses its wearer, and soon it's going back to Spain."

"How do you know where to mail it?"

"The address is on the box it came in. I thought we might take a trip and deliver it in person."

Angelica jumped up from the couch and threw her arms around her mother. "We're going to Spain?"

"In two weeks. Aunt Diane's going, too. I asked Grace—she can't go, but Thomas and Katrina are going. I'll show you the dress now."

Nora heard Angelica's feet dance behind her as they made their way to the bedroom. She pulled the box from a nook in the closet and watched her daughter's eyes sparkle. Nora removed the carefully folded dress, nestled in tissue paper that made a swishing sound.

Angelica ran her fingers across the fabric. "Soft as a baby's blanket."

She slipped it over her head and twirled in the mirror, which reminded Nora of the first time she'd tried it on. She could tell that her daughter longed for the dress, the way she stroked the fins, gills, and eye sockets of the fish skeletons then moved on to the swirls and crisscrosses in the pitch-black sea of fabric.

"That's enough, honey, time to put it away. I'll hang it in my closet for tonight, but tomorrow it goes back in the box."

Later that evening, Angelica tucked her mother in bed and planted a light kiss on her lips before heading to her own bedroom. Through the walls, Nora could hear her daughter toss and turn, and knew she must keep a close watch.

Perhaps the pull of the dress or Angelica's innate desire brought her tip-toeing into Nora's room. Pretending to be asleep, Nora opened one eye as Angelica silently removed the dress from its puffy satin hanger. Unbeknownst to her daughter, Nora followed her back to the bedroom and hovered silently outside Angelica's door.

She heard Angelica tear off her nightgown and whisk the dress over her head, twirling and swirling. Suddenly Nora heard a flapping sound.

"Ow!" Angelica squawked.

> MY DEAR, IT IS ONLY A GENTLE SLAP.
> LOOK WHAT THOU HAST DONE.
> DID THY MOTHER NOT SAITH THAT THE DRESS
> WOULD FIND THEE IF IT IS MEANT TO BE?

Angelica yanked the dress over her head and heaved it to the floor. She jumped back in her bed and hid under the covers.

The voice of the dress came at her like a tossed sea.

> DISAPPOINTED, I AM, AT SHOWING THY NEED
> FOR INSTANT GRATIFICATION.
> 'ME, ME, ME' AND 'NOW, NOW, NOW,' TIED
> TO THY ADDICTIVE NATURE.

Then its voice turned calm like the ebb tide.

> THAT IS THE CHALLENGE TO OVERCOME, MY CHILD.
> WHEREFORE I HAVE ASSIGNED THY MOTHER TO
> TEACH THEE TO LIVE A FULL LIFE. BE SO KIND AS TO
> RETURN ME TO HER CLOSET.

Nora opened the door a crack and watched Angelica peek out from under the blankets. She heard Angelica's muffled sobs and felt helpless when her daughter said, "I'm sorry, I didn't mean to disrespect you or my mother. Sometimes I can't stop myself from doing what I don't want to do."

Nora stole back to bed before her daughter sneaked the dress back into the closet.

In the morning, when Nora was in the kitchen brewing coffee, Angelica shuffled in and hugged her tightly. "Did I ever tell you you're the best mom in the world?"

"Did I ever tell you you're the best daughter in the world?" said Nora, hoping that Angelica would take to heart the dress's warning about her addictive nature.

Over breakfast, they reviewed their plans for the trip to Spain. Nora felt excited at the prospect of actually standing before the statue of the Virgin Mary, patron saint of the village of Mijas. But she also felt relieved to be returning the dress to its proper place, lest she be accused of stealing the dress. She knew she wasn't a thief, after all, Rosie had told Nora that the dress chose her.

Just then, Grace burst in through the kitchen door with a hearty hello. She hugged Angelica and poured herself a cup of coffee.

"We're going over the itinerary," Nora said. "I wish you were coming with us."

"Me too, but I have to work."

"Are you sure that's the real reason?" Nora asked, rubbing her chin.

"What do you mean?"

"If Thomas weren't going, I bet you'd come with us."

Grace stared into her coffee.

"Are you okay about my inviting him on the trip?"

"Why wouldn't I be?" Grace said, shrugging her shoulders.

"Come on, Grace. You two still love each other."

Grace made a face. "Where did you get that idea?"

"When Thomas came over to tell me Mrs. Carver died, he also wanted you to know, which says a lot about how much he needs your support, especially in a crisis. He admitted he loves you."

"Who said I still love him?"

"Remember the Early Bird sale and how the two of you kissed under the mistletoe at the Lobster Claw?"

Grace began to blush, then said with a smirk, "How about you and Kirk? If *I* should go, then *he* should go, too."

Nora scowled. "He walked out of my life, and we haven't talked or seen each other since. I'm over him."

Angelica, who'd been quietly studying the map, raised an eyebrow. "It sounds like you both still have feelings for them."

Nora handed the itinerary to her sister. "Take this in case you need to reach us."

"Angelica's right," said Grace, "I *do* miss Thomas."

Chapter 28

Following a seventeen-hour flight and two layovers, they touched down in the Province of Malaga on the southeastern coast of Spain. Nora and Angelica led their party off the plane, with Diane, Katrina, and Thomas following close behind. "Come get me when the baggage arrives," he said, "I'll be at the bar."

An hour later, the women retrieved the suitcases and found Thomas. They expected him to say, "What took you so long?" but instead he raved about the smooth flight, although the girls hadn't thought so.

"How would you know?" Katrina quipped. "You slept the whole way."

Out front, they found the bus to Mijas and crammed their belongings in the side racks. The driver loaded the line of passengers for the first leg of the trip. Nora, Diane, and Angelica squeezed into a small bench seat. Katrina and Thomas sat right behind them. Angelica clutched the straw bag that held the dress, Marguerita's journal, and the map.

Nora wondered if the crystal archangel Uriel that she'd given Angelica was in the bag. Known for powers of healing, forgiveness, and release of karma, he would be the perfect companion to complement the fish dress, with its similar healing powers. She hoped that her daughter had brought it.

The bus lumbered along the Mediterranean coastline, offering breathtaking views of the cyan sea with yachts and vessels pushing through whitecaps. On shore, flat arcs of golden sand spread across the beaches. Nora marveled at the way the early morning light streamed through the window, casting an iridescent glow upon Angelica's face.

Nora's eyes grew heavy, and she started to doze off. She dreamt of walking on the beach, wearing the fish dress, carrying a woven straw basket full of fish...

"Mom, we're about to switch buses."

Trying to remember the unfinished dream, Nora kept her eyes closed for several more seconds, but it slipped away. When she finally opened them, Angelica was staring at her. "Are you okay? You look stoned."

Nora interlocked her fingers and stretched her arms above her head. "I was having the most wonderful dream." Nora gazed out the window. "According to Rosie, the past, present, and future are all happening at once."

"Do you believe that?" asked Angelica.

Exhaling, Nora said, "I'm not sure."

The bus turned off the main road, leaving the sea behind and passing along lush, grassy fields dotted with wildflowers. It came to a rolling stop in front of a stone archway in the middle of nowhere. They exited the bus, retrieved their bags, and waited to board the next one.

"They call this a bus station?" grumbled Thomas.

Nora rolled her eyes. "What do you expect, the Ritz?"

"A bathroom, at least," Katrina said.

"How long is the next ride?" Diane asked.

"About an hour," Nora answered. "I think I hear it coming."

A weather-beaten bus with a loud muffler spewing black smoke rumbled to the archway. The travelers reloaded their bags and climbed the steps, again squeezing into seats like sardines. "This better be the last one," Thomas groaned as the bus backfired on its way out. "I don't trust it. Looks like an old hippie bus, with those flowers painted all over it."

Nora smiled, accepting that it was part of his personality to be a complainer. She turned around and gave him a teacher stare, telling him to knock it off. Then she heard him mutter to Katrina, "She acts like she's still in the classroom."

Nora gazed out the window, taking in the rolling green hills covered with avocado groves that Diane had read about in the tour book. Miles later, distant snow-capped mountains glowed purple, rising behind the hilly terrain. "You're looking at the famous Sierra Nevada Mountains, with the highest peak in Spain," announced Diane. A distant memory flashed through Nora's mind, disappearing in a blip. She shivered with a sense of déja vu.

"Look," Angelica shouted, "I see the white villages. We must be close."

"Almost," said Diane, "We're still climbing. The elevation of Mijas is 1,184 feet. It's built on the side of a mountain."

"I'm glad somebody prepared for this trip. Leave it to the librarian," Thomas said, giving Diane a thumbs up.

As the bus climbed a steep, narrow road, a large open truck loaded with potatoes came barreling down toward the bus, which veered sharply, nearly crashing into a ravine. The bus driver blasted his horn and swore in Spanish. Diane gripped the seat in front of her, while Nora and Angelica clung to each other. Thomas called out, "Jeesh, this is a suicide mission."

"Stop being a wuss," Katrina squawked. She turned to the others. "If we don't find a bathroom soon, I swear I'll be sitting in a puddle."

Thomas groaned, "Oh no you won't, not with me in the same seat."

"Don't get your panties in a bunch," Katrina said, snickering.

"All I know is that my panties better not get wet."

The bus pulled off the road and stopped in front of a large sign with unfamiliar words and a photograph of white stucco cottages with terracotta roofs.

"What does it say?" Nora asked, turning to Diane, who was the only person in their group who could read or speak Spanish.

"Welcome to Mijas, Land of the White Villages."

Thomas cried out, "It's about time!"

A white-washed building stood nearby. Katrina spotted a picture of a toilet on the front door and sprinted off the bus ahead of the others, disappearing into the building. After they regrouped, the travelers walked a half-mile up the hill, dragging their suitcases in the hot sun. They finally reached the villa where they would be staying. Like most of the architecture, it was a whitewashed structure with a terracotta roof. They were greeted by a large yellow tiger cat with a smile that looked painted on his face. He rubbed up against their legs.

"Bienvenidos al Casa Tejon," a friendly voice shouted from the open-air porch. The man came out to greet them and helped bring the luggage through an arched doorway and into the lobby. A short time later, they were relaxing on

the veranda of their suite, inhaling the strong sweet smell of potted sage on the stone railings.

"This place is gorgeous," Diane exclaimed, scanning the view of red rooftops and church spires below.

Even Thomas looked like he was enjoying himself, a peaceful expression on his face.

They could see the plaza with its stone courtyards, gardens, and fountains. "I want to go there," shouted Diane.

Thomas grabbed his stomach. "Let's do it. I'm starving."

Nora pointed beyond the village and said, "If you look out that way, you can see the Mediterranean again." It mesmerized her, the way the water glistened and sparkled like sapphires in sunlight.

"I read that we're almost 1500 feet above sea level," said Diane.

"Where's the church, Mom?" Angelica asked.

Nora pointed toward the mountain range behind them. "Not too far. The gypsies live in caves way up there, but it would be too rugged a trip to take."

"Is everyone ready?" Thomas asked, tapping his foot against the tile floor.

"I need to freshen up first, if that's okay with everyone," Nora said.

The girls stepped inside the suite. Nora dug in her suitcase to get a change of clothes. She took out a small pink velvet bag and handed it to Angelica. "This is for you."

From the bag, Angelica lifted a silver locket on a slender chain and held it up to the window, where the sun glimmered on it. "It's beautiful!" she whispered.

"Open it," Nora said, biting her lip.

Nora watched as her daughter carefully slipped a fingernail between the two silver hearts, and the locket opened. She held it to her lips. "Mommy!" she shouted. "It's Daddy and me! My true father!"

Nora gently clasped the locket around Angelica's neck, where it settled perfectly on her throat chakra, source of communication and expression.

When everyone was ready, they walked toward the center of town. Suddenly Diane started gagging. "What stinks?" she squawked, pinching her nose.

Angelica looked at the map. "It must be the burro taxis and the donkey carts."

Sure enough, they were standing near a cluster of burros and donkeys tucked into makeshift wooden stalls, the animals' hind parts facing them. The smell was strong, intensified by a warm breeze and a scorching sun.

"Watch where you walk," warned Nora.

Thomas shook his head. "We have to ride stinking jackasses to get around town? Now I've seen everything."

"We're in the historic quarter. It's a tourist thing," Diane explained.

"Not this tourist," he mumbled.

They trudged past the stables and around to the front, where more donkeys stood tethered to metal railings, their tails lazily swishing flies away. The animals wore fancy bridles decorated with bright-colored strands of yarn and matching blankets draped over their backs. Nearby, peasant women sat on overturned wooden crates, busily weaving and chatting in Spanish.

"Maybe we can talk Thomas into taking a ride later," Nora confided to Angelica.

Katrina patted a donkey on its forehead. "You poor thing, you must be sweltering. Look, he's winking at me."

"She's so hard up she's flirting with the donkeys," Thomas said.

Katrina gave him the finger as they moved past the animals and entered what felt to Nora like another world—the antithesis of the smelly, dirty donkey world they'd just left. The Plaza de la Peña looked surprisingly cosmopolitan, with its gleaming stone courtyard bordered by double-decker whitewashed buildings ranging from stubby to tall. Stone steps wound from one level to the next, with crowds of people milling about, shuffling in and out of shops and restaurants. Others relaxed on mosaic stone benches scattered around the square, or stood by the circular fountain that spouted water twenty feet in the air. Guitar music floated across the plaza, which was edged in brick, with chartreuse grass and clusters of fragrant flowers, splashes of rainbow colors.

"This is more like it," Katrina said.

"Why don't we just grab fast food for now so we can explore the village, and then later we'll go to a nice restaurant," Nora suggested.

"When are we taking the dress back?" asked Angelica.

"Later today. Father Diego's not there now."

"Whoever he is," Thomas said.

"He's the keeper of the sanctuary where the shrine is," replied Nora.

Thomas led the way to a food stand where they ate fish and chips and burgers. Afterwards, instead of staying in the center of town, Diane led them down one side street then another, meandering through the arteries of Mijas.

"This place is like a maze. We should stay close together," Katrina said in a high-pitched voice.

"Scaredy cat," Nora teased. "Do you think the bogeyman's going to jump out of a cubbyhole and snatch one of us away?"

Thomas gave a jolly laugh. "I like this area, it's quaint." He pointed out the cobblestone streets, the white stucco houses, and the fancy wrought-iron gates.

Katrina looked at him and said, "Since when do you like *anything*?"

"I'm really enjoying this!" he exclaimed, his eyes twinkling.

"You all should be," Diane spouted. "Rocky Harbor doesn't have the character of Mijas. This is medieval history—the Moors, with fortress walls still standing. And the Christians. Look at the arched doorways and fancy tile inlays. Beautiful stonework and carvings—are those lions?"

They wandered deeper into the labyrinth, with Nora and Thomas following behind. Streets turned into alleys with scruffy-faced men propped against the front steps of rundown storefronts. Barefoot boys, too young to be roaming the streets by themselves, rode makeshift bicycles.

"Not my cup of tea," Katrina said, turning to Diane. "You got us here. Now get us back to the plaza."

"I wanted to see how the common people live. The plaza's for tourists, with its crowded shops and fancy restaurants," Diane said.

"Who do you think *we* are?" Katrina demanded. "That's exactly where we're headed. I want to pick up some souvenirs."

"I could use a bite to eat," Thomas said, his voice sounding pleasant.

As Diane led them back, Nora couldn't help but notice that Thomas walked with a bounce instead of dragging his feet. *This trip is doing wonders for him*, she thought.

But Nora noticed that Diane was walking with a slight limp. "Are you okay?"

She rubbed her knee. "I'll be all right. Just find me a shady spot and a cold beer and I'll be happy."

"Me too," Katrina said.

Back in the plaza, they bought cold beverages and sat on stone benches in the courtyard as they watched crowds of people walk by. Out of nowhere, Nora heard a familiar voice shout her name.

"Oh, my God, look who's here!" Angelica screeched. "It's Auntie Grace!"

What? Nora spotted her sister jumping up and down like she'd just won the lottery. "I can't believe you're in Spain!" Nora shouted as they all rushed to greet her.

"We've been two stops behind you the whole way. It's about time we caught up," Grace said, throwing her arms around each of them, including Thomas.

"What do you mean, *we?*" asked Nora.

Grace looked around. "I thought he was right behind me."

Suddenly, Nora's knees buckled, and she held onto Angelica. "Oh my God, it's Kirk!"

She felt his body tremble when they hugged, then he stepped back and gave her an awkward, lingering smile. She introduced him to Diane and reintroduced him to the others. It surprised her how he seemed to cling to Angelica, and she to him, as if they were long lost friends.

"You're lucky to find us," said Thomas, chuckling. "We've been through every nook and cranny in Mijas, except for the part where normal tourists go."

Grace laughed. "Not chasing Margo, I hope."

"What?" Nora shrieked.

"Just kidding. She's in good hands with Miss June."

"I'm ready to eat," announced Thomas, pointing to a salmon colored restaurant with pink roses hanging from the balcony.

"I've *been* ready," Katrina said.

A gentleman greeted them and led them up a flight of stone steps to a brilliant sunlit veranda with a bird's-eye view of the plaza. They sat at a large round marble table inlaid with tile. Nora was not quite sure how it happened, but she and Kirk were sitting directly across from each other, and Grace and Thomas were seated right next to each other, Thomas ordered two bottles of wine, a pitcher of beer, and a lemonade.

Katrina suggested they go around the table and offer a toast. She raised her glass. "To the handsome Spaniard I will meet tonight."

"In your dreams," Thomas said, joking with Nora.

Katrina narrowed her eyes. "What did you say, Thomas?"

"Sweet dreams, the best to you."

"Salut!" they cheered each time to the sound of glasses clinking.

Katrina shouted, "To making it out alive through the bowels of Mijas!"

"Thomas lifted his glass and smiled. "I want to thank everyone for this wonderful trip and for our close friendship." He looked around the table, pausing at Grace before turning to Nora. "And to the return of the fish dress. May we never hear about it again," he proclaimed, laughing.

"You mean *imminent return*," Nora reminded him. "It's still with us."

Katrina shaded her eyes with her hand and looked around the table. "Who's next?"

Angelica raised her glass of lemonade. "To my mother for her love and patience, and to my aunties for being like second moms." She teared up as they raised their glasses.

"*Salut!*"

Nora, misty-eyed, said, "To all of you for being in my life but especially to my daughter, whose courage and strength are unsurpassed. Congratulations on her new job, she starts as an advocate for domestic violence victims when we get back home."

"*Salut! Salut!*"

"And one more toast." She cleared her throat. "To Kirk, in the name of forgiveness for those we love, and for those we want to love." The rich tone of her words echoed across the table long after she'd spoken. Nora glanced in his direction and thought she saw his eyes water.

His voice wavering, Kirk said, "I also have two toasts." He looked at Angelica and raised his glass. "This is to the most determined young lady I know." Angelica grinned. Then Kirk turned to Nora, his glass teetering high in the air. "You're an amazing woman. Thank you for showing me undeserved kindness."

Then he reached in his pocket and pulled out a folded and refolded piece of stationary, fumbling while opening it. He cleared his throat and began to read, as the paper shook.

Dear Nora,

Where do I begin?

Almost six grueling months have passed since we've been together, and they've been the loneliest days of my life. I thought I knew what I was doing when I walked away, but I now realize what a coward I was. I'm deeply sorry for betraying you.

Please forgive me for making such a stupid mistake. I wasn't the brave knight you thought I was. Instead of defending and supporting you through your crisis, I ran away and hid.

Do you remember our first date at the Chinese restaurant, and the fortune I got about the rose? I was supposed to protect and defend you, not turn against you.

Will you give me another chance?

KIRK

He looked up at Nora. "I love you, Nora!"

His words hung in the air as Nora searched for the right words to say.

Grace spoke next. "I will also make two toasts. First, to my daughter, Eve. If she were here, she'd raise her glass to spending time with family and friends. Unfortunately, she's 6,500 miles away in Hong Kong."

"*Salut!*"

"Second, I'm going to follow in Nora's and Kirk's footsteps, and be brave. She turned toward Thomas, took a deep breath, and announced, "To the man I want to spend the rest of my life with."

Everyone's glasses froze in mid-air.

You could hear a feather fall, waiting for Thomas to say *something.* He leaned closer and nuzzled against her, his face beet red. "Grace, will you marry me?"

"Thought you'd never ask." She burrowed into his neck. He lifted her chin to his and they rubbed noses.

"It's settled. Grace and I are officially engaged." Thomas snatched a red carnation from the centerpiece, twisted it into a ring and gently slid it onto her finger. "You're my mate. I promise we're going to travel and have fun relaxing."

"*Salut! Salut!*" Everyone stood up and clapped as if they were watching the climax of *Breakfast at Tiffany's,* where the couple seals their love with a kiss for eternity. Then came a synchronistic moment when a mariachi performer joined them at the table, serenading the happy couple with a love song.

They feasted on gazpacho and tortilla omelets made with sweet breads, potatoes, and peppers. Next came fried fish and sardines on skewers. Giddy from too much beer, Katrina blurted out, "I know this little fish can't possibly fit a penis in its mouth, at least none that I've seen."

Nora gave Angelica an apologetic look. "Katrina, must you, especially in front of my daughter? Don't you remember the night at the Ark when you promised Thomas you'd never bring up the fish dress again?" As soon as the words *fish dress* came out of her mouth, Nora regretted having said them. Surely Angelica would want to know about the sexual connection to the dress, but for now Nora had no intention of explaining its deeper symbolism.

Thomas rolled his eyes. "That does it, time to go. Let's get rid of the dress right now." He leaned over and kissed Grace. "We'll come back to the plaza for a donkey ride and a wedding parade." He waved his hand in the air. "*Garcon,* I'll take the check."

Along with the bill, the waiter brought a tray stacked with candies. "Turrón?" he asked, winking at Katrina, who gracefully batted her eyelashes, replying in her sexiest voice, "*Gracias.*"

Everyone popped Spanish almond nougats in their mouths like grapes, then descended the steps to the plaza.

Chapter 29

"We have to climb *that* mountain?" Diane asked. "I'm not sure these legs can handle it."

Grace threaded her arm through Thomas's. "It's not as bad as it looks; we're walking on a dirt road, not rock climbing."

Angelica walked alongside Diane. "I'll help you."

Nora, still recovering from Kirk's letter, heard a soft whistle and recognized it as Kirk's. He edged his way over and they walked together. "So, how are you doing?"

"Pretty well, thanks. How about you?"

"Doing okay. Busy with work, wooing the old ladies so they'll buy hearing aids, and hanging out with my daughters and the pups." He was talking fast.

Nora took a deep breath. "Your letter—it stunned me, so beautiful—I couldn't speak."

"I meant every word of it," he said.

They stopped and looked at each other. Kirk reached out and held Nora's hand as they continued up the hill. Nora broke their silence. "In your letter, you asked if I would give you another chance. My answer is *yes!*" She threw her head back and laughed. "You can hang with me if you're tough enough."

With a smile across his face, he bowed before her, gripping an imaginary sword. "Yes, I *am* the brave knight." He took her hand and kissed it. Still holding hands, they walked along the dirt path, grinning. Nora felt young again, unbound by any number-of-years designation, with no limitations on her aspirations.

Kirk said, "I'm really glad Grace asked me to come to Spain. I guess we both were on a mission."

"A love mission, maybe?"

"We have a lot of catching up to do, Nora. I want to know everything about you."

"Well, I'm writing again. Are you still playing music?"

"Yes, it's my therapy. What are you writing?"

"A novel, it's *my* therapy."

"What's it about?"

"It's called *The Fish Dress*. It's—"

"Isn't that the chapel?" Angelica pointed to a grassy embankment in the distance.

Nora left Kirk's side and grabbed her daughter's hand. They sprinted over rocks and through bushes and brush, while the others trailed behind. There, at the top of an old stone staircase built into a knoll was a stone chapel, its arched wooden door beckoning.

"It's the Chapel of *la Virgen de la Peña!*" Nora cried out.

They all stood in silence as she lifted the bronze cherub knocker. The door creaked open, and they were greeted by an elderly gentleman, hunched over, thin and balding except for a halo of gray hair. He looked like a bell ringer, dressed in a brown hooded cloak that brushed the ground when he moved toward Nora and bowed low. "*Mi nombre es Padre Diego, eres Nora?*"

"Oh my God, it's Quasimodo," Katrina whispered.

"Pleased to meet you," said Nora, hoping he hadn't heard Katrina's remark.

"*¿Sabes inglés?*" Diane asked.

Padre Diego shook his head. "*Lo entiendo, pero no lo hablo.*"

"*No hay problema,*" she replied. "*Voy a traducer.*" She turned to the others. "He understands some English but doesn't speak it, so I'll translate."

Padre Diego ushered them inside, lit a row of candles with an iron prod, and babbled in a tongue they'd never heard before. He made the sign of the Trinity and blessed them, pointing toward the altar. Nora recoiled at seeing the statue of the Virgin Mary.

"*¿Porque le tienes miedo?*"

"He's asking why you fear her," Diane said.

"It's n-not that," she stuttered. "She's lovely. I'm just overcome by how she looks so full of pain. Her sorrow makes me sad." A weighty lump settled in her throat."

Father Diego replied, "*Como todos los santos, ella es una true martyr, sufriendo para que ostros puedan ser redimidos. No hay autocompassion en ella.*"

"He says she suffers that others may be redeemed but there's no self-pity in her."

Nora felt a nudge. "What about the dress and the journal?" Angelica asked, holding out the bag.

Nora handed Sister Marguerita's diary to Padre Diego. He gave her a stern look and raised his voice. "*Todavia queda el asunto de la mortaja.*"

"He wants you to give him the shroud," Diane said.

Nora addressed Padre Diego directly. "I'd like to return it to la Virgen myself."

His face clouded over, and he turned to Diane, spouting a long explanation of why that would be unacceptable. When he finished, Diane explained to Nora, "He said you must recall what was in the letter. It said that Padre Diego would secure the shroud in a safe place until the Higher Order of the Sisters of Charity could verify its genuineness. The last time, when Sister Marguerita returned the shroud to *la Virgen,* it became linked with rumors of human sacrifice, and then it vanished."

Nora looked at Padre Diego. "What do you mean?"

He narrowed his eyes. "*Algunos piensan que la iglesia escondió el vestido por miedo a la magia vudú. Otros creen que los gitanos lo robaron por temor al poder cristiano. Esta vez no puede haber ningún error con un talismán tan poderoso como el vestido de pez, como tú lo llamas. Insisto en que me lo des ahora.*"

Diane's eyes widened. "My God, he's saying that some people think the church hid the dress out of fear of voodoo magic. Others believe the gypsies stole it out of dread of Christian power. He says this time there can be no mistake with a talisman as powerful as the fish dress, as you call it. He insists that you give it to him *now!*"

Padre Diego held out his hands.

The dress buzzed in Nora's ear.

*DO NOT CLUTTER THE MIND WITH RELIGION IN ANY
OF ITS FORMS THAT BE PUZZLES, RHYMES, AND OF
HUMAN LYRICS. STAND UP TO THAT FEAR-BASED
VENGEFUL TRADITION.*

Clutching the dress, Nora moved closer to Padre Diego and looked right in his eyes. "This is the Virgin Mary's shroud, and I'm going to return it to her myself," she said, feeling the strength of her voice. She turned her back on him and started to walk toward the altar. Hearing footsteps, she looked behind her, expecting to see Padre Diego, but it was her daughter.

"Please, Angelica, go back," she whispered. "I'll explain later." She kissed her and watched her disappear into the arms of Grace and Kirk.

Nora tiptoed down the aisle to the altar where La Virgen de la Peña stood, her arms extended as if waiting to accept the shroud. Nora's eyes met hers, and this time Nora didn't recoil, for she saw joy emerge from sorrow. She placed the folded dress in the Virgin Mary's hands and knelt before her, folding her hands in prayer position and bowing her head. "I bring you back your sacred shroud."

THOU HAST DONE WELL.

Nora slowly walked back down the aisle. She would miss the dress and all that it had revealed about forgiveness, love, and self-worth, although the journey was at times wretchedly painful. She had learned how to navigate through the illusionary nature of life to discover what is truth. She no longer needed the dress to guide her, for that small, still voice was now inside her, and no longer silent. Perhaps, as Rosie suggested, there *is* something to past, present, and future happening simultaneously in a timeless universe containing the realm of all possibilities. She smiled to herself as she made her way to where the others were clustered.

"We've got a problem. Padre Diego's hiding under a pew," Thomas said in a low voice.

"What happened?" Nora asked, still in a daze.

"I think he's on the brink of a nervous breakdown," Kirk said.

Nora took Angelica's hand, while Grace and Diane walked toward the pew and tried to comfort Brother Diego. When he emerged, his body was shaking like a willow in the wind.

Unable to look at Nora, he circled around her, wringing his hands. "*Las Hermanas de la Caridad me dio órdenes estrictas de asegurar el vestido y mantenerlo separado de la Virgen hasta que podamos tomar decisiones oficiales. ¿Quién sabe qué terribles consecuencias han desatado tus acciones? Por favor, solo vete. Te veré afuera.*"

"He says the Sisters of Charity gave him strict orders to secure the shroud and keep it separated from *la Virgen* until they can make official decisions. He worries that our actions have unleashed something terrible, and he wants us to leave right away."

Nora lowered her head before Padre Diego. "We're very sorry for any trouble we have caused," she said politely.

They filed behind him, resembling a class of disobedient schoolchildren. Angelica and Nora stayed to the rear, lingering to take a last look. *Am I hallucinating?* thought Nora. *Does Angelica see what I see?* It wasn't the face of the Virgin Mary but that of Sister Marguerita, just as Nora had first seen her at the secondhand shop—a white cloth hooded bonnet framing her oval face with its high cheek bones, walnut eyes, small mouth, and straight nose. But instead of the distant side gaze Nora remembered, Marguerita looked directly at her and mouthed the words *mucho gracias*, then held a finger to her lips.

Marguerita's face faded, and the Virgin Mary reappeared. A beam of light fell across her, casting a glow in her eyes and a faint smile on her face.

"*¡Ven ahora!*" Brother Diego's voice grated from the doorway.

Feeling faint, Nora managed a final goodbye as they exited the arched doors and began their downward trek. No one said anything.

"Mom, what just happened back there?" whispered Angelica, trembling.

Nora wrapped her arms around her daughter. "No need to be frightened. Marguerita thanked me for what she was unable to do—break the vow of silence—and the Virgin Mary acknowledged her part in our journey."

Angelica smiled and whispered, "Thanks, Mom, for showing me the way."

They caught up with the others and heard Thomas shout, "Who's ready for a pre-wedding donkey cart ride?"

With a round of cheers and a high-spirited *hee-haw*, they completed their descent.

Thomas acted like the mayor of Mijas, barking orders and taking charge of the donkey carts, choosing only the most festively decorated ones. Each cart had a driver. Grace and Thomas led the parade, their cart draped with fuchsia flowers and silver bells. In the next cart, sat Diane and Katrina. A handsome Spaniard sporting a leather vest and a matching cap, hopped into the driver's seat. Katrina did a double take. Angelica, Kirk, and Nora clattered behind in a cart dragging brightly painted tin cans.

Diane called out *"Boda!"* the Spanish word for *wedding*, and soon *Boda! Boda! Boda!* echoed throughout the plaza with locals and tourists joining the parade. Scores of people clambered onto donkey carts to form a caravan, and the village erupted with Spanish guitar music, joyful song, and lively clapping. Flamenco dancers rushed into the streets, twirling their red ruffled skirts and black satin capes under the crimson sky and setting sun.

While riding in the cart, Kirk presented Nora with a single yellow rose. She reached for it with care, to avoid the sting of its thorns. It reminded her of Kirk's fortune cookie message to withhold thorns from his lover. The rose also reminded Nora of her mother's sweet-scented roses that once climbed the trellis in the backyard. Just as she had forgiven her mother, it felt liberating to forgive Kirk.

He put his arm around her, affectionately squeezing her shoulder. "Nora, if it's one thing I regret, it's turning my back on you. It was stupid, immature, and selfish. And now I've chased you across the world to tell you how much I love you. I promise to be true to you forever."

He reached into his pocket and pulled out a small square box.

Nora blushed. "What's this?"

"Open it, Mom."

Nora's hands shook as she removed the lid. It was the necklace Kirk had given her for Christmas, the one she threw at him when he left her. Kirk lifted the necklace from the box, its stone no longer shattered, and its links no longer broken, and gently clasped it around Nora's neck.

She rubbed her fingers over the crystal. "Thank you, Kirk," she said in a soft voice.

"It's beautiful," said Angelica. "It looks like the moon."

Nora rubbed the crystal between her fingers. "It's moonstone, the traveler's stone, offering protection on journeys. Also brings love, passion, and wisdom."

Kirk handed Angelica a tiny pouch.

"For me?" she asked, holding her hand to her chest. Angelica's eyes lit up when she saw the pink quartz crystal earrings in the shape of crosses, a second later they glistened in her ears. "Thank you," she said, kissing him on the cheek.

"I almost forgot," he said, turning back to Nora.

"Me? Again?"

He dug in his pocket once more. "Just a little something." He held out his hand, with his fingers curled shut, then looked over at Angelica. "Is it okay with you if I ask your mother to marry me?"

Angelica blushed. "It's not up to me."

Kirk stood up in the cart and knelt on one knee in front of Nora, whose skin began to tingle. "Nora Jenkins, will you marry me?" he asked, in a strong voice.

She clung to his words as shivers ran up and down her spine.

Kirk extended his fingers, revealing a sparkling diamond ring in the palm of his hand, waiting for Nora to say, "Yes!" She placed her hand in his and felt the sweat of their palms rub together, the jewel pressed between them as if branding them.

Nora hesitated. Inside, her breath hurt, and the words were difficult when they came out. "I do love you, Kirk, but I'm not ready for marriage." She gently removed her hand from his, leaving the ring behind. "I'm afraid all I can promise right now is the moment."

Kirk's body stiffened. "Nora, what does that mean? Is it over between us?"

"Of course not. I just need more time to digest everything that has happened. Angelica and I are a family again, and she's starting a new career. I need to finish my book. I'm not the same person I was when you met me."

Kirk nodded and gave a deep sigh. "Nora, I'll wait as long as it takes for you to marry me."

Nora saw the look of determination in Kirk's eyes. She reached her arms around him and kissed his lips. "I do love you, Kirk, and I want us to be together."

A rising full moon in a cloudless sky lit the way back to Casa Tejon, with lighthearted laughter echoing throughout the hills. Nora, Grace, and Kirk walked together; Kirk told them he was thinking of moving closer to Rocky Harbor, and they chatted about how fun it would be to take a whale watching cruise and see the Tall Ships come into the harbor later in July.

Back at the inn, the evening belonged to Grace and Thomas. They all gathered on the veranda and imbibed in the cool sweetness of sangria while snacking on fresh avocados, black olives, and goat cheese with bread. They counted the stars in the sky and reflected on the magical day they'd shared, then drifted off to sleep in the cool night air wherever they happened to stretch out on the terrace.

****

Nora awoke at sunrise—she was the first, except for the smiling tiger cat lounging on the tiles, licking his yellow fur. She tiptoed to the railing and looked out over the village, observing the vendors crank open their awnings as the sweepers tidied the sidewalks and courtyards.

Her gaze stretched far beyond the village's steepled churches and dome-shaped mosques, coming to rest on Mediterranean waters of deep blue, gold and olive green. She imagined herself as a mermaid waving her fish tail up and down, skimming across whitecaps and gliding through sea foam. She felt a kindred connection with mermaids that morning. As a child she'd read stories about their intuitive abilities and large capacities to heal the human heart.

Nora stared in amazement at Angelica, a picture of innocence asleep on the settee. Nora vowed to never again let her daughter slip into isolation, as she, herself, had done. That cavern of disconnect that could easily lead to self-destruction, especially with Angelica's history. *She's on her own journey*, Rosie had said. Nora reached over and kissed her daughter's forehead. Angelica half-opened her eyes and smiled, then drifted off again.

Kirk stirred. Nora tiptoed over to him and lightly rocked the hammock he was in. "Good Morning," she whispered. "Mind if I join you for a minute?"

Kirk's eyes opened. He was grinning.

She squeezed onto the edge of the hammock. "I've been thinking about the ring," Nora said.

He raised himself up. "And?"

"Why don't we store it in the treasure box I gave you, for safe keeping." Nora could feel Kirk's eyes upon her as she left his side and moved toward the balcony railing. The cool terrace tiles felt grounding, while the sea breeze whirled through her hair, blowing it everywhere. For so long she had wanted to escape from the prison of her thoughts and emotions, and now she was free.

Closing her eyes for a moment, Nora imagined herself back home in Rocky Harbor, leaning over the wooden railing of the footbridge and gazing at the open ocean, as she'd done many times before. It had always been a mag-net, pulling her toward it, spellbinding her with a wish to cloak herself in its strength and renew her spirits. No longer would it be just a fantasy.

Nora couldn't stop thinking about the fish dress. Had it really talked, or was it her imagination? In the end, did it matter? The work was done, and the inner voice now belonged to Nora, although she would never disregard the nuns nor the Sacromontes. While they worshipped different deities, they both had loving spirits, opening their hearts to Marguerita. One thing was clear: Christian and Pagan energies had united to heal Nora's heart, her mind, and her soul. She silently thanked the dress for teaching her the importance of con-nection, forgiveness, love of self and others. And letting go of the past—the old stories she had told herself for most of her life— about inadequacy, self-sabotage, and defeat.

Nora was ready to begin her new life!

RECOGNIZE THE TRUTH OF WHO YOU ARE BECOMING: DEEP, RICH, AND STRONG LIKE THE SEA.

THE END

For Discussion

1. What does the dress symbolize in Nora's life?

2. How does the author transform the dress into a character?

3. Nora has always felt pulled toward the ocean. Living in a coastal tourist town, she senses a rhythm to life. What role do your surroundings play in your life?

4. How do Angelica's home life and her school experiences contribute to her subsequent behavior? Could her mother have done more to protect her?

5. Who is your favorite character and why? Least favorite?

6. Discuss the "vow of silence" and its influence in the story.

7. What do you think Rosie means when she tells Nora there's a thin line between truth and illusion. Rosie also says that the past casts a long shadow. Relate these statements to the book and to your own life.

8. Share your views on reincarnation, past life regression, time travel, and karma.

9. Which character changed the most over the course of the story, and in what ways?

10. Do you think Nora made the right decision about Kirk at the end of the book? What would you have done?

11. What would you say are the major themes in the story?

Acknowledgments

So many people to thank...where do I start?

With **my family**—all of you—for encouraging me to find my voice and go for my dreams. Siblings Cindy Snow, Nan Barter, and Rick Walsh. Sister-in-law Christine Walsh and brother-in-law Brad Snow. Nieces Kim Snow, Erin Valenzuela, and Shannon Walsh.

My friends, without whose support I might have given up. Talented writers Lynn Wilcox and Dan Pope, Geof Fowler and Al Bower. Fine Art Photographer Rosylyn Carrier-Brault. Beta Readers Sally Jordan, Alimatu Busari, Angela Peart, and Chris Field. Dr. Mel Tavares and Kingdom Writers.

Brand strategist Jiayao Chen. Web Designer and Marketing Consultant Lauren Middleton of Forest City Marketing.

Barbara Ellis-Uchino, Vice President, Unicorn for Writers, steadfast, comprehensive editor of The Fish Dress, and my confidante.

Publisher Alexa Bigwarfe of Kat Biggie Press, who gave me the opportunity to share my story. Her team of experts—Assistant Nancy Cavillones, Instagram Unicorn Raewyn Sangari , Cover Designer Michelle Fairbanks, and developmental editor Kasie Whitener.

Abigail McGrath, founder of Renaissance House, a residency program for artists and writers in need. Poet Mary Wheeler. Thank you both for helping me write through a painful season in my life.

All this would not be possible, were it not for the grace of God. Thank you.

About the Author

New England-based teacher, mother, and writer, Carol Parker embraces spirituality, the outdoors, the Arts, and is dedicated to improving the lives of those affected by drug addiction.

The Fish Dress is her debut novel.

You can learn more about Carol at https://www.carolparkerauthor.com/ or join the discussion about the book on Instagram: @carolparkerauthor.

Made in USA - North Chelmsford, MA
1207605_9781948604703
12.07.2020 0748